Selected Pieces

Ezra Williams

TSL Publications

First published in Great Britain in 2023
By TSL Publications, Rickmansworth

ISBN: 978-1-915660-62-6

Cover & photographs courtesy of :
Mike Wells

for Eli, as always – my son, my Actual

By the same author

Fiction

Losing Henry

Fairytales and Oddities

Poetry

Seven Unquiet Shouters

Poet's Pleasure

Orphans of Albion

Contents

Foreword

In March 2020, the thing we call world took a lurch. It wasn't a political thing (say, the assassination of the leader of the free world), and it wasn't a religious thing (say, a terror attack of the scale of 9/11) and *of course* it wasn't an artistic thing (don't be so vulgar). It was nevertheless an astonishing thing.

I have written about it in print before, so shan't waste time talking about the myriad ways Covid-19 – and subsequent mutations of the virus – affected us all. But one inarguable positive was that it gave time and space for certain personal consolidations. It provided me time to write my fifth book, although technically my second, as the first three were youthfully solemn bullshit – and nobody read them anyway. And it gave me time to gather some old journalism together with a view to a collection: indeed, the sleek volume you hold in your hands.

But there were unexpected problems. I quickly realised that much of what I had contributed to magazines, journals, periodicals and newspapers over the years didn't merit being published in a book, or even published for a second time. Besides, journalism was itself a dying prospect since the advent of Social Media.

What *was* truth? Did truth even exist anymore? Or was *belief* – 'this is what I feel, so it's true to me' (and *ergo* must be respected by *you*) – the way of the future? I had long thought, indeed since the late 90s while still in education, that journalism was dying. I was exactly primed to see it: I remember the introduction of email, and I watched as it was sent: the very first email, on TV. Yes, it was filmed for TV. And I know it probably wasn't the very first, and I know TV isn't real, but that's the point. Even then, as a child, I thought: this means everyone is connected now. It means the death of history: it means we can *all* just make it up. It heralded the birth of Manifestation.

In the young 2000s, among my literary friends, *fake news*, or *false reporting* as it was then known – although the two are, in fact, different – was regularly bandied about in public, in our private residences, over late night phone calls, and even, horrifically, in *pubs*.

Why pubs so horrifically in particular? Well, first a word on the difference. *Fake news* is a fairly recent term, much associated with the 45th President of the United States, Donald Trump. As far back as July 26th, 1920, H. L. Mencken wrote in *The Baltimore Evening Sun*:

> As democracy is perfected, the office of the President represents, more and more closely, the inner soul of the people. On some great and glorious day, the plain folks of the land will reach their heart's desire at last, and the White House will be adorned by a downright moron.

That's damningly harsh, on the American people, I think, more than the office itself. And yet... *fake news* was Trump's inarguable get-out-clause – out of everything – just blame *those* guys for it. It's all just... *Fake news*. And it was stultifying.

Our use of *false reporting*, or occasionally, after drinks, *coffin journo*, had the opposite effect, that of rejuvenation. And it wasn't the same: fake news was just fake, but false reporting was provably false... Until one day it wasn't anymore. Journalism had died. And we watched it go, over our glasses of pruno, and our two-day-long arguments about everything in the world. Suddenly, it wasn't there; it had been replaced. Now the masses had a voice, and it was new, new. What was the point of *us*?

Pubs are, or were, an important part of the British male psyche. We used to be able to smoke in them, for a start. At that balmy time, I was spending much time in them: with authors, composers, artists, musicians and lovers. Pubs were where politics, literature, music and life took place and took shape in the early thousands. We met each other, talked and argued and smoked. And everyone respected a different viewpoint. *In company*, it was called. 'You look like shit, were you in company last night?'

Yes, yes, sorry about that. I was *in company* last night, and everyone was smoking... and the company was extraordinary. My apartment (2002 – 2013) in Notting Hill, on Westbourne Park Road, became for a while a hotbed of intellectual activity.

It boasted a dartboard.

Later (when I got rid of the bed), a pool table was brought in, and then we went the whole hog and had strobe lights fitted, painted the place black and red and put in booths, for privacy, but mainly for cleanliness: it was easier to clean separate tables rather than one big one, even if the one big one had once been owned by Larry Hagman (and signed by him and Oliver Reed, among others.)...

And the intellect came and kept coming. I hosted novelists, musos, opera singers, playwrights, fashion models, the occasional drug dealer, business owners, journalists, political figures (it was predominantly Labour then), actors, philosophers, toy makers, tinkerers, ice cream salespeople, one sculptor – the only person to ever get thrown out – and many others. Then I got married, moved, and it all disappeared. And I didn't really live there, except at the beginning. I lived with my ex-partner Helen C (who makes a cameo later in this collection), a lady who was in the publishing world, and wryly indulged my and my friends' wild antics for many years.

And I mention this because several of the pieces herein were written there, and one was even written *while* the place thronged around me. I wonder if you can identify which that was...

****

I promised myself (and publisher) that I would not *rewrite* anything, as that would be dishonest. Hence certain pieces were immediately thrown out, as being inappropriate in the current thought-climate, even if they were well written at source. Also, I reserve the right to change my mind. A simple thing, you might say, but not so, or *not so at the moment*. So, I haven't changed the text – merely tidied up some jolting shifts in tense, re-jigged the occasional minor false quantity, got rid of several inferior interior chimes – yes, *those* – and consolidated the punctuation: tightened the commas, polished the full stops.

Being uncomfortable, I always felt, is how one grows. And that will reappear, I'm sure, but I rejected the anti-Theistic stuff (and not on the grounds of pandering to a new Puritanism) and likewise most of the stuff about sex – my experiences of *that* belong in yesteryear. I say that with deep and pregnant melancholy, but my love belongs there. Still, it's impossible to get rid of it *all*, or I wouldn't be me, and you, perhaps, wouldn't be reading me.

So here I present – and I hope it entertains – selected pieces from approximately 2007 to the present. Why 2007? Well, that was the year *Losing Henry* was published, my first solo literary endeavour. I was then working as a reviewer for a magazine in Highgate, where I now live, in a preternaturally warm flat at the very top of a building hidden at the end of a silent cul-de-sac...

Thus I hope you find something entertaining, dear reader, in the following. They are not presented in order (for aesthetic reasons), but they span a big part of my life. From the carefree, sexy, twenty-nine-year-old to the overcast (but hopefully still humorous) forty-six-year-old, who no longer necessarily believes in love – from the childless to married father of two – through cancer and divorce, opera and literature, success and failure, losing my soul and finding my voice. I hope you'll excuse me for including some pieces that should have found a home at the time but did not, and some that were written solely for personal reasons.

And naturally, although I'm ashamed to have to say it, everything that follows comes with large bullet-pocked signposts, all reading TRIGGER WARNINGS AHEAD.

****

Lastly, a word on the title: I toyed with *Titbits With Williams*, to tie in with the reportage section in *Fairytales and Oddities*, and also with my online Isolation Sitcom or Covid-Comedy of the same name, but as some of the work dates from much earlier, I briskly discarded that idea. Also, having one's own name in the title seemed too self-referential, humourless and Kardashian-esque even for my post-modern sarcastic impulses.

There were undistinguished co-habitations with *The Collected Journalism* and, starkly, *Selected Journalism*. But who was the journalism bit really for? Who needs such soulless nonsense?

Selected Pieces seemed to fit for several reasons: firstly, the most obvious, musical one. Pieces are what I *do*, and have performed my entire adult life as a musician. Whether conducting a fully-staged opera, giving a piano recital of delicate ballades – what whimsy – singing Puccini arias at football World Cup events and West End award shows, or accompanying a suburban ballet school as the kids dance their routines, I just magic up the pieces. And magic is the correct word. I have always felt immense pride in having a job where joy is conjured from nothing, from sound in air.

Secondly, *Selected Pieces* allowed me to do what I alluded to above: including personal things. I wanted to include them because the dedicatee of this book is my son. He's eight, so won't be reading this (or anything by me) for a good while yet, but when he does, they'll be there, waiting for him. And there are further reasons to do with decorum, artifice, and what is still to come, in my life and in yours, on which more later...

So *Selected Pieces* it is. Let the curtain open.

Maspalomas, January 2022

In December 2021, five months after the publication of *Fairytales and Oddities*, I was invited to contribute my thoughts on what Christmas meant to me to a magazine with a Christian-slant, that has since (unsurprisingly and unsorrowfully) gone bust. In the end (at the end?) they rejected what I sent them. Perhaps, if they had published it, they would have survived, but gods work in pesky, mysterious ways, and we'll never know. Yet here is my offering, long and proudly uncut.

An Advent Calendar of Cautionary Tales

(To be read to children at bedtime...)

1.
The gingerbread man sits in the gingerbread house. All is gingerbread: he is unsure of anything. *Is the house flesh?* he ponders, *or am I merely house?*
He screams and screams but no one comes. No one ever will. No gods hear the shattered gingerbread cries of the ignored, forgotten gingerbread man...

2.
What was my best ever Christmas present?
Let me think.
Yes, it was a dog, definitely a dog.
Now, I know what you're thinking: a pet is for life, not just for Christmas. And that's broadly true. But, to be fair, the vet had literally given this dog a month to live. And I made that dog – let's call him Lucky – very happy for that month. It was the happiest fucking month of that dog's life. And at New Year's, when Lucky passed away, I took him out to the garden, and he joined all the other dogs I'd got for Christmas. So it goes.

3.
No son, I can't sleep with you. I have to sleep in my own room, and this is *your* room. I *want* to sleep in my own room. What's that? You think there's a monster under the bed? Well, yes, there *is* a monster under your bed, but it only wants to eat you. So let's not involve me, shall

we? Good night now, go straight to sleep, and don't make me use my opera voice.

4.

'I expected someone, I mean something...'
'Taller?'
'Well, yes,' said the knight looking down at the dragon.
'I'm afraid a dragon's size is proportionate to its hoard.'
'I heard your hoard was huge. Thousands and thousands and thousands of books...' said the knight, with glittering cruelty.
'It is.'
'But?'
'I went digital,' the dragon said, showing the knight the SD card they were both standing on.

5.

ONE DOOR CLOSES ANOTHER ONE OPENS
ONE DOOR CLOSES ANOTHER ONE OPENS
ONE DOOR CLOSES ANOTHER ONE OPENS
That's me steadily eating my way through a chocolate advent calendar...
It's also just what doors do. They open, they close: so no need to cry.
And tonight it's either serial killer documentaries or Christmas flicks.
We either slayin' or sleighin'.

6.

I'm a Santa-Truther parent, and it's time. Today I'm going to go down to the soft-play area with a megaphone and shit is gonna get real.
Are your kids misbehaving? For £100 I will come to your house dressed as the Grinch and throw your fucking Christmas tree out the fucking window.

7.

I was digging in our garden the other night, when I came across a chest full of gold coins. I was about to run straight in and tell your mother about it, but then I remembered why I was digging in our garden in the first place.

8.

With my blood pooling at his feet, the mugger bent down and began to turn out my pockets: wallet, travel card, bookmarks, tissues, Covid facemasks...

He started having second thoughts when my dark blood began to creep up his legs.

9.
Q: Why do ducks have webbed feet?
A: To stamp out forest fires.

Q: Why do elephants have flat feet?
A: To stamp out burning ducks.

10.
I live in a hot house to protect me from the cold outside. Inside my hot house I have a smaller cold house to protect my food from the heat of my hot house. Sometimes I take food out of the cold house and put it in an even smaller, much hotter house so that I can eat it.

11.
Twenty years from now you'll select an old jacket from the very back of the tallboy in the back of the backroom, and a facemask will slip from the pocket and fall at your crusty, twisted feet. As you retrieve it, you'll smile with fond resignation and think: Ah, those were the days. Covid-19, eh? Alpha? Omicron? Delta Variant? Monkey Pox? Yes, those truly were the days.
Then you'll sheath your machete and set out across the scorched hinterland in search of provisions, moving mainly at night to avoid the roving cannibal gangs.

12.
Thoughts of Nature:
While most birds are motivated by food, the woodpecker is motivated by its unrelenting hatred of trees. On a happier note, the Mandarin Chinese word for penguin literally translates as *business goose* – swings and roundabouts then, or the natural order of things.
Plants: I'm waving my genitals in the air...
Humans: Mmmm, fragrant.
The very fact that we know chameleons exist proves that they're worthless idiot failures.
...the paragon of animals... Shakespeare, *Hamlet...* but not the stingray that killed Steve Irwin. No, that one's a bastard.
I walked past the Build-A-Bear shop in Westfield shopping centre yesterday, sighed, shook my head sadly and thought: What heartless

bastard would build a bear into the world in the state it's in right now?

13.
2019 – AVOID NEGATIVE PEOPLE

2020 – AVOID POSITIVE PEOPLE

2021 – AVOID PEOPLE

2022 – A VOID
2023 – You may as well go ahead and pronounce the *l* in salmon. Nothing matters anymore.

14.
Sally prayed for a White Christmas, and that's what Sally got. God is good. But Sally's White Christmas was followed by a Red New Year, a Blue Easter, and a Green Halloween: few survived. Thanks for nothing, Sally. Thanks be to god.

15.
Mary knew a little lamb
With fleece as white as snow
But everywhere that Mary went
The lamb was sure to go.

It followed her to school one day,
So Mary told a cop...
Arrested with non-lethal force,
The lamb was told to stop.

16.
Christian thoughts:
Christianity is the best way to cure gayness. Of course it is, sure. Get on your knees, take a sip of wine, and allow the body of a man into your mouth.
I'm not sure about the whole abortion thing. While I like the idea of killing babies, I'm unsure about giving women the right to choose...
'My religion says I can't do that' – 'Fair enough.' – 'My religion says you can't do that.' 'Fuck off.'

'When God put a calling on your life, He already factored in your stupidity'... This is simultaneously the most disturbing and yet comforting thing I have ever heard.

There is a book, if I remember correctly, where there are two tangible characters, both naked, until a Big Brother-type authority shames them into wearing clothing. These characters have premarital sex, produce two sons, one of whom kills the other, and there is no record of them ever marrying. It's full of violence, murder and torture – it's a bestseller. I recommend it.

Ship's Log: Captain Noah. Life on my Ark is hard, but we all persevere. Still, unicorn steaks are very tasty...

17.

A friend in need... is a friend you could help.

When in Rome... eat pizza.

Fool me once... that's rude.

If it isn't broken, it might break at any immediate time...

Whatever doesn't kill you makes you weaker and kills you later on.

What doesn't kill you... disappoints me.

18.

The universe is an ongoing explosion. That's where you live, where *we* live: in an explosion. Also, we have absolutely no idea what *living* is, or any idea of time. Sometimes atoms arranged in a certain way just get very haunted by religion.

When the explosion is big enough, dust wakes up and thinks about itself.

That's *you*. Dust to dust.

19.

Some days you will feel like complete and utter trash. But when that happens, tell yourself: 'No, I am not trash. I am a stressed-out lump of coal on its way to being a diamond.'

Because you're a huge piece of coal-y potential right now – if a kid got you for Christmas, in that blackened stocking over the mantelpiece, you know that that kid would have had to have done something really impressive – like stealing jewellery off his dead grandmother's corpse, or something like that. The top level of huge – that's you! – go you!

People will criticise your dreams. 'You can't marry the moon.' 'Being sad is not a real job.' 'Stop summoning the devil.' Ignore them. Be real. Be yourself. Start a cult.

20.
'Can I get chips with my burger please?'
'Sure,' I reply, a thin expensive smile playing on my moistened lips.
'Will that be eat in or take out?'
'Piss off you nonce.'
I love working in the prison canteen.

21.
... And thus Odysseus set sail for Ithaca. As they rode the combers and breakers, Odysseus began his customary voyage pep talk.
'We now venture forth on our odyssey...'
A young sailor, raising his hand, gently interrupted: 'Excuse me, sir, what's an odyssey?'
'A long journey named after the only survivor.'
'Oh, ok. Wait, what?'

22.
'Did you know there are infinite parallel universes?'
'Yes...'

'Did you know there are infinite parallel universes?'
'No...'

23.
'I am ready to make the announcement.'
'Yes, Sir Isaac Newton, and we are ready to hear it.'
'I like them thicc af.'
'We cannot write that, Sir Newton...'
'Then let's go with: The greater the mass, the greater the force of attraction.'

24
All of a sudden you realise that it's all true... that dingo really did eat that baby, there really are crocodiles living in the LA sewers, those Sri Lankan conjoined twins really are a god, alien lizard people walk the earth among us (and eat whole guinea pigs like on that TV show V from the 80s), the Loch Ness monster, Elvis and Tupac are well and thriving, the sasquatch has long since been accepted into society and is living quietly on benefits, the CIA didn't kill JFK, his head just did that, acid rain, the hole in the ozone, climate-change, global warming,

killer bees, they're all still coming, Y2K zapped us after all, Nancy Spungen and Courtney Love are the same person, rock and roll is the devil's music, masturbation will make you blind, or at least nuttier than squirrel shit, Jesus loves you, everyone will be famous for fifteen minutes, the truth will set you free, punk and poetry aren't dead, Obama was white after all, love wins, hope is a good thing, we all got Mad Cow's Disease back in the fresh hundreds, the world is our fever dream, your pretty face is going straight to hell, and we're all on our way to the apocalypse.

Just blink your eyes if it's okay with you.

25.

Happy Christmas, all.

At the very least, start the day off with a smile and get it over with.

The Mysterious World of Randonautica

I first came across Randonautica, not through friends' recommendations, or my phone's App store, but through YouTube. The videos were sleazily compelling – murder victims found, mysterious messages, abrupt epiphanies, freaked-out (predominantly American) teens... I *dug* it all.

For those not in the know, Randonautica is technically a computer game. It is billed as such by its creator, Joshua Lengfelder, who launched it on 22nd February 2020. Apparently randomly, it generates coordinates that the user can travel to in a spirit of exploration of their locale, and report their findings via social media. The creator(s) intended it as 'an attractor of strange things', and that's precisely what he (they) got. Many people found highly disturbing things at the coordinates they were sent to, and the fact that the Randonautica logo features an owl didn't help things. Or rather it did: the owl is seemingly a reference to the OWL-Experiment and has close ties with the frequency illusion.

The frequency illusion (or frequency bias) is simply where one, after noticing something for the first time begins to see it everywhere – the term was coined in 2005, by Arnold Zwicky, a professor of linguistics at Stanford, and later Ohio State University. In an email he stated that: 'I consider the illusion a process involving dual cognitive biases – "selective attention bias"...' where we notice things that are pertinent to ourselves and disregard the rest, 'and "confirmation bias", where we look for things that support our hypotheses while disregarding obvious or potential counter-evidence.' So, being human. It is naturally mostly harmless, but has been noted to cause the 'worsening of symptoms in patients with schizophrenia'. Of course, too, there are legal implications, since 'eye witness statements and accounts of memory' can be influenced by the frequency illusion.

Before 2005 and Prof Zwicky, it was referred to as the Baader-Meinhof phenomenon, because in 1994 a man named Terry Mullen wrote a letter to the *New York Times*, in which he referenced the long-defunct West-German terrorist group as an example of an unusual word, phrase or idea that, once you come across it, recurs again for you within 24 hours. The next day others began writing in about the phenomenon, all using the catchy new moniker, and the floodgates could not be closed. Here we should briefly mention the Mandela Effect, where huge numbers of people collectively misremember facts or events. Paranormal researcher Fiona Broome coined the term, when, after reporting she had vivid and detailed memories of the great South African anti-Apartheid leader Nelson Mandela dying in prison in the 1980s, received thousands of letters from people with the same memories. That seems sketchy at best, but better examples include 97% of people asked believed there to be a hyphen in the brand name Kit Kat; almost all *Star Wars* fans remembering C-3PO as being all gold – he isn't, he has a silver lower right leg; the line 'Play it again, Sam' occurring in *Casablanca* – it doesn't, although the line 'Play it once Sam, for old times' sake' does, etc. There are dozens of famous movie ones. So, a poor cousin to the frequency illusion perhaps, but both phenomena share a similar birth.

And the OWL-Experiment was a reference to John Hopkins Hospital in Baltimore, where research on owls' brains (which has since been deemed sincerely medically unsound), in order to better understand why humans with ADHD struggle to focus, apparently involved forcing owls to look at dots on a TV screen or listen to sudden bursts of noise.

How does one get an owl to focus on anything? I reasonably wondered, *with their rotating heads?* And they were barn owls, common ones, those used in the Hopkins experiment and, while the owl on the Randonutica logo has its head inverted, although not under-the-wing, it is not obviously a barn owl. An exuberant design, it gazes out at you with upside-down eyes, and could clearly be perceived as creepy, much as the surrounding golden star could be perceived as being redolent of the occult.

I was also hazily aware that the owl features heavily, as a symbol of evil, a 'watching bird of darkness', in the magnificent depictions of hell by the painter Hieronymous Bosch.

****

A novelist friend expressed genuine concern when I described Randonautica and writing this piece to him. He called it a *grunting at the urinal* kind of thing to write about (and I saw his point, but a job is a job, and *Nature Human Behaviour* is a fine publication), but this didn't phase me when I downloaded the app and perused the options. I quickly realised that there was more to this than the glossy public surface…

The official website was headed by the aforementioned logo, followed by an arrow to a clearly different owl encased in what resembled a guitar pick. I made a mental note to check the significance of that later... Directly underneath it was: RANDONAUTICA is the world's **first and only** quantumly [sic] generated Create Your Own Adventure app. Beneath that was *Explore the world you never knew existed*. The Bold font and italics (and lower case) are all from the welcome page. Then follows a circular, white-bordered rendering of what I presume is meant to be the world, but looks like a pulsating brain in X-ray, labelled – 'quantumly random'.

What's with all the quantumly? I thought. But the website had that covered: the coordinates, your personal coordinates, were generated by personal electronic information – from social media, map locations, buying habits, and much more. In short, your online footprint would be fed through a quantum supercomputer in Australia (although the site promised more than one, as it grew) that would send back a place for you to visit, based on the digital information it received and subsequently processed.

Before I began any earnest Randonauting, I scanned the rest of the website. It was all New Age guff like Break Out Of Your Reality Tunnel, and... your mind is your guide as you... Set Your Intention to view the world differently... Yawning, I scrolled until I found this – The 9 Tenets of Randonauting. Oh, this should be worth a giggle, I realised, pressing on. I present them as they appear on the website (it's faster than paraphrasing, and the layout is theirs):

seeing in the dark
Dedication to exploring the uncertainty and blind spots of the world around us.

venture mindfully
Paying attention, practising safety and situational awareness.

be sincere
Show compassion and willingness to understand oneself and the community.

high vibes intent
Be luminous in thought and strive to radiate a positive mind set.

value inner life
Appreciation towards the self as the catalyst for an effect on the external environment.

bridge cultural gaps
Share experiences to assist in understanding the beauty of shared global consciousness.

transform and shift
Curiously test the theory of quantum randomization and the possibility to change a life path or shift into a new, better space and time.

bring a trash bag
Be respectful of the environment and always leave the place you travelled to better than what it was before.

synchronicity
Diving into randomness to find connections and meaning for both the individual and the community. Using serendipitous occurrences to guide you on your path.

I was hooked. The Americanisms were clear (trash, randomization, that comma before better space and time), and hopefully need no pointing out from me, but what about that *seeing in the dark*? and the amusingly tabloidal *luminous in thought*? Not to mention that *shared global consciousness*, and its unimpeachable ambition. These guys wanted it, wanted the whole world, and I found that I minutely admired that. I had an issue with *synchronicity*, which clearly didn't mean what they thought it did: but that was tiny barracuda compared to what came next.

I went Randonauting.

Set Your Intention. I requested an 'emotional' connection with where I was sent. I could request a 'memory', or a 'potluck', or even a 'make your own' future.

Feverishly, I typed in my name and filled out the details.

– LOCATION REQUIRED –

I put in my location.

– What are you looking for?

By now with somewhat bloodshot eyes, I tapped in MEMORIES.

And then an interesting thing happened.

Randonautica sent me to a famous author's old abode – understandable, since I had bought a book by the same author on Amazon recently – so the algorithm recognised that. It sent me to a place where there was a connection of some kind. Cool. It's *quantumly* working, I thought, as I gathered myself to go to the second suggested place.

Then a curious thing happened. It sent me to a place that even *I* didn't remember, until I got there, or almost there. I approached the old school, Barrow Hill, and suddenly memories flooded back. Of E.T. picture books – yes, it was that long ago – and not being allowed to leave class to urinate, and bottles of milk – I'm guessing 1987 and mid-Thatcher Milk fiasco... Yet no one alive knew that I had ever even attended that school for a couple of terms when my family first moved to London. My mother had been dead since 2015, and my father since 2011... But that Aussie quantum supercomputer found it and picked up on it and took me back there. It was... unnerving, yet exciting.

After a dizzy weekend, punctuated by genteel bursts of weak paranoia, I asked the parent of a child whom I routinely took care of, if I could take the (then) nine-year-old boy, Giuseppe, randonauting with me. His mother, understandably, asked: 'What on earth is that?'

I hastily explained.

'So what's up with it? You haven't needed my permission before to take him anywhere...'

I replied that randonauting had suffered some bad press of late, and that I would be grateful if she could Google it before giving me the all clear to take her son, no matter how well-acquainted we were... She went away to check...

****

Randonauting had led to finding money (Andy Bidwell found £70,000 in a bag at his coordinates in Scotland in July last year) and drugs (a vacationing couple in Missouri was sent to a cocaine stash worth over $1,000000 in December), but nothing was as infamous as what happened when a group of US teens headed out to a beach in Duwanish Head, Puget Sound, West Seattle, on June 9th, following their Randonautica route, and came across two suitcases that contained the dismembered bodies of two people.

I doubted the verisimilitude of the story as much as I doubted the cloudless mental health of American teens recounting a road trip. But it was true, and I watched the suitcases being found on YouTube – it is there still. *That* was my introduction to all this. The bodies were those of Jessica Lewis, 35, and Austin Wenner, 27, and their landlord, Michael Dudley, 62, had been detained and held on a $5,000,000 bail. He has not been charged, so I cannot comment on him, but I can comment on details that the police have released. Before being chopped up, Austin Wenner had been shot in the back of the head once, but Jessica Lewis had been shot many more times, and also stabbed. You don't need me to point out the implications of this, and we await the findings of the trial…

****

Later that night Giuseppe's mother texted me possibly the only sane thing about the whole situation: If the boy agrees, then that's fine. Just make sure you're back by 7, for dinner as usual.

Thus a few days later, after picking him up from school, I explained Randonauting to the boy (who seemed agreeable so long as we could stop at his favourite health food shop on the way back and buy almond milk), leaving out the gruesome murder stuff, and we put in our location – somewhere near Finsbury Park – and our intention – EMOTIONS – and then we were off, trundling along the blue line on the unspooling map.

The first coordinates sent us to the middle of an empty field in Highgate Wood. I asked, 'So is this an important place for you?'

'No, this is just rubbish,' he said. 'Can we get almond milk now?'

'Look around. Anything important? Right here. In this spot.'

'No, absolutely nothing. I don't know what you guys [adults] care about half the time. What was all that chess club stuff about? And I never even *wanted* to be head of the debating team…'

'Ok, *fine*. Let's go.'

The second coordinates – our intention this time was MEMORIES – led us back down the hill, and gave us time for sweet reflection.

'Where's the almond milk shop?'

'Sorry, we missed that *waaaay* back…'

'This is total shit,' said the kid.

'Can we watch that language, please, Giuseppe?'

'Why?'

'Because swearing isn't cool at your age.'

'But *you* swear.'

'But not in front of you.'

'But you *swear*.'

'And?'

'Where's the fucking almond milk?'

'*Jesus*. But firstly, no, it's not just about your age. Hey, look: we're here…'

Randonautica had brought us to a stop along the Heritage Trail known as Parkland Walk South. We paused. The kid looked decidedly non-plussed, so I suggested, 'Do you need a pee?' Indicating a clump of dense shrubbery over yonder, I said: 'Just go behind there…'

But something had happened to his eyes that I took a moment to register. They had changed from the tired, trusting schoolroom brown to a tele-visual horrified stare.

'What on earth's...' I began, but he lifted an arm and pointed at something over my head. I swivelled, half expecting the axe of a serial murderer to swipe my bonce in half, but there was nothing.

'Did you do this to make fun? That's unkind. It's *cruel.*'

'What? Do *what*? Of course I would never be cruel...'

Then I noticed something nailed to the tree, a piece of wood with something carved on it. My eyes were obviously not any competition for his, so I craned and squinted to read... There was a name I didn't recognise and underneath, a date I didn't recognise. 'I don't know what you mean...' I began, as I turned back, but by then his face was a mask of tears. How had there been time for so many tears?

We descended from Parkway South the mostly muddy way and went to Café Tit-Ti Burger on Highgate Hill. Through the sobbing, oh god, and several hot chocolates, oh god, and then over a comfort/ sympathy pizza, oh god, he spilled it all out. His father had died serving overseas... It took me a full painfully disjointed hour to work out what had happened.

The name on the carving was his father's. And the date was the date of his father's recent death.

Flabbergasted, I delivered young Giuseppe home, with many a gracious gulp for his unsettled condition, then sprinted back, but the wooden plaque was gone. I jumped up to see where it had been. The nail hole was there, but nothing else... I walked home slowly, stunned, under mineral stars, and went to bed and fitful sleep.

The next morning I called Joshua Lengfelder.

****

I explained the gist of this article to his adorable secretary, Amy, but was forbidden access to the mighty Lengfelder. Amy was charming incarnate though, all husky-toned and loftily amused, and despite being on different continents, I lost no time in gallantly asking her out. After exchanging personal details, and promises of a long-distance Zoom-sex relationship – post-modernity at its erotic zenith – I tried another way to get to Lengfelder. He had been releasing videos on YouTube himself, as Watch With Josh, under the username Randonautica App.

Watching Josh, on camera, was uncanny. The only one who could feasibly explain any of this was a twenty-something dude with a ginger beard and untidy black haircut that was most often constrained under reversed baseball caps or slogan-ed bandannas. Josh favoured plaid and cotton pastel shirts and talked fluently about Randonautica, selling its great points – the freshness of the format, the innovation of exploiting randomness, the beauty of the vision... but it was all flimflam, and no substance. He didn't want the whole world and everything in it, as I had at first presumed: he was a charisma-bypass, an insight-vacuum. I listened for almost two pleasurable hours and learned, pleasurably, nothing, nada, zilch, 0. He talked with the self-awareness of a crayon. Yet I warmed to him. It's as if everything beautiful was at his fingertips, and then humanity moved in, and it was all instantly frittered away. The whole world globed in a wine glass.

I DM'ed his channel repeatedly; Lengfelder never got back to me. But Amy did, oh yes, but for other reasons...

****

So, whither Randonautica? Well, nowhere, as it turned out. It all just withered. The app disappeared from iOS and Android, the founders' YouTube livestream ceased in October 2021, and all that remains online is what we say about it.

Giuseppe returned to school, hopefully not too traumatised, Jessica Lewis and Austin Wenner are still murder victims, chopped up, their bodies discarded off Duwanish Head, Arnold Zwicky got tenure and is still ploughing on, my novelist friend's latest got shortlisted for many major literary prizes, the owls still hoot, Michael Dudley awaits sentencing, the supercomputer whirrs quantumly on, Terry Mullen (remember him?) is surely long dead, and Amy sends nudes.

But it was highly diverting while it lasted.

Nature Human Behaviour, 2021

Brenda Williams (1948–2015) was my mother, but more importantly she was a poet. Her early work was technically glittering and intense, and she didn't shy away from the Big Themes of the day, tackling racist issues, the-battle-of-the-sexes (this was the 80s), OPEC, Thatcherism, Gaddafi (the first time), the Rushdie Affair, MAD nuclear proliferation and much more. Back then she wrote stream-of-consciousness, almost Beat, little punctuation, no apologies. The prosody was clear enough; it read easily.

In 1984 her classic work *Death and the Maiden* appeared. Telling the dual story of her mother Kathleen's death from tuberculosis in the 60s alongside her own coming-of-age, the long poem crystallized her talent. I don't think she ever bettered it, but that's just my opinion: after all, who else's would it be?

She was mesmerizing on the *Death and the Maiden* tour, or perhaps I loved her. At just six, one of my most vivid memories is of her reading that opening line in some bookshop or other: *the café by the water was becoming shabby*... The *in medias res* and use of the neglected 'shabby' created, to my mind, a perfect opening sentence – morally, technically, and structurally. It gave me an early appreciation of rhetoric.

But Brenda's star wasn't to last. Some talents explode brightly and wink out of existence like a knuckleclick. Hers wasn't like that; it was painfully slow. Her downfall was mental-health, a depression so thorough that it killed her at least three times. First, it killed all of us – family, acquaintances, neighbours and carers... Then it killed her talent: by the end she was simply versifying old hatreds and birdcalls from the hospice window... And then it physically killed her. But it also killed a hundred other, less significant things in her life before the final one. Nothing could be done for her by then: depression was all consuming, and all controlling.

But the birds still sing...

An extra: I used an online App to calculate the time between the 10th December 1948 and the 15th May 2015, Brenda's dates. Both were Fridays. I was born on Good Friday, 1978. My brother was also born on a Friday, in 1972. My mother lived for 24,262 days or 66.43 years. She lived for 582,287 hours, or 34,937220 minutes. Or even this: 2,096,233,200 seconds. She made a billion, in one way.

****

Almost a year after her death, a Memorial was held in St Martin-in-the-Fields, on London's Trafalgar Square. I was expecting a modest gathering, but nearly two hundred people turned up that gorgeous

April afternoon to remember Brenda. Here is the eulogy that I gave for her that day.

Eulogy

Thank you all for coming. I'm Ezra, Brenda's son. It's wonderful to see so many old, and some new, faces here today.

You proceed by quotation, or so the reviewer is told. This is sound: it's what's *there*. The words are what there is or what's left. And in a way I am asked to review her life. But of course the work isn't all that's left – I am here and my brother Isaiah, I am a writer and she was a writer, so there will always be a part of me that examines the work to locate the person. I never met Nabokov or Bellow, but I *know* them, or the best of them. This is also sound. The best is what goes on the page. Perhaps that's even truer of poets than novelists, given the inimical intimacy of the form, and the choice.

But she was my mother, and this is where the difference lies. It's extraordinary to me now, reading her, because I was actually there when most of it was written. Playing with my Lego around her feet – in those days she used to stand at a window to write. Later, irritating the piano at the end of the corridor, later still having youthfully solemn sexual dramas over the telephone... by then her headphones would be in. This is important because, even though I was a child, and didn't feel the weight of words keenly, lines such as

The Return

in St John's Wood evening comes slowly to the listless trees
listlessness much the same as that at the edge of Wychwood
only the difference matters and the diurnal form from
which the night takes hold they do not disappear vestigial
here their substance smokes on the skyline reality is
memory the forest trees they do not disappear and
dark is the light within and dark is their hypostasis
though darkness firstly comes to the topmost forest fragments
light comes lastly to the darkest the difference is within and
the difference between futility and despair is the
tree in apparition and the way the night takes hold and
futility is eternal and is not of this world

and lines such as

Oxford from a Prison Cell

after seven days and you come as a faithless woman
though the sun coloured iris hurts it breaks towards the sunlight
Caltha palustris unearthed closes only to the dark
the body will fight to the death for its own dignity
while the mind more able to imagine a walled up tomb
than a room with a locked door the eternity of one
and the time of the other where the mind free wheeling can
recall only the absurd I sat once with my back to
another door learning Greek for the first time and the last
time learning Greek then you came with cups of kings you cannot
help me now let's go on together turn and turn about
I will make the songs and you shall grind them out

... they take me back instantly to when I first heard them, indeed
where I was standing, or what I was holding in my hands when she
first read them to me. But why should I remember that, if the work
isn't worth it:

(A sonnet from The Pain Clinic)

I want to leave something behind that will
Tell of the days and nights alone with fear,
To emerge from the inexorable
Instinct just to quietly disappear.
And I wished to retrace a narrative
From the outline of footprints on the way,
Somehow to keep going, I tried to give
Back to language and was able to say
Something of the joy that it gave to me
Beyond the chaos and the far street cry
Answering an echo and endlessly
Pursuing me demanding a reply,
Ineffaceable, insignificant
As graffiti lingering on a wall.

Well, I can tell you, Brenda, the poetry will survive. You will be read,
Plug, or Pluggs, my pet name for her. She liked to claim that this
stemmed from her ability to plug everything up, and that may be true,

I don't recall, but more likely it came about because a childhood speech-impediment caused sudden plosive sounds to erupt from my throat: Mum, Love, Lug, Above, Plug... Anyway, Plug it was.

There are so many wonderful stories about her I could tell you. She was such a vivacious soul during my early years. And later, when depression gripped her, our relationship became a deeper one. But I guess I have to boil it down to a few poignant moments.

So I'll not tell you about her embarrassment at mistaking Messiaen for Handel – her mind was elsewhere, elsewhere by some 250 years! Or the hilarity that ensued when, to cope with a sick cat's bladder problem, I resorted to stealing toilet paper en-masse, from my school. Or even about the time Isaiah came home from Vietnam and his suitcase turned out to contain a preposterously large insect that had inter-Continentally hitched a ride. The words 'Die!' and 'You Bastard!' were used, as well as the heel of a shoe.

These are all good. But the two most perfect moments, or at least the ones that inform my heart of who I am, are these:

Gertrude Falk was a character. Two others shared the Nobel Prize based on her research. She was Professor Emeritus at UCL, and a fabulously aloof and kind old Jew. It's fair to say I adored her from the start. She and my mother had a very serious relationship: talks, tea, tragedies. But when she was with me Gertrude unleashed her quietly anarchic side. I'd ply her with red wine and we'd laugh and argue about the default stupidity of people, volcanoes, the War, natural selection, UFOs, horticulture, Shakespeare, languages, and Jewishness – of *course* Jewishness. Usually we would be sober to meet Brenda, but just this once we got carried away in The Roebuck pub in Hampstead, on Pond Street. We both, Gertrude (81) and me (31) looked suitably shamefaced until my mother said: 'Gertrude, if you were 50 years younger you could be my daughter-in-law!' It was one of the great moments of my life.

And then this – I was briefly playing jazz piano in a restaurant in Bayswater that has still not been replaced, I must unsorrowfully add, after more than a decade... But Brenda came, to hear me and have a free meal. I don't remember what I was playing, probably something by Bill Evans or Errol Garner, but apparently the people on the table next to her were complaining about the amplification. When I finished my set and sat down beside her, she pointedly announced: 'Some people have absolutely no taste.' I never forgot that loyalty.

I also admired her resolute refusal to admit that her postcode was NW8 ZERO-A-R, and not NW8 OAR, as in the oar of a boat... A poet for the little things...

It should also be mentioned, her looks. She was a very beautiful woman. Her grandson Eli, whom she only met a handful of times before the end, once pointed at the TV and shouted: 'NANA!' And on the screen was the beautiful actress Courtney Cox.

Her voice, too, was a source of life. The mid-sentence salutary lilt followed by the contrived contralto looping-drop... Most of you here know me, if not only as Brenda's son, then as an opera singer. Of course I was studying when we lived together – in a sense she learnt alongside me – and you'd be surprised the interest she took in voice. We'd watch and discuss Orson Welles' Macbeth and how he cadenced each speech... She was an avid Domingo fan, although like a true connoisseur, preferred Aragall in *Tosca*, and she would often listen to Bach, Elgar, Mahler, Eva Cassidy, Bob Dylan, Herbert Howells and many more.

When I was awarded the Howells Prize at the Royal College of Music Brenda was in attendance and stayed all day. She didn't congratulate me or kiss me, but she did something she never did: she bought me a drink at the bar. And she knew that I knew that she was proud of me.

****

I recently took a trip to the Hollies [a wood in Leeds], a place she loved with abandon. It's much the same as when she took Isaiah and me there as children. I hope it doesn't change. Her spirit is there if it is anywhere, and her spirit is quite a spirit.

A friend remarked recently that I must miss her terribly, and I thought: Of course. But the truth is, she's all over my study, on my shelves, on my desk, she's in the faces of her grandchildren and in the phrases they use, so how can I truly miss her? She's still *here*.

But it does surprise me how much she can be suddenly on the mind. I was on the way back from Marrakesh recently with my family, and I thought *she never flew*. She never experienced that simple miracle of human invention, being above. She only went abroad once, to Holland, with me, by Jetfoil. I was a boy singer at the opera house and she played my unwilling chaperone. We took canal trips and visited the Rijksmuseum, but not Anne Frank's house. That was too close to the heart. Being entombed and writing was something she came too know all too well.

I made her alternately laugh, frown, scowl, shake her head, laugh, cringe, look resignedly at the floor, look steadfastly out the window, and finally laugh when, on a train journey across the famously flat

Dutch landscape, I tirelessly shouted *VATCHTOWER!* when we passed any structure over three storeys high. We also got fabulously lost in the Red-Light district, got almost sick on white chocolate and petted the tame pigeons that seemed to enchant her. And I guess they would be enchanting, with nothing to compare.

And so, Brenda Williams, poet, campaigner for justice, protester, my mother, I wish to offer you thanks and love. You would often say to people – forcefully – how I had *introduced* you to certain music. But it's an inverted truth. Let's be clear. I would never have been the musician or person I am today if it weren't for you. I would probably never have even heard such music if it weren't for the strength of your conviction that I should somehow... create. My brother and I are men today because of you. And there will be generations to come who will know who you were and what you stood for and stood up for. And I remember your father Cyril, and your mother, Kathleen Smyth of Attymass, County Mayo, Ireland.

I would like to end with a poem and a quick story that Brenda enjoyed telling. The story concerns the mighty Robert Lowell, drunk and slurringly belligerent at a book reading... A woman in the audience asked, 'Mr Lowell? Where does your writing come from?'

Here one imagines Lowell taking a long drag of his cigarette before replying, 'From my balls, madam, from my balls.'

Then the woman asked: 'And what colour ink do you use?'

For The Union Dead

The South Boston aquarium stands
in a Sahara of snow now. Its broken windows are boarded.
The bronze weathervane cod has lost half its scales.
The airy tanks are dry.

Once my nose crawled like a snail on the glass;
my hand tingled
to burst the bubbles
drifting from the noses of the cowed, compliant fish.

My hand draws back. I often sigh
For the dark downward and vegetating kingdom
Of the fish and reptile. One morning last March,
I pressed against the new barbed and galvanized

fence on the Boston Common. Behind their cage,
yellow dinosaur steamshovels were grunting

as they cropped up tons of mush and grass
to gouge their underworld garage.

Parking spaces luxuriate like civic
sandpiles in the heart of Boston.
A girdle of orange, Puritan-pumpkin colored girders
braces the tingling Statehouse,

shaking over the excavations, as it faces Colonel Shaw
and his bell-cheeked Negro infantry
on St Gaudens' shaking Civil War relief,
propped by a plank against the garage's earthquake.

Two months after marching through Boston,
half the regiment was dead;
at the dedication,
William James could almost hear the bronze Negroes breathe.

Their monument sticks like a fishbone
in the city's throat.
Its Colonel is as lean
as a compass-needle.

He has an angry wrenlike vigilance,
a greyhound's gentle tautness;
he seems to wince at pleasure,
and suffocate for privacy.

He is out of bounds now. He rejoices in man's lovely,
peculiar power to choose life and die –
when he leads his black soldiers to death,
he cannot bend his back.

On a thousand small town New England greens,
the old white churches hold their air
of sparse, sincere rebellion; frayed flags
quilt the graveyards of the Grand Army of the Republic.

The stone statues of the abstract Union Soldier
grow slimmer and younger each year –
wasp-waisted, they doze over muskets
and muse through their sideburns…

Shaw's father wanted no monument
except the ditch,
where his son's body was thrown
and lost with his 'niggers'.

The ditch is nearer.
There are no statues for the last war here;
on Boylston Street, a commercial photograph
shows Hiroshima boiling

over a Mosler safe, the 'Rock of Ages'
that survived the blast. Space is nearer.
When I crouch to my television set,
the drained faces of Negro school-children rise like balloons.

Colonel Shaw
is riding on his bubble,
he waits
for the blessèd break.

The aquarium is gone. Everywhere,
giant finned cars nose forward like fish;
a savage servility
slides by on grease.

April 2016

With reviewing, the rules are: stay away from anything you're unlikely to warm to, proceed gently and by quotation, and try not to ruin careers. These days I adhere strictly and almost charmingly, to all three: but the following pieces date from 2004 – 2006, when I was a spiteful literary brat (my first full book, *Losing Henry*, was still to appear), and didn't care less what anyone thought. I don't care today, it's true, but for very different reasons.

Why was I working for a poetry magazine? Well, we know *that*, don't we? A poet for a mother, and a poet for a namesake – Ezra Pound. It could be pointed out that mentally ill people naming their children after other mentally ill people could be seen as falling at the first hurdle...

These reviews all come from a single magazine – *Poetry Express* – and were chosen from the throng for apparently being the funniest ones, and those with most heart. Reading them now, I see why they were chosen, but a patina of shame sullies them for me. It's a beautiful day, sure, but one with heavy expectations of slate-coloured clouds and the dredging snore of thunder. Trip-wired and booby-trapped, they were written with a sense of lit purpose, and are included here with the caveat of non-judgement – you were young once too, remember?

Book Reviews (Part 1)

Eamer O'Keeffe – *Esnesnon a collection of Nonsense Poetry & Proze*, Matrix; Debjani Chatterjee – *Jade Horse Torso – Poems and Translations*, Sixties Press; Zebrakilla – *Mannish*, Ephesus the Conquering Lion; Anno Birkin – *Who Said the Race is Over?*, Laurentic Wave Machine.

It's hard to dislike Eamer O'Keeffe, not least for her name. Like a zanier and often cleverer Wendy Cope, her poems abound with linguistic pirouettes and delicate rhythms. In a reader she inspires what all writers aim for: a reluctant smile, then an unreluctant one. I first encountered her work some years back in a series of small books (approximately fourteen centimetres by ten) that showed her to be an accomplished visual artist as well as poet. This ability also plays a part in her new book *Esnesnon a collection of Nonsense Poetry & Proze* [sic]. In a way, prose isn't quite right – even the un-scanned pieces (and there are really only three in a book of over thirty) are poems of a sort, with in-rhymes and elegiac sentence structures harking back to some of the better 'Beat' work and, more recently, the glorious patter of John Hegley. My two personal favourites are *Retreat* – which perfectly demonstrates O'Keeffe's love of language – and *Understanding Poetry*, a lovely justification for the end of a relationship. Recommended all round.

Likewise, Debjani Chatterjee's collection of her own poems and assorted translations, *Jade Horse Torso*, is an open jewel-box. There is the occasional dud – *Cat's Purr*, a sentimental ditty in memory of a pet, hinges on clichés such as 'crisp salad days', 'warm summer days' and the entirely tabloidal 'purr is purrfect' – but there aren't many more. Of course the Rabindranath Tagore is extraordinary, numinous and prescient, but it was a pleasant surprise to read some living Indian writers, Safuran Ara, Usha Verma and Naggar Khan included, whom one doesn't get the chance to enjoy very often in this country. Sixties Press – more please! Chatterjee's own poems seem to stem from a deep vein of human understanding and her referenced sources of inspiration reflect this: William Carlos Williams, *Star Trek* and *Birdwatching on Inland Fresh Waters*. If I hadn't read the book, I'd find this amusing. I have however read the book, and I think it's entirely apt.

I can't say the same for Zebrakilla, whose new book *Mannish* shows no details of by whom or indeed when it was published, or of any hint of copyright. I opened it with some trepidation. Within two pages I developed a coruscating migraine and went to bed. When I next tackled it, half an hour was all it took to hospitalise me with a ruptured spleen. It wasn't Zebrakilla's fault, but lines such as: *To penetrate the crowd / To liberate the crowd / BLOOD!!!! / BLOOD!!* can't have helped. (And what is it with those hicuppy exclamation marks?) However, Zebrakilla's poems would work if set to music and rapped, and in the book he does describe them as lyrics.

Don't be fooled by my facetiousness: I did have enormous fun with this book. There are lovely comic moments, such as when Zebrakilla rewrites the Ten Commandments from the viewpoint of 'a sick twisted sista', Ms D, an author surrogate *par excellence.* Number 6 is: *Thou shall not touch me or stare at me too long.* Fantastic, as are the knowingly overblown yet curiously beautiful section headings, *Oblongata Rhinestones, Euphoric Entanglements* and *Stratospheric Lamentations.* Uplifting feelings are created too, notably in *Suicide Letter* and *The Phoenix*, but to quote them would spoil the effect. I would say though that this book is worth the price of admission alone for the genius of All I Want For Christmas, a poem so obviously brilliant and funny that one wonders why it hasn't been written before.

And let's get one last thing clear: Zebrakillas's use of the 'n' word... An author photo adorns the back of the book, and the author is demonstrably black, and fine-looking fellow to boot. Thus his use of the word is of the spiritually reclaimed variety, not the street-parlance variety, and means, in this case, *how people see me*. As 'urban' – a miserable term – writing, it works and certainly doesn't jar. Especially *Fever*, an indictment of small-time drug dealers, and *Dreamer*, where Zebrakilla imagines for his children a life without prejudice. Oh, if it could be that way...

Anno Birkin could, and should, have been a great writer. However, he died in 2001 at the age of twenty-one, and the world's talent base dipped slightly. In Bruce Robinson's foreword – he of *Withnail and I* fame – Birkin is described as 'a great poet... and we can only be amazed by what he could do with half a yard of ink'. His book *Who Said the Race is Over?* (his title or one given posthumously?) struck me in various ways.

Firstly, the writing is terrifically frank, an often admirable quality but one that can, as in *Terrorist Attack*, written for September 11th 2001, lead to a certain sentimental bias: *Don't get me wrong – I long to know a / time that knows no pain, but there is / only gain where there is empathy. / I hunger for the fantasy that all men know each other.* And doesn't he mean sympathy not empathy? Yet this is an introspective frankness and not the self-obsessed knowing frankness associated with many twenty-something male writers. Perhaps this is a bad example too, since 9/11 reduced even the most seasoned poets and novelists to myopic wrecks. A better one might be: *So with eyes to the floor I stand, sorry and sore, / and I long for that sleep to defeat me, / so the whole world may breathe me as you did so easily, / silent in moments of knowing.*

Secondly, examine this beautiful stanza:

> To you, my pages may seem insignificant,
> pointless and vain. So be it. Treat them
> not as a meaning or a collection of
> words, but as a spear, parting the flesh
> so that it may sting the core of self –
> so that it may release its venom into your
> system and stop at nothing to tear apart your soul.
> Read again my friend, watch how the words bend.

He wrote that in 1996, aged fifteen. Fifteen! I confess when I opened this book and at the bottom of the page read 'aged 15', I groaned. Then I read the poem. Note the Shakespearean linkage of 'word' and 'spear', the four-word-long anaphora in lines five and six, and the nod to the reader, breaking the Fourth Wall, 'my friend', in the final one. Not even Larkin was doing that at fifteen, and as a teenager, Auden was busily plagiarizing everyone he'd ever read.

Thirdly, my original impression of the illustrations and varied doodlings that adorn the text in myriad colours was that, although undeniably fetching, they only served to distract from the real purpose of the book. I thought they had been included either because the publishers were frightened that page after page of shining pain and gilded beauty would put the average reader off, or because his family felt they contributed to the understanding of the poems. They don't. But they do contribute to the understanding of Birkin's psychological state, something that infuses the work anyway, thus rendering the pretty scribblings redundant... However, it all makes sense at the end when, shatteringly, what he wrote in his final hours is printed in full colour facsimile. It isn't an easy journey, dear reader, but it's worth getting there.

I remembered what Henry James said: Tell a dream, lose a reader. I mention this because Anno Birkin sure does recount a lot of dreams, not to mention daydreams, musings, visions, meanderings, flights of whimsy and tangential imaginings. In fairness, James was talking about prose, but the quote applies equally well to prosody, I feel. Yet the voice we are presented with is so fresh and energetic that its powerful reverberation carries you through. In other words, the dreams aren't a problem.

Quotation is the only real evidence the reviewer has, and one proceeds by it. But quotes bring to mind other quotes and thus allusions. It's easy, though perhaps ill-advised, to judge a writer by their allusions to others, but they can help locate the genesis of the talent. I spoke about Shakespeare earlier (and some would argue he's the only one that counts), but notice the homage to Donne here:

> He comes like morning, when he does come,
> unsure and unspecific,
> with opal and magnetic eyes,
> with handsome and intrepid hands,
> with open arms like velvet web.

Touched reads like a Bob Dylan lyric and thrums with sharp acoustic rhythms. *Zie Punk Volk* takes us to the Blues, and *Dreams of Waking* contains wisps of Bukowski. A strange final thought: I suddenly imagined looking back through this piece and counting all the adjectives to see if they would add up to twenty-one. I think they would add up to so much more.

R.I.P. Anno Birkin, you beautiful, sad, sad soul.

****

An aside – when I wrote the Anno Birkin book review [see above], I was literally reviewing what the magazine, *Poetry Express*, put into my hands to review – I would turn up each month at the offices in a squat cube of a building, after huffing my way up the stubbornly steep hill, and the editor, Simon, would dump a pile of books, pamphlets, manifestos, un-versified diatribes at this or that, single scrawled sheets on the death of a pet (complete with photographs) and much more straight into my open rucksack, with the cheerful directive: 'See what you make of some of these.' Such is the state of poetry. A Millennial scallywag, I read the books and reviewed the ones I chose to, without undue background research: for me, in those days, it was about the words and only the words.

A little under five years later (in 2009) I attended a swanky party in Kensington with a girlfriend who was on the cusp of fame, something she was later to modestly achieve. At that party, around midnight, I found myself drinking at the bar next to an elegant older lady who didn't seem to want to be there any more than I did. A beer with lime slices for me, a Negroni with floating fruit for her. After a gulp of time I turned and sighed: 'Which one's yours?' I was referring to the various charities that were being represented that evening... She laughed and we set to chatting.

Jane, as she introduced herself, was there representing Anno's Africa, a charity that runs educational arts projects for children living in slum conditions in Kenya and in cities and towns in Northern Malawi. As she talked, impulses began to slowly fire in my brain, and I made the necessary connections: of *course*.

I had been drinking with Anno's aunt – the famous one, Jane Birkin, who sang all those French songs. After we overcame the coincidence, of both meeting at all, let alone the fact that I was one of only a handful of people who had actually reviewed *Who Said the Race is Over?*, we had a good natter, and a great evening. When I left, the air around me felt suddenly spacious and exuberant. And I never saw her again.

But let's progress on, without regret, and into the second sheath of reviews...

****

Alan Dent – *Town*, Smokestack Books; G.S. Sharat Chandra – *Immigrants of Loss*, Hippopotamus Press; William Oxley – *Namaste: Nepal Poems*, Hearing Eye; Pascale Petit – *The Huntress*, Seren; Pascale Petit – *The Wounded Deer*, Smith/Doorstop Books.

Urb Versus Rus could be a fitting alternative title for Alan Dent's new long poem *Town*. Besides being long (fifty-eight pages of startlingly small print), it is also mysteriously devoid of commas, although apostrophes appear to cut the mustard. This does beg the question whether one needs a full stop or question mark at the end of a twenty-eight-line sentence, especially when it's followed by a line space before just continuing in a different font.

Ah, yes, the fonts: Dent uses five and each conveys a different voice in the presumably autobiographical family narrative, although these overlap and change at moments of high emotion. In fact, the voices use such similar language, word-ordering and figures of speech that they're really one anyway, and if that's the point then it works well, giving a unifying structure to a challenging conceit. And while the vision of urban grime and deprivation pitched against rustic innocence is far from original, it doesn't grate and is, at turns, both beguiling and unobtrusively affecting. However, one does find oneself thinking, to paraphrase Rossini's alleged comment about Wagner, that there are some brilliant moments and some rather poor quarters of an hour.

Immigrants of Loss is a volume that combines the startling imagery of Updike – every other line an extraordinary metaphor or construction – with the visionary scope of Ondaatje. The front flap informs us that G.S. Sharat Chandra 'takes what he needs' from the cultures of India, British India and the USA and 'conjures a world of ethnic diversity and linguistic flexibility'. If I were him I'd fire my editor: this work isn't constrained by boundaries and would read as well anywhere on the planet so long as literature was still appreciated there.

'Nibbled eyes', '...dips absurdly into the juggled air', 'nomad in a mist of grapes', '...watched / on the wall my shadow / straightening its sparse hair...' Most poets would kill for these throwaways, and many novelists too.

Sharat Chandra's kind of writing transcends not only race and country, but seemingly the page itself, in so far as it is impossible to peg down to any style and genre except that of the exceptional. I don't want to spoil the languid story with its tingles-up-the-spine finale, so I'll merely quote a stanza and urge to procure this book any way you can.

> He'll clear the transgressing blades,
> alone even if it be for a moment
> to hold the deep dear face,
> speak uncomplainingly of links
> in speechless, human grace.

Remaining in the same part of the world, William Oxley's little book *Namaste: Nepal Poems* with its pretty inside cover design of grooming chimps (courtesy of Emily Johns at Aldgate Press), doesn't seem so good. The comparison's unfair though. This is a far sweeter publication that conforms to Western views of exoticism, Goddesses whose mere mention seems to require exclamation marks, and mystic temples too ineffable for syntax. In *Durbar Square* there is a good example of this: 'Oh, look at that poor doggie' a child cries upon seeing 'a black cur' crawl forth to die. This is what I'm talking about. This is a characteristically Western insult to Indian street dogs who are highly distinctive creatures – they look like abruptly promoted rats, bemused by their sudden elevation, and quietly pining for a return to the rodent kingdom. Hit and miss, in other words.

Much travel writing suffers from this problem, but this is a book of poetry and is thus doubly indictable. Still, the longer pieces here are well worth a look, notably *Seeing Not Knowing*, and *The Real Skirting The Unreal*, and, if you can get past the dogs in the opening line, *Nepal*, a fine poem that deserves to be read and then read again with a little less expectation.

I came to Pascale Petit's *The Huntress* expecting something quite different, not least because I thought she was a he. It may have been stupidity, or tiredness, or an existential crisis – can I write anything anymore? – but I felt that that first Gallic *e* confirmed nothing. Thus you can imagine my discombobulation upon reading lines such as: *A daughter must put out her hand / and touch her mother's muzzle...* and *Every molecule in the room / told my eyes to look away / but a daughter must meet her mother's gaze*. It must be stylistic post-modern poetic quirk that had passed me by, I thought. What was going on?

Petit is in fact a very serious poetess [I would never use such a word now: this is a good example of how little I have changed] and *The Huntress* does her voice justice. It is not a narrative, but loosely tells the story of a girl's childhood dominated by her mentally ill mother and flips this against the discovery of the New World. It's a big undertaking and there is a tendency in the reader to wonder at statements such as: *Like Cortés, I found her...* and *Then... she's Xochiquetzal / in her Butterfly Palace* and, even better, and my favourite, *She's the stalagmite Madonna... white as ECT.* How much can a writer mythologize a person before they lose their own identity and become a figment or a paragon? Clearly deification helps, but Petit somehow loses sight of the end result: the reader must still be able to identify with this person, and she lost me twenty pages in.

However, the poetry itself is almost uniformly excellent, something that *The Wounded Deer (Fourteen Poems after Frida Kahlo)* brought home. Naturally, one thinks of that other depiction of painting in another art form, Moussorgsky's *Pictures At An Exhibition*, famously orchestrated by Ravel, who when asked about the paintings that inspired the pieces, replied: 'This is about music.' It's the same situation here. Much though I admire Frida Kahlo's work, to compare the paintings with the poems is to miss the point of the book. And what poems! It's a shame there're only fourteen of them, but they're perfectly judged, something that eludes most slimline collections of this kind.

The title poem, while not the best by a stretch, is a tasty anthropomorphization of the eponymous animal, and *Self-Portrait With Monkeys* is a pyrotechnic exercise in beauty of descriptive language. That could be a good way to categorise the book – as Petit's love affair with the English language. Take this stanza about her eyes, and her dog's:

> His are the eyeballs
> underworld dogs wear.
> Mine are of such transparent stones,
> it's like wearing a string of sunny days...

or this, as an image of sunrise:

> He sits on my bedside table
> like an orange spider,
> entangling my still life in his rays.

Poetry Express, 2004 – 2006

In Memoriam Pierre Boulez

Two nights ago I found myself shivering in a back garden of a large house by the Thames up past Putney, giving a radio interview by mobile phone about Pierre Boulez, who died on January 5th [2016]. I was in the garden because I had had to leave a rehearsal I was taking in the living room of the house to do the interview; I was doing the interview because I was the only person the radio presenter could find who had actually known and worked with Maestro Boulez.

So what did I say? I told a few anecdotes, talked briefly (while fumbling to roll a cigarette in the freezing air, phone cupped between ear and shoulder) about serialism, and at more length about the musical institutions he founded, which happily continue to thrive: the Lucerne Festival Academy [in Switzerland], Ensemble intercontemporain and Cité de la Musique, and perhaps most importantly, IRCAM (the Domaine musical, Institut de recherché et coordination acoustique/musique [in Paris]. He'd have wanted them mentioned, I felt.

The radio interview was fifteen minutes long, so I wasn't worried about running out of things to say, despite not having seen Boulez in person since 1998. Still, when I went back inside, the singers (who had been enjoying their break with cups of tea and Jaffa cakes) all noted that I looked somewhat upset. And it was true. I loved Boulez very much, and not simply for the work he did with me and other composition students at the Royal College of Music – although there *was* that – but because I admired him so greatly, perhaps even more than the other legendary musicians who had come to give us masterclasses and lectures: Maazel, Haitink, Solti, Rostropovitch, Menuhin, Domingo and many more. So that's certainly saying something. And genius itself is very lovable, the act of creation is within itself an act of love, and Boulez himself was cuddly, so let me start with his genesis as a genius.

My father, who died five years ago, failed as a composer (or so he felt: he destroyed all his scores and recordings, so I have nothing to compare) and thus crystallized into a recording engineer who particularly championed contemporary music. According to him, at the Maida Vale studios in the mid 80s, Messiaen once kissed *me* on the forehead, and I whimsically imagine the baby me not being washed for a week... My dad recorded Andrzej Panufnik – whom I do remember – Cornelius Cardew, Graham Fitkin's first works and many more. It was through him that I first encountered Boulez's music. My dad didn't record Boulez, but he stocked his CDs in a little music shop in a basement in Islington that he ran. And I was hugely taken with the uncompromising quality of the work. My favourite at that time was probably *Notations*, first the piano pieces and later the orchestral expansions.

In 1990 I began attending the Purcell School of Music, where I studied the Darmstadt School. Like the Second Viennese School, this was not an educational institution, but rather a group of composers who shared aesthetic values and certain compositional attitudes. The members of the Darmstadt International Summer Courses for New Music in the early 50s to 60s included, alongside Boulez, Bruno Maderna, Luigi Nono and Karlheinz Stockhausen, to mention just three. Now *there's* a line-up.

Of course serialism itself developed as a reaction to the Great War. Ravel's *La Valse* premiered in 1920, and utterly skewed the waltz, a famously Germanic form, to the point where it was twisted into a 4 across the bar, pah pah pah pah, and not the waltz 3, or *um* pah pah. And notice the title: that *La* was a wonderful reaction to and flipping-off of everything Germanic, never mind what the music itself did. The Second Viennese School (and there wasn't really a First, although some musicologists like to be gumptious windbags on the subject) grew out of the same disillusionment with the political situation in Europe. Arnold Schoenberg, its symbolic father, came up with twelve-tone music as an almost anti-racist movement in sound: no note was to be considered more important, or possess more privilege than any other, and each note was not to be used again before any other was granted a second use. Admirable, we nod together. Understandable given the countless millions that had so recently perished.

Schoenberg's major pupils, Anton Webern and Alban Berg, continued the tradition and developed it. Of *course* they developed it – such a system could not survive on its own for long, because the harmonic language was obviously limited. By the advent of the Second World War, Schoenberg, who was Jewish, had fled to America, Berg died in 1935 after contracting sepsis following a wasp sting, and Webern, who had stepped outside his door to have a cigarette, was shot in error by an American soldier in 1945. You couldn't make this shit up. Schoenberg died in LA in 1951, having witnessed not only the Holocaust, but also the deaths of his best and brightest pupils.

Expressionist is arguably the best word for The Second Viennese School, and most of their works are still performed, most notably Berg's Violin Concerto (1935), and operas *Wozzeck* (1922) and *Lulu* (posthumously premiered in 1937). To readers unfamiliar with

Webern's *oeuvre*, I recommend *Five Pieces For Orchestra:* the Funeral March alone will harrow your soul and bring your heart to breaking. Georg Büchner [1813–1837] wrote the play, or 'scenes' (*Woyzeck*) upon which Berg's opera is faithfully based, and oddly, if you go into any bookshop today, the main English translation is by John Mackendrick. Now, I never met John, but he was in love with my mother, and she always used to say that she wished Mackendrick had been my father, but she refused to have a child with him due to his various personal issues, which you can Google if you wish to know more about. Still, she used to say, 'he was very, very nearly your dad'. So, if I wasn't already feeling involved in all this, I was super-totes chuffed when Pierre Boulez first walked into that classroom.

Regrettably, that class began at 6 p.m. and I had been in the college bar since 1 (when it opened) until 5.30 (when it closed). So I was far from my best that evening in Room 208b in the bowels of the RCM, facing one of the greatest musical minds of all time. In fact, glancing at the music on my desk, I rapidly ascertained that I could no longer coherently read it, or indeed any music. The notes were certainly ink, but the ink didn't make any sense. To justify my inebriation I had concocted a get-out-clause: which was, at least, true. My dad was dying of a flesh-eating disease, my mum was having another indulgent faux-psychotic break, my flatmate had been found dead 'under mysterious circumstances', and my girlfriend had only eaten lettuce sandwiches for so long that her periods had stopped and her teeth were crumbling… I had had finer days… And there was mould collecting in the high corners of Room 208b, which I found obscurely disconcerting…

In 1976, Pierre Boulez conducted the *Jahrundertring* at Bayreuth, Wagner's own opera house. I hadn't been born. The *Centenary Ring* was celebrating the centenary of both the Bayreuth Festival and the first performance of the complete cycle of the *Ring*. Wolfgang Wagner directed (of course) and the first performance caused a 'near-riot' for the brash modernity of staging, yet it established a standard, called *Regietheater* (literally director's theatre) that has stood the test of time not only for that production, but for all opera productions everywhere. That *Ring* was revived every season for many years. And musically, it was all Boulez, being seminal in his slow tempi and setting a precedent for future Wagner wannabes. Solti's Ring in the 60s boasted better singers – primarily Windgassen and Nilsson – and actual horses in the recording studio (they're on YouTube in all their majesty), but Boulez took an intellectual approach, and it paid off. Here I feel I must share an anecdote…

The story goes that both Boulez and Messiaen wrote dissertation-length analyses of Stravinsky's *The Rite of Spring* – Messiaen's focussing on the harmonic (the aggregate chords, the modal progressions) and Boulez's focussing on the rhythmic (the sudden stabs of sound and metric modulations). Stravinsky read them both and said: '*Wow*, I never thought of any of that. I just *wrote* the damn thing.'

That day in class, Dr Boulez recognised a soul in pain, and didn't ask me any questions, although he certainly noticed me, roiling and sweating like a wizard in the front row. I have always been grateful to him for that. I imagine he viewed me with indulgent pity – a dourly typical English student wasting their time on a class clearly over their heads. But I *wasn't* one of them – I was secretly seething and brooding and wishing I could actually read the music all aglitter yet encysted on the page in front of me in knots and liquid shapes...

As a conductor Boulez was Music Director of the New York Philharmonic (my favourite conductor Bernstein's old position), Chief Conductor of the BBC Symphony Orchestra, Principal Guest of the Chicago and the Cleveland orchestras, and guest of the LSO, and Vienna and Berlin Phil(s). That is an extraordinary legacy. His recordings span four decades. Bernstein is the only comparable contemporary, but he veered toward the Romantic rather than the new. His Mahler and Beethoven were Boulez's Stravinsky and Carter.

A ridiculous perfectionist, Boulez revisited his old compositions systematically, going backward – updating the latest first, as if perhaps the juvenilia was not worth his attention. I later studied with George Benjamin, the great French composer (yes, I *do* mean French composer), and he taught me a great deal about how Boulez's *Notations*, in orchestral form, conformed to 16th Century counterpoint. It was perhaps the best music lesson I ever had. And it brings this article full circle, like *Notation 3*, a rhythmic cell that generates its own harmony.

Straight after class I rushed to the toilets, locked myself in a cubicle and, snarling with disappointment, quietly sobbed. Some time later – it felt like four and a half minutes or so of silence – I left the RCM and slunked home.

Today, twenty-four years later, I walked the same halls for a recording session with an Italian cellist. It has changed, of course – the bar is on a different floor, the interior square is gone – and the toilet where that ridiculous child sat, bawling like a goblin, is cordoned-off, for building work. But I paused anyway, remembering the brilliance of Boulez and what he taught me. Finally, with a last glance back, garnished slightly with regret, I went on, and in to the new rooms to record.

One final anecdote: I had forgotten about its existence, but a colleague from those young days, having heard my radio interview, emailed me a photograph late last night. In the black and white image, from left to right, stands Prince Charles, Sir Georg Solti, Pierre Boulez, and myself. The event was some prize-giving at the RCM circa 1995... *They* are all wearing black tie, and I am wearing (deliberately) ripped 501 Levi's jeans. I am also wielding a plastic cup, a *skiff*, full of that horrid gassy beer Caffreys, which was popular at the time...

But that wasn't what caught my eye. What caught my eye was this. Boulez was flashing his wide-brimmed, Brando-esque mega-watt smile, and he had his right arm around Solti's shoulders, and his left arm around mine.

That's what I'll remember, other than his genius: the generosity.
Maestro, Requiescat in pace.

Upbeat, 2016

Crete: Bougainvillea and the Bull

Grief defines us. The daily, hourly losses, revisions, reversals.
What we do with it can be cathartic, healthy, artistic, murderous, but
we have to do something with it. I find most people run away from it;
redefine it; shove it, like dust, into a corner. Go mad with grief if you
must, but dance with it; make a friend of it. Grief will be the
companion by your side all your life. Life is the dealing with it.
– Harold Pinter –

Two and a half weeks ago I received a cursory email from an Italian
filmmaker's 'people' enquiring if I might be interested in a role in her
new film. Curious, but always cautious, I checked her out online, and
she was the real deal: an ex-ballerina and performance artist (with
diversions into the fashion world) who had directed several short
films and gaudy music videos. The role I was up for was a minor yet
memorable one: that of a homeless person who, after the two main
characters unseeingly passed him in a grimy subway tunnel, would
gaze after them and softly begin to sing the tenor aria *Una furtiva
lagrima*, from Donizetti's *L'elisir d'amore*. The character apparently
symbolised everyday ignored beauty. Ah, so she needed a tenor – this
made things clearer. And everyday ignored beauty? Hell, I was a
goddamn authority on *that*.

Feeling full of vim, I blurted out a reply and attached some of my
recordings of famous tenor arias. This seemed to do the trick, as two
days later I virtually met with her and her 'people' in a Zoom meeting.

'Ah, Willllllliams, you are "the talent", as we say'... '*Si*, you would be
indeed perfect fit for thiiis.' Two days after that I flew out to Crete to
meet them on the set of a project they were finishing up out there –
something that involved mountains, from the little I could glean,
although that certainly made sense as I flew in. There were mountains
everywhere below...

I had an ominous throb on the flight however, because the child
next to me slept for three hours with her eyes wide open. It was
certainly a medical issue, as the mother occasionally deposited eye-
drops – left, right – at regular intervals, and gratefully and longsufferingly nodded at me each time she did so, but it still gave me the
heebie-jeebies. This feeling was compounded when I got to my hotel,
a tiny place with an incongruously grand name – an Imperial Plaza,

say, or Real Luxury Palace, with its 22 rooms and grand-piano-sized (and grand-piano-shaped) pool. It just all felt... slightly *off.*

I was aware that the tourist season had just ended and that the hotels would only stay open for one more week while they cleaned house and snatched some last-gasp cash from dwindling stocks, but I had not expected to be the only guest, and nor had I expected the town itself to be shuttered and silent. The place felt anaesthetised – an unnatural slumber, as of walking past a psychiatric hospital at midnight and feeling the weight of all that medicated sleep.

I had worked in film before, and knew never to believe, or put one's trust in, any aspect of the alchemical process, but I was floored to wake the next day to an email telling me that they'd given the part to someone else... Not even a thank-you-for-your-interest, or a sorry-to-drag-you-all-the-way-to-Crete... Ah well, I sighed, there's another bonkers story to add to the lurid Williams life files...

But, dismissing all thoughts of myself in the third person, I resolved to enjoy my remaining time in Crete, even if I must do so alone – which is how I liked it, to be honest, having never been a fan of rabid crowds or collective (and forced) enjoyments. But... hold on... while I hadn't been to the country before, I knew a girl who lived in Heraklion, who would make a fabulous travel buddy... Thus my phone's Contacts page flashed into view, sharp as a Cretan spear, and I called her. One of the things I had always admired about D was her uncomplicatedness: she said what she thought, she thought before she spoke, and there would be no discussion, if she had nothing else to do. As I dialled the number, I found I wished more people possessed this quality or ability. After a brief conversation, I found myself skipping across the travertine stone plaza toward the front desk of my Glorious Hotel Of All Gods, or whatever it was called, to pay for an extra guest to be added to my room.

The irony of Brexit wasn't lost on me when, in the hotel's foyer, really just a glorified smoking space, Pomme's *Göttingen* began playing – a song in French with a German title playing in Crete to an English listener – at that moment I felt truly European, and proud of it to boot, goddamn.

****

Knossos was my first stop to tick off, and I met D at the curved black gates. After embracing with a warm *frisson* of nostalgia, and limbs going at awkward angles like birds in a crosswind, we repaired to a modest faux-wooden bar diagonally opposite – fake palm tree here, karaoke machine there – and caught up over a pair of hasty drinks: beer for me – you can't go wrong with what you know – white wine for her, and raki for us both, as it's a marker of friendship in Cretan culture, in fact a signifier of old Cretan nobility.

D (how my fingers twitch to tap out the triple-syllable of her forename) was a musician friend a few years my junior, whom I hadn't seen for over twenty years, but she laughed the same wide-brimmed and unselfconscious laugh I remembered from all those years ago when I told her the story of why I was in Crete, and it was no time at all before we were back to being old 90's conspirators.

It's not exaggerating to say that D had the bone-structure of a goddess, but with eyes lit as if from the bottom of a barrel, unstructured and fragmented though the slew. Slyly glinting. An alluring humour to her personality, tiny feet, and the nails on one hand grown longer than the other: testament to her brilliance on the classical guitar. A gaze that tweaked you to consider whether you were on the right path in life, but didn't judge. Warmly dark, with a fine untidy dusting of angel-strands along the hairline, she was 165 centimetres tall, minus heels, and if it were possible, exuded even more elegance clothed than unclothed. But I felt she was burdened, and put it down to our being so much older since our last meeting. I asked her to compare a William Carlos Williams poem:

> According to Brueghel
> when Icarus fell
> it was spring
>
> a farmer was ploughing
> his field
> the whole pageantry
>
> of the year was
> awake tingling
> near
>
> the edge of the sea
> concerned
> with itself
>
>
> sweating in the sun
> that melted
> the wings' wax

                    unsignificantly
                    off the coast
                    there was

                a splash quite unnoticed
                    this was
                    Icarus drowning

with the final verse of Auden's telling of the same story:

In Breughel's Icarus, for instance: how everything turns away
    Quite leisurely from the disaster; the ploughman may
        Have heard the splash, the forsaken cry,
But for him it was not an important failure; the sun shone
As it had to on the white legs disappearing into the green
Water, and the expensive delicate ship that must have seen
    Something amazing, a boy falling out of the sky,
    Had somewhere to get to and sailed calmly on.

D paused, looked me full in the eyes (and I realised how seldom people ever do that), and snorted: 'Oh, come *on*,' and scuffed the heel of her left shoe on a gaudily painted clay plant-pot, '*everyone* knows the Auden is better.'
    'Urb versus Rus.'
    'No, ha! Cold War versus new minimalism.'
    'American or English? Or just us?'
    '*Rus*. Ohmygodohmygod.'
    I laughed, D smiled as if at a private joke – although I was still detecting that inward burden – and we left the bar and went on through to Knossos Palace, a place that must have seemed like a structure from the heavens to those who first saw it. And that was the point, I guess.
    Imagine yourself for a moment in the position of a peasant in 12AD. You have wood houses and stone to build with and grasses and farmland to cultivate, and suddenly this monolith appears. *I* could worship, in such radiant and primitive circumstances.
    D headed the expedition as if I were a less-than-reputable helper, who had problems with certain cheeses and couldn't be relied upon to lead anyone anywhere. That was fine by me. But as I followed I realised, suddenly, that that was one of the things I'd missed about her, her *not to need any* justification. She walked as if she belonged. She had always done that, everywhere she went. But then, she *did*

belong here, she was their's, and *I* was other. It was a young feeling to me, something fresh, perhaps even gently abstract, but not unknown. Still, something nagged inside. Her eyes looked mournful in an unlocatable way, like those of an animal imprisoned behind glass, an old great ape who had grown up in the jungle and seen his family flower and grow, but whose current territory was measured in meters and not miles.

Over her shoulder D called and clapped her hands, 'Are you coming? Gallop. Come. Chop.'

An aside: some years earlier I had played a character named Icarus in an opera called *The Open Cage*. And yes, it *is* the Icarus you are thinking of – the one who flew too close to the sun and, dripping wax, fell into the ocean for his vanity. The libretto of the opera *The Open Cage* was written by two poets... Generally one poet is bad enough, but two? No good could come of such an arrangement, I felt... Eventually, nearing performance, I met them both and gently expressed my opinion that their libretto was almost *too good* for music, too rich and well written to be set to music. They both – Adam Donen and Adam Horowitz (son of Michael) – pooh-poohed my suggestion. And why would they not? I was just the singer in the show. They didn't know me as a writer. And it wasn't my place to tell them. *The Open Cage* is available to watch on YouTube to this day. In it, Icarus (me) and my father Daedalus (the exemplary baritone Alistair Sutherland – a voice of rare supple elegance, and a singer unafraid of the unrelentingly high *tessitura*) – fashion wings with which to escape the labyrinth of the Minotaur, who appears as a computer-generated Pac-Man visual projection, relentlessly chomping away until he reaches us, his prey.

O Roaring soul, I was walking in the footsteps of my character! I attempted to tell D this, and she yelled something like: 'But you always have.'

I didn't understand, or didn't properly hear, but as we were the only ones there, D put a blindfold on me, and we crept around the ruins, her voice as guide. The peacocks chased us, but without conviction. *Those humans are the only ones here today, so we ought to at least hassle them...* But peacocks are not frightening. Nothing so ridiculously designed could be frightening; they are not bulls. Then we walked back and toured it all again sighted, and we laughed more and more and more. Eventually D asked: 'You're going to write about me, no? In a book. Oh, I know.'

'I wasn't particularly going to, but I probably will now, yes.'

'Make sure you write a thing from me, one: it is more painful to grieve, you say mourn, for someone who is alive still rather than one who is dead.'

'I promise I'll write that.'

'Promise me.'

'I do.'

'You say it.'

'I'll write *it is more painful to grieve for someone who is still alive than for someone who is dead*. Is that what you meant?'

'Just write it. Tell my story.'

I was beginning to wonder if there was some agenda I wasn't privy to, when she brightened, took my hand and said: 'Come! Choppy chop. Are you hungry? We go now.'

D loved the present tense and used it whenever possible. Her grasp on English was undisputedly excellent, and when we had attended college together in 1997 I recall she spoke it like a native, indeed with a slight South-London tang that I always found irresistible. But even then she favoured the present tense, marking that Europeanism as a verbal thumbprint whenever available. ('Where do you see your guitar career in ten years?' 'It is successful.' 'Did you have a good time at the end-of-term ball last year?' 'I am having an excellent one.')

We went for dinner that night and I had to ask what, if anything, was wrong.

'I married badly,' she replied, with a sorrowful incline of the head and a candour that surprised me, as she skewered a stray piece of chicken that was nearing the plate's edge.

'You were married? Wow. I didn't know. Never knew. When did this happen?'

'Two thousand and the oh two.'

'So you were...' It took me a beat. 'You were just twenty-one! What happened?' Noting her hesitation, I added, 'you don't have to tell me if you don't want to.' I was nodding in all the correct places.

'Will you write my story?'

'Of course, anything for you D, you know that. Say whatever you want or as little as you want. Entirely yours,' I said, shovelling down a spoonful of soup and coughing lightly as a sliver of garlic excited my vocal cords.

'Yes. I do know. I trust you.'

'Cheers.'

'Only a little.'

We ate on for a while in silence while she considered. The restaurant was a place named *Avli*, just off the main traffic artery in

Malia, opposite an ornate church with toffee-twisted minarets. Over D's head, on the wall, was a history of the place. The same family had built it, still owned it, and had had Presidents dine there as their personal guests. A waiter noticed me reading the blurb and, catching his eye, I nodded appreciatively at the wall while simultaneously miming culinary satisfaction with my elbows and cutlery.

'Ok,' D said, finally, as dessert arrived, 'I married a religious man. I was young. Too young. That was it.' Then, very quietly, she added, 'he took my son.'

I was enjoying my tiramisu and didn't really process what she had said (I *am in* the process! Perhaps the present tense had something going for it) until I found myself saying, over a forkful – oh, disrespectful implement – 'are you saying your husband kidnapped your son?'

By this juncture her eyes were a firewall of private pain and girdled with the intensity of guitar strings tuned deliberately sharp. When she continued, D didn't keep her voice steady or pretend to be sane, and as she spoke her fork, this time fist-held, seemed to be pointing directly at her teeth. She said,

'I didn't understand, at that age, what it meant. He is a Muslim [the present again], I was a Greek, almost a *Jew*' – here other customers began to glance our way and the waiter deftly stepped forward. I batted him back with a hand below table height as she continued, 'and he took my son to Libya and now I am nothing.'

This was all getting a little dramatic, and becoming a tad embarrassing (what a social snob!), thus I signalled for the cheque and quietly drew D out of the place and onto a stone bench. I rolled two cigarettes and offered her one. She declined, but I did the faux-cinematic gesture where you light two at one go and offer the lady the one not still in your mouth. As she quietly sobbed she took the cigarette and smoked it in little fitful breaths, a puff here, a puff there, none properly inhaled, and she became after a fashion, self-conscious for that and stopped crying, which was the intention.

'Let's go home,' she said.

'Do you mean the hotel?'

'Yes, to the Majestic House of Wonder.'

'I thought it was the Perfect House of Athena.'

And D smiled. And that smile was a wonderful thing, a thing that carried the vanilla and woodsmoke of the restaurant with it, a smile in which one could get lost, if one had not studied the map beforehand, and planned which pretty pattern of streets to take.

It was a ten-minute walk back, under a nailclipping of moon. D leaned into me and asked: 'So I guess we're going to do this again?'

'No. I think it's best if I put you to bed,' I replied. 'Sorry. I have three massive beds in there. Just take one. I don't give a shit, *woah*, careful, mind your step. And we'll get up tomorrow all glitterous and...'

'Glitterous?'

'Yeah, glitterous, it's my new favourite. And we'll have lunch, maybe hit the beach. There'll be no one there...'

D smiled again, and relaxed on my shoulder, but I was inwardly roiling. As we staggered up the slight hill together before over the crest where a little Taverna – *Serpurva* – divided the street in two, I found myself thinking about sex. How could one not? When you already know the body of the person, being with them again years later is a double-luxury, as if the knowing makes it all the more enjoyable and illicit, every caress a *what if?*, every sigh one of loss.

There was never love between us – I want to make that clear. We briefly dated at college (not at school) and had moved on with no ties or regrets or longings. I think, even at that time, we were both damaged enough to understand that friendship was the more important inclination. So I put her to bed in the lounge area of the hotel room that adjoined the kitchenette and drew the sliding door to my own bedroom as quietly as I could, or until it softly clicked into some invisible socket one could only identify by touch. I waited a few moments to make sure she wasn't stirring, and then went onto my balcony and enjoyed a snippish fag. As I sat there in the chill air – it was well past midnight but my smoke was making such pretty shapes against the frothy grey sky – I began to experience a discomfort in my chest.

The chair was so warmly cushioned, and all terrestrial life just a breath away from cardio-vascular collapse anyway, and the moon, now a full sliver of raw onion, was so vibrant and pretty, that I didn't move. I resolved to wait the pain out, while considering what D had said. The religious angle was interesting. But what did *almost a Jew* mean? I don't think that's debatable, being Jewish. It's matronymic, I thought, and D's surname was certainly Greek. And what of the strange remark 'and now I am nothing'? I was musing on these, and other thoughts (What good are feelings here? Who needs them now?), when a throaty blast of some immense exhaust pipe drew my attention back into the room. Upon re-entry it seemed that my ears had lied, until the petrochemical tang of D's fart came under the door and entered my sinuses. Oh, poor girl! What did I feed you?

I went to bed shortly after, and her farts punctuated my sleep all that night. Who knew so much air could be held in such a slender container?

****

The next morning we paid the hotel manager to make us breakfast (no chef was old Faustus!) and over sloppily fried eggs and inexpert paninis, the conversation continued, as it always had, always did, and always would. (Always will! D added in her beloved present tense, or perhaps: Always shall.)

I asked, 'Look, listen, we had both...'

'Yes.'

'...*Quite*. We had both had quite a lot to drink. And you said some things that were... are... concerning.'

'Aaaw, Israa Wheeliams, what am I going to *do* with you?'

'You've gone full Greek again.'

I sometimes think that humans haven't quite grasped the idea of humanity. What good are feelings anyway? Who cares? I held up my hands, palms heavenward, in a complicated gesture, combining I-don't-know and who-really-gives-a-shit. D leaned toward me and, after a flirtatious pause filled with epic calm and promise said: 'Let's go back to the room.'

What was I to do? You. Tell. Me.

There followed several hours of acrobatic sex, the kind one always has after funerals, when life impulses need to be fortified, when one cares only about what is to come and not what has gone before.

Following this unexpected diversion, we visited the grave of Nikos Kazantzakis on the outskirts of the city. Disembarking from the bus, I was immediately struck by the sight of a man, comatose and face down on a bench right by the bus stop. I resolved to check on him when we got back, as the route was circular.

D was in fine fettle, all exhibition and feathers, so I asked her: 'Do you want to talk about yesterday?'

'You hear that song?' she said.

'No, what? What song?' but I turned to where she was looking, and there, across the street was, on the screen of a shopping centre, Pomme singing *Göttingen* with orchestra. The ominous throb in my chest started up again, burning in earnest...

'I love that song! It's so... European! It's so... *us!*'

'Whatever you want, D.'

Now, I knew Kazantzakis as the author of the book of a film I'd seen when I was a child – *Zorba The Greek* – but I had honestly forgotten that he'd also written the contentious *The Last Temptation of Christ*... His grave was reached by a series of concrete walkways that wound around a hill, or appeared to – they actually wound around on themselves on just one side of the hill. Feeling tetchy by the top, I faltered, and D grasped my arm.

The grave on the top was a grass plateau dominated by a large cross. I was grateful for this because the Cretans had honoured a man who had been excommunicated by the Greek Church for his writing by placing him on the top of a hill that was literally, by metres, above the old walls of the town of Heraklion, their capitol. Apt, I felt. His grave overlooked his domain. A place that respects its artists in the face of implacable gods deserves recognition for it.

Every city has those areas, mini-ghettos, where youths congregate to drink, smoke and let loose with cans, canisters and butts. Used condoms are always there. It's where character is built, where morals are lost, where we all go when we are young, or we should. The Kazantzakis stairs were one of those areas. Adorned by pretty constantly-changing graffiti, young people watched us pass up and then down, but didn't spit or curse, as they might have done in London or Zagreb... They were polite and even moved aside. I wondered if this was because of whose grave mound they were reclining on, or because of the woman who was accompanying me, oh gorgeous, glorious D! Who cares? I'd happily take it, either way.

When we got to the bottom I checked on the derelict again. He was in the exact same position. Face down on the bench. The bus was due in 12 minutes, and for each of those I wondered about calling an ambulance. He didn't stir once, despite the traffic volume. I turned to D and asked, 'Should we?'

She shook her head as the bus arrived. Recognising her superiority as a resident, I boarded with a backward glance. Would he stay that way until someone came? Would he wake up and be as new? Was he already dead? I would never know, but at least someone cared, even if it was just me.

****

Next we went to the beach in Malia. As it was off-season, we scrounged the last dinner going from a Pirate-themed restaurant and ate on the sand. I asked, over mouthfuls of fish, 'So come on. We have to talk, no?'

'These years?'

'These.'

'Common sense, walk in, walk out. Who cares?'

'Well, me, *I* do. I have need-to-know eyes. Look!' And I pulled down my lower lids and rolled the irises upward while thrusting my tongue out at an abstract angle.

'You don't want to know *really*,' she said, and I understood this was different. The beach suddenly felt like a vast interrogation room, all blue tops and clear sides, and sand running in left, right. 'You like me now because I give you something of you, and we have the sex, but you I want you for something else for me. I want you to write.

'My son was my whole life,' she continued. 'He was all I ever had wanted, really. And his dad took him away. Zooosh.'

Feeling sure a Zeus pun would be unwelcome, I replied, 'I do want to know really. Can you tell me something about it? Anything I can write *about*? When did all this happen? Start there. Start somewhere. *Fuck.*' I cracked open two beer cans and handed one to her as she began, this time in full-Greek mode, replete with mispronunciation, and, I felt, deliberate misunderstandings of language. What a wonder was D! Such a puzzle of a person, an emotional conundrum.

'I married young. I was twenty yawning [all in]. Not twenty and ones as you say. What that did *I* knew? I married Mohammed because he offered me life. House,' here she threw her hair back as if carefree, 'security.' [se-curr-ee-tee] – we both waited a few breaths before it came: 'A child.'

'D,' I said, smiling with half my face, 'every guy who dated you back in college at some level imagined a kid with you. Genetics. I know I did. That's life, sorry, the impulses are...'

'I understand,' she replied (with a lovely emphasis on the first syllable – *un*-derstand. Whee! A trapeze of a vowel), stop being such a Nazi-factionist.'

'I beg your pardon. *What* did you call me?'

And it would have all ended right there, had not she explained that she meant narcissist, but in the Greek voice it had come out as Nazi-factionist. I explained the old tale of Narcissus and its relevance to modern life via that old chestnut psychiatry...

****

Agios Nikolaus was our last stop that day and save for a mild fracas between D and the bus-driver which involved some hurling of k's and g's and a little light luggage, by noon we were at the lake, cheery cherry milkshakes a-hand. Good times. O Halcyon, salad days: this was *it*. This was what I had stayed for – not to mention the mountains and olive groves and the glorious bougainvillea... For those readers who don't know what bougainvillea is... It is the gloriously droopy pinkish-red flowering bush that had, over centuries, been trained into a pervasive vine. Many writers had mentioned it in their work, and some had used it as a symbol of love...

As I leaned back in my expensively cushioned lounge-seat – off-season, I had my choice of the best – I imagined what books I would write... Perhaps a long War Novel where the symbol of the man's love is the bougainvillea, and he spends 400 pages getting to see it, but finally dies as it comes into sight... Had that *been* done? Perhaps *Doctor Zhivago*? Or what about a thriller where a guy breaks into a famous art dealer's penthouse apartment, only to find himself trapped, locked in, with the bougainvillea the only way of communicating with the outside world? *Ha*, that would be something. I supped my milkshake through a straw and naturally thought of Derek Walcott... I met him once, the poet of the islands – different islands – still... Or what about a novella set *here*, in Crete, where a rowing boat and its crew can only be guided to shore, not by a lighthouse, but by the bougainvillea.

I was shaken awake by D. Apparently I had been making noise. Night terrors, or dream terrors, had long plagued me – even collegiate girlfriends reported me crying in my sleep. But lately it had become worse: I'd started to *scream* in my sleep. Apparently not fully screaming (and I was not able to bear witness), I thrashed and began to moan in a high pitch. This is what D had woken me from.

'Have this,' she said, and handed me a tumbler of something suspiciously alcoholic in texture.

'Aw, thanks, I didn't mean to...' But I wasn't complaining.

'People are moving away from us.'

'You mean the people who are still here. "And they all moved away from me on the bench there!" Thanks, but come on.'

'Drink.' D drained hers.

'Arlo Guthrie,' I murmured, cloudily concluding that these drinks had been purchased while I snoozed.

She put her elbows on the table and smiled. We drank together. The cliff face was behind her and, after a while, kids crowded round the edge of the lake, to see the flocks of black arrows dart in to eat what the waiters threw out. A pizza slice would vanish in twenty seconds. They dipped their fingers in and mock-screamed as the fish flocked, then went back to doing their imitation of childhood as the fish continued on in their fish ways. Refulgent as perfect shoeshine they darted in, then away. Look there, see, and there, see, *see*.

A feast of a sunset was settling in, all red anticipation and wind and the expectation of being deliberate. But suddenly her face cleared, the forbidding look passed, and she coughed. 'It wasn't *you*,' she said, 'just so, *so* much to decide.'

I drained the remnants of my cherry milkshake and then what remained in the tumbler and looked up, up to the pale stars now coming through. Were they proper stars or mere shadows of stars? And were stars any good anyway, given their proximity to chaos? Who knew? I didn't. A handful of certainties lay ahead. I decided to wait for her to say something...

...Imagine the day-trippers in their sunhats and glorious disregard. Imagine any single method of disposition! It is decidedly pleasant here, and I do not much want to move... Christ, I'm taking on her present tense characteristics, I thought. Suddenly... She said: 'You are a narcissist, no?'

'Don't you have to be, a little bit, just a little bit, to write? I mean, even the hateful characters, the murderers, racists, hell, even the *musicians* have to have just enough of yourself, the author, in them to make them believable...'

'Did you ever love me?'

And both tenses met in my answer: 'I always did, always do. I called, remember?'

A tiny crevasse in her thinking opened and spilled out some unexamined thoughts. Her face absorbed them, and distorted accordingly. One eyebrow raised then dropped, an expensive ear clearing itself.

'But go on,' I said, and leaned in, patting her hand. For gossip or misogyny? We cannot tell. 'What is all this about?'

'I learned a thing...'

Awesome, I thought, things are looking up!

'...about my soul.'

Aw, shit, forget what I just said.

D continued: 'When he took my son to Libya I did everything I could. I went and begged at appropriate embassies. I went to the courts, the judicial system (jew-diss-ceel), they do not care.'

Interrupting, and feeling somewhat naked, I asked: 'So where in Libya is your son?'

She told me her story as we walked the markets and bought several olive oils (in 100ml containers for high-flying me) and huge luxurious bottles (for the ground-stung.). Hot Chilli, Greek Salad (obviously), Garlic Infused, BougainX (it tasted wonderful on the sample spoon), Clear and Plain, Rice Spice. She had married a religious person. Ah, belief, that most overrated of virtues. Pregnant at nineteen, she found herself forced into marriage. And why not? The sad cries of clustered children in a local playground helped her somewhat throughout the pregnancy, but, as a woman, she was the bearer, the vessel, and below dignity. When the child came, a little boy, Mohammed – she had wanted an unusual name, or one 'with a ring to it,' but was soon disabused of such a stupid notion – was the completion of a perfect mixed-race household. We are proud of this. We wanted this.

When D decided that Allah had allowed her enough beatings and had then allowed her to muster enough mental courage to leave, praise be, she did so via a bathroom window from a motel in Nevada, where the family were holidaying. D, cut from the glass and the fall, had to leave her son in order to run and get help from emergency services. By the time she located a phone, it was too late, Mohammed had disappeared with Mohammed. Ten weeks later Mohammed and Mohammed were located in Libya by Interpol, to a street, to a house, to a single door on Google Maps. But there was absolutely nothing that could bring D's son back. He was gone, into Libya, into a street, into a house, behind a single door on a screen that would stay open for years.

'Oh,' I said, heartlessly, 'this can't just be because you want me to write about it. There are a billion Mohammed stories I could tell. Or write about you. Or spin. There has to be more.'

'You are perfect for me now to write. You understand?'

'I get that, I do. I really do.'

'Then write this. Take it down.' I dutifully, but not without resentment, got out my notebook and readied my pen. 'What others do to you is terrible. But what they make you do to yourself is worse. And when you willingly, yes, accept what is being done, then you have done it to yourself, and that is unforgivable. I can't get over that. I *squander* my love.'

'I understand,' I said, and I did. Twirling a toothpick between 1 and 3 RH, I called a cab to take us to the village of Krassi. There was something there that D might appreciate, I felt.

Krassi is tiny. No, no, recast the sentence. Krassi is a tiny.... and I was about to type village, but caught myself. Krassi is lonely and beautiful. I took D there for one reason: a tree. Yes, I took D to see a tree.

As we alighted from the taxi (only metres from the tree, but behind a wall), I took D's arm, and slurred her body into mine. That's a totally terrible way of saying: I got out of the car and, with a gentle and graceful movement, our lips met. Yeah ok, go with that. I can't write romance, or recast romantic sentences – romance renders my pen limp. Anyway, *I* knew what we were going to see just over that wall, but D, despite being technically Cretan, did not.

So I kissed her and told her to close her eyes.

Up a slight incline and one harsh step (which I warned her about), and we were there. I released the blindfold.

D gazed forth. Her eyes travelled up the marvellous trunk of the famous Plane tree, wider than ten average men, over 2400 years old, travelled back down to the modest little marketplace where Schiller, Lermontov, Kazantzakis and many other great writers – look, there is a plaque about them, if you need it – all sat, debated, drank, argued and wrote. It's a place of genius. It has that strange sheen of brilliance while still being just a fucking tree.

Here I got down on one knee, and selected from my rucksack a tattered copy of Yannis Ritsos and regaled D with a full opera-voice rendition of the Best Of. By the end she wasn't just D, she was G, B, F, indeed all the keys!

We dined together that night in a taverna in a neighbouring village that boasted being a movie set. And one could see why – the church was 'perfectly preserved Mexican', the square, where we ate, was clearly adaptable for filming if one removed the tables and chairs. Very cheap. So we ate pizza and smoked and laughed. Laughter is the most important, I'd say. Even if love is gone, still laugh, or try to. We ate where Antonio Banderas had fired film guns and where Claudia Cardinale, one of the greatest beauties, if not the greatest actress, of her time had strutted and fretted her stuff. And D finished her story:

'Yes, and I'm glad you asked. *Of course* I considered suicide. But that would be *his* victory, no? Mohammed's victory. Because everyone would die along with me – I'd kill everyone along with myself.'

'I think I get it...'

'You *know*...' D said, and grasped my right wrist in her left hand. And what an enticer! How dazzling was she then?

I understood. Having to mourn someone who is still alive is perhaps worse than having to grieve for someone who is dead. A promise ought to be a promise, yet I owe you, dear reader, a brief explanation. D and I were at school together, over twenty years ago and had little in common, save for music. And that's normal in this case, because we were at The Purcell School for Young Musicians. D appeared to come from a history of wealth – army officers et al – but she wasn't *like* that. Or rather, she didn't act like that: family of heroes.

She went on: '... What you do is: you run it past your soul. See how it fits. Me and my son are the same person, so that loss is like having your arm ripped out or your leg torn off while your spirit is already drowning but can never die. There is no... what do you call those limb replacements?'

'Prosthetics.'

'Yes. There is no prosthetic for that. The damage that causes is massive, the shockwaves are immense, and I wonder just how much damage we have sustained. How much I can do more.

That day when that man flew to Libya with my Mohammed I lost more than I could bear, more than I *can* bear... and grief is a black hole that sucks everything into it and it can destroy everything. It's not a pleasant place to be in, but it's also a fascinating place to be in. It's unmissable, in a way. I just hope one day I can laugh out loud, and laugh again and again, until I hear myself start living again.'

That evening we sat out in sagging deck chairs in the gardens of The Incandescent Boarding House Of Royalty (or whatever it was called), next to an apple orchard, bordered on the far side by a bougainvillea hedge trained around a long spindly trellis. In between was a field of peaceful cows, but by the fence stood a lone bull, like an angry afterthought, staring at the sad human couple five metres over yonder, sipping drinks and smiling, always smiling as if with some moral obligation, despite it all.

There was only one thing left to say.

'What's your son's name?' I asked.

Purple Patch, 2022

The Curious Case of Jennifer Mee

... In fact, this ought to be *The Curious Case of Jennifer Mee Followed By The Even Curiouser Subsequent Case of Jennifer Mee*, but that would be a title screaming to be recast. Very seldom – this is one such case – I know I want to write about a story upon first hearing it. With this, which feels like something out of a John Irving novel (or perhaps I just don't fully understand), I knew in a nanosecond. Two words were all it took: hiccup and murder. But let's be systematic.

****

Jennifer Mee first entered public consciousness – if we can reasonably call it that, without sarcasm – in 2007, when during a science class at school, she began to hiccup. She was fifteen, and as an averagely intelligent girl she likely understood – just like we all do – the mechanism of a diaphragm having a tiny spasm, and then relaxing, and the hiccups going away. Except in her case they didn't go away. Mee tried to relax and focus on her teacher and on the science lesson, and on the science, but fifteen minutes later she was in the nurse's office... Five hours later the hiccups had only intensified, she was in hospital, and her troubles had only just begun.

Back then she looked much like my sister did at the same age. Oval face bordered by brown straight hair, no adulthood in the eyes yet, a gawky yet charming demeanour, and a definite eagerness to please authority. And very much still a child: a face that seems, to a healthy-minded adult, completely recognisable for a second or two, but then instantly dismissed in less time than that.

So it was easy for the public to empathise when she appeared on their screens and radio stations, appealing for help with a chronic hiccuping disorder. Daytime TV audiences rallied, offering advice, support and even trips to water parks... The press christened her 'Hiccup Girl', and, for weeks, she captivated the nation, unbelievably generating headline stories day after day.

This is an American story, obviously (hence that use of christening above), and us British can comprehend a teenage girl perhaps captivating a nation, a singing sensation, say, or a courageous assault survivor... the Austrian Natascha Kampusch had escaped captivity the year before –but we don't have the zeal Americans have. We're not believers. A hiccuping medical mystery would have barely managed the local papers and airwaves. Still, captivate the US Mee did, and she was pedigree headline news.

Over the following several weeks viewers and listeners waited on updates of her visits to pediatricians, cardiologists and neurologists... Doctors ordered numerous blood tests, conducted CT scans and MRIs... But no one could explain why Jennifer Mee's hiccups wouldn't stop.

Before you scoff, dear reader, consider this: she hiccuped around 50 times a minute, every minute of every day and night, for over a month. This causes significant distress. Mee suffered deep chest pain due to the constant pressure, breathing issues, coruscating heartburn, and could only eat soft foods, like 'applesauce and Jell-O'. She needed medication to sleep and had to drop out of school.

After weeks of discomfort, Mee was understandably distraught, depressed and desperate for answers. And as any teenager in the late '00s would, Mee sought them on the Internet. From sipping iced water, to holding her breath, to having people scare her – Boo! – Mee tried remedy after remedy to no avail. Nothing lessened the symptoms or cured her affliction. And so, finally, with Jennifer's physical *and* mental health declining, her mother, Robidoux – I am guessing she was of French Canadian extraction – turned to the media for help.

The Tampa Bay Times answered her pleas, and Mee's story went viral. Robidoux said they received '30 to 50 calls' from media outlets competing for interviews. *Today* – for English readers, an NBC mainstay, on air since 1952 – offered to help by coordinating a meeting between Mee and gastroenterologist Dr Roshini. This was going well until the hosts, for whatever reason (TV is TV) decided to turn the segment into a comedy. Upon observing that Mee stopped hiccuping when she spoke, male anchor Matt Lauer quipped: '... there's the solution right there! Don't stop talking.'

Still, Mee continued, with her mother, to campaign for help, and professionals suggested Lamaze breathing techniques, acupuncture, a modified Heimlich manoeuvre, and even swallowing tablespoons of peanut butter. Regardless, the hiccups persisted.

If you look at the girl in interviews around this time, there is clear desperation behind the eyes. She has been taken from childhood and placed in something alien to all of us: not celebrity, since there was nothing to celebrate, not fame, since she just wanted a cure, not infamy, she'd done nothing wrong... But she looked the same age as her own mother.

Finally, Jennifer's hiccups stopped. After five full weeks Mee was finally cured. I have spoken to the doctor who claims he cured her, and I'll say this: he still works successfully in St Petersburg, Florida to this day. But this is not about him, and to be fair, in a radio interview in Florida after she awoke to that soothed diaphragm, Jennifer credited her recovery to several things: a specially designed drinking cup (no further details given), a chiropractor, a hypnotist and an acupuncturist. When asked what was the most exciting thing about her newfound comfort, Mee answered: 'Monday, I'm going back to school for sure. That's the first thing I told my mom, that I want to go back to school.'

And that would have been that, a Beautiful American Tale, had it not, almost immediately, become a Classic American Tragedy.

****

We know power corrupts. But what does fame do? For someone thrust into it, without warning – Jennifer Mee didn't have any film to promote or song to plug – it must have been terrifying. Add to that someone who was struggling to breathe and suffering chronic heartburn, not to mention sleep deprivation and anxiety. And add to *that* being a teenager who is already immensely insecure about their appearance, and I think it's safe to say it was a very cruel hand Jennifer Mee was dealt that day in science class in 2007. But where lies the blame? Her mother was only trying to help, as we all would try to help our children. Was it Matt Lauer's fault for being an insensitive cur? Or was it nobody's fault? Is this just how the cookie crumbles for certain folk?

Whatever it was, the end of her hiccuping signalled the start of serious personal problems. Unable to adjust back into her old life, Jennifer Mee began using drugs and dropped out of school, while astonishingly managing to conceal this from her family until 2010, when her stepfather discovered her MySpace account, where she alluded to drinking alcohol, smoking weed, and visiting strip clubs. (I can't help wondering what her stepfather was looking for, but let's give him the benefit of the doubt, and pretend a tab was accidentally left open on a laptop.) As punishment for both participating in and posting about unlawful activities, Mee's parents had her phone disconnected.

A furious Mee ran away from home.

And now she was in the headlines again.

Imagine how *that* must have felt, your still-teenage flounce-out making front-page news. Your private humiliation now public humiliation; your every move distained and disregarded.

Robidoux [the mother] gave an interview and informed the press that Mee's 'time in the spotlight' had *changed* her daughter. She believed Mee wanted 'freedom without boundaries', and that her brush with fame had 'exacerbated the situation'. *Which* or *what* situation? Always a little rebellious, being on 'national TV and brain medicines' had given Mee the impression that she was important and no one could tell her what to do, 'including her parents'. Please ignore the *brain medicines* bit, because the best, or worst depending on your dependence, is yet to come: 'we believe this set her on the devil's path...' It is worth noting also, that she would not be a minor in Britain, so our view is slightly *off*.

Still, what is provable, what we know definitively, is that Jennifer Mee, eighteen years old, began hanging out with similarly disenfranchised young people and met her boyfriend, Lamont Newton, among them. In pursuit of freedom and independence, Mee moved in with Newton, his friend Laron Raiford, and Raiford's girlfriend, who doesn't feature again, but who happened to also be called Jennifer. None of the young adults had criminal histories, although drug use was rife. According to her diaries, Mee would go days without sleep due to 'mixing ecstasy, weed and cocaine', a combination that made her feel 'invincible'. I must say something here – that is a highly illogical ordering, but could mean nothing at all.

Still, what is provable, what we know definitively, is that when money for substances ran dry the group delved into petty crimes, often staging minor robberies to fund their next supply, a mugging here, an unattended cash register there. Not that I am condoning this behaviour, mind.

Still, what is provable, what we know definitively, is that at some point in October 2010, the roommates began focusing on a man Mee was already talking to on the Internet.

On October 23rd, Mee asked 22-year-old Shannon Griffin to meet her in person. The pair had been speaking online for a few weeks and, according to Mee, they arranged to meet under the pretense of Griffin buying weed. Griffin's cousin told the court that the young man left his house excited at the prospect of taking Mee on a date. 'He liked that bad white girl thing she had going on,' he said, adding, 'Shannon [pronounced Shan-oohn] was never gonna get in no trouble.' [sic]

We should add that by this point Jennifer Mee did not look at all like the schoolgirl from 2007. Her pictures look like the lady you'd avoid at the bar. She no longer looked like her mother. She looked like her *mother*'s mother. She looked like her grandmother: the grandmother that was dead. Sallow skin, eyes that travelled an inch into the world before stopping, a constant dampness about the brow, distinct sexual cunning in the eyes, but not yet sporting the neck tattoo that was prominent for her prison interviews. I have the four printout photos in front of me on my hotel desk. Of her at 15, at 17 and a half, at 18 – and it's terrible to say, but there it is, in the eyes – the recognition, and the resignation. But if there's a better advert for how drugs can rob you of personality, I'd like to see it. The pre- and post-meth photos you see online are generally of people already with no hope. Jennifer Mee wasn't like that, apart from in one obvious way. The fourth photo? We shall come back to that.

Robbing people wasn't new to Mee, Newton or Raiford. This was true. They had a history of using social media to lure targets on fake dates and drug trades. And, as always, Mee used herself as bait. She told Griffin to meet her at a vacant house across the street from her own, then led Griffin down an alley adjacent to the home, where Newton and Raiford were waiting. The pair assaulted Griffin, intent on beating him up and running away with his money. Unfortunately for them, it was impossible to tell how big someone was from a thumbnail on the Internet, and Griffin was six-foot-three and built of athletic alabaster. One woman whose window overlooked the alley told police: 'Oh, he wasn't going down. They kept coming and coming at him, but he was fighting hard. He was winning.'

By this point, Mee claimed she had fled from the alley. She was halfway across the street when she heard the first gunshot. She panicked and kept running. Six shots were fired, three of which, according to the coroner, could have claimed Shannon Griffin's life. The coroner couldn't say which one had done the final damage.

Shannon Griffin was murdered for less than $60.

This we know.

When friends didn't hear back from Griffin after his supposed date, they involved the authorities, and Griffin's phone activity was rapidly traced to Raiford, as Mee had used his phone to set up the meeting. The trio were instantly and easily apprehended, and evidence connected to the murder, namely Griffin's wallet, license and work ID were found with them, moreover, Mee's fingerprints and DNA were on Griffin's belongings and Raiford's .38-caliber revolver was found next to Griffin's body. The trio was immediately taken into custody. Upon questioning, Mee said she 'truly [didn't] know or understand what took place for [Newton and Raiford] to do what they did.' She claimed she had 'no idea a gun was going to be involved', and [that their] 'plan never included murder'. Her family rallied around her, saying Mee 'would never hurt a fly' but admitted she was 'naïve' and 'easily misled'.

Look at that proliferation of clichés. As a writer, I'd never use something so tub-thumpingly tabloidal as *would never hurt a fly* unless the person had actually done it. But this is real life, or was real life, and *easily misled* didn't sway the prosecutors.

John Trevena, Mee's attorney, went for an angle – he believed Mee was a victim of manipulation and mental illness. He told the jury Mee was manipulated into coordinating the meeting and urged them to remember she had no idea a gun was involved and was not at the scene of the crime at the time of the shooting. He argued that Mee's biggest fault was associating with the wrong people, which, he asserted, could be a symptom of Tourette's, along with Mee's hiccups. Trevena didn't think the diagnosis could be used 'as a direct cause for what occurred, but it might help explain her errors in judgement'.

A life defined by hiccups. This is an extraordinary thing. This is worth writing about.

Trevena went on to reveal that Mee was on Thorazine, a medication used to treat psychotic disorders, and he claimed she was schizophrenic, without any professional diagnosis. Now, this may strike you, dear reader, as an odd thing to claim, but in fact he was merely angling to remove the death penalty from proceedings. A judge, however, determined Mee was of sound mind to stand trial.

Newton and Raiford were charged with first-degree murder and sentenced to life without the possibility of parole. Mee's trial was a little more complicated. The jury had to determine if Mee was the mastermind behind the plan or if she was a bystander who didn't know what would happen when she led Griffin into the alley on October 23rd.

The defense argued Griffin would still be alive if he hadn't got involved with Mee. She was the one who developed a relationship with him – albeit a virtual one – and orchestrated a meeting, fully aware it was going to end in robbery. The jury's decision came down to this, a very sad, or very stupid, confession. The night she was arrested, Mee called her mother from jail. In the recorded phone conversation, Mee said she [had] 'set everything up', and that the robbery 'went wrong... it just went downhill after everything happened'.

So that was it. Hiccup Girl had, to use language her family might understand, thrown herself under the bus. In language we might understand, she had condemned herself.

Mee was the catalyst to Griffin losing his life. She facilitated the ambush, fully understanding she was bringing Griffin into a situation meant to cause him harm. The fact that Mee claimed to have run away during the fight had no bearing on whether she could be held accountable for the outcome. Under Florida's murder felony law, Mee didn't have to pull the trigger or even know a gun was present to be found guilty of murder in the first-degree. Participating in the crime was enough, and the jury knew she participated because she confessed to her mother.

Pinellas County Judge Nancy Moate Ley sentenced Mee to life in prison without parole.

Mee has attempted to appeal her sentence, but the request was denied.

I reached out to Robidoux but got no response.

There was this though: while I was finishing this piece, or at least artlessly typing it up, in a basement dive on 5th Street, New York, a barman got talking to me about the case. I asked for a refill, and as he refilled my glass, said: 'Those two n****s sure did that pretty white girl.'

I was speechless. The barman was African-American. I spluttered, 'What, who, do you mean? *What*? Huh? The victim was black as well.'

He sighed: 'I know. *Look* at her. She didn't do it. We did.' And he richly frowned as he poured my drink then shook his head and added: 'You English lot. You'll never understand us. Enjoy your afternoon, brother.'

White Noise, 2022

Goncharov: An Uncommon Story

On Sunday evening, after a day spent musically moaning into my pillow, faculties of taste and smell pendulously obstructed and my gut feeling like the shallows of a tropical swamp, I rose, in a noble spirit – and took a copious piss. The midgy dusk seemed to press in around the house as if radiating quietly relentless disapproval of my stricken condition. Boy, it was bad. In a state of craven brittleness, I examined my eyes in the mirror. Distinctly puffy lids, a sure childhood sign of illness (according to my now octogenarian mother), still applicable in adulthood... hints of punk colours in the irises, the chemical, graffito taints of pink, yellow, teal... a faint twittering of neural madness. Boy, was it *bad*.

Feeling royally martyred, and tight in the core as if hundred bowel movements behind the usual, I flushed and grimly shuffled back down the hall to bed. Lost, a forgotten piece in a shadowy and unwinnable game...

But suddenly I was assaulted from both sides: the mobile by the bed began to scream and the doorbell began to buzz and rattle aggressively...

With colossal effort, and, I felt, immense forbearance, I pressed the ENTRY button and inwardly groaned. I hadn't ordered anything, or couldn't remember having done so. I groaned again, and through the hole, watched the delivery guy ascending, phone to ear. As I turned the keys he took the phone away from his ear, pressed a button, and *my* phone stopped ringing. A sallow-skinned teen with several upper teeth missing, and garlanded by contrails of skunk, he handed me a slim parcel and, brandishing the handheld verification machine at collarbone height, said:

'Yo, dude, defo need a name for disun. Dey sayz. Important, innit.'

I signed his little screen with a (swollen) finger and accepted the parcel while muttering vague thanks that hopefully didn't sound threatening.

'You okay, man?' he asked, dubiously, as if I could not possibly be trusted with his delivery.

'Yeah,' I coughed.

We both stood for a few seconds, cottony darkness pressing against our eardrums. I was acutely aware that, save for a teal towel tucked round the waist, I was technically naked, and that he was probably aware of this, too. But in any case, the motion-activated communal hall light suddenly popped off, and I found myself wondering what good could come from being in such a situation with a pubescent druggie... But then we were back in the light, and I coughed again:

'All good. Cheers. Yeah.'

'Well, if you sayz so. *Enjoy*.' And he withdrew a spliff from the breast pocket of his uniform – the one directly under the company logo – and backed away.

When I saw him leave the building from my balcony window – the faint thud of the front door was as welcome as the ascultation of my child's heartbeat *in utero* – I repaired to bed and turned the parcel in my hands. Slim as a poetry collection yet, if anything, less forgiving to the touch, I angled the bedside lamp so that it was unsteadily illumined, and tore open the packaging... And O, dear reader, right there in the sweaty carwash of my sheets, I almost passed out, or passed away, in sheer pleasure of anticipation... I made a sound like a dying computer's final sigh, a distant heave, or electric *diminuendo*... For there, there, *there* in my hands, in my quivering dewy mitts, was a DVD of *Goncharov*. Was this merely a luxury of the addled mind? Oddly, I felt compelled to grab a tissue and wipe the plastic cover repeatedly. Not exactly unsteadiness, but a sense of general insecurity assailed me as I regarded it.

This was *Goncharov*, the 1973 Martin Scorsese-directed classic gangster flick, that had been (for reasons we shall come to) deleted from circulation. Copies were notoriously difficult to come by, particularly on DVD, and I had forgotten that I had half-heartedly ordered several copies (on VHS and DVD and even the soundtrack) online over a year ago, and later attempted to illegally download it from several different streaming sites, which cost me three laptops to incurable viruses. It was a no-brainer. I gave up on trying to find it.

Yet here it was, and, *no*. Wait... It could just be a blank DVD... I could have been scammed... oh, the *horror*....But I had been released from my illness, shot out from it into full consciousness – with *Goncharov* as my provisions for one. No longer roiling in my own foul moisture, I made the living room in two bounds and, cursing the modern world, fired up my laptop and shook with frustration until the *Ta-Dah* of the Apple save-screen came, as if led by a leash, from bottom right to top left.

I thrust in the disc and with the same movement dropped to my knees on the tussocky rug. I had a second or two to think that this was all too good to be real, and another few to consider where this DVD had come from, and still a few more to feel simultaneously very frightened and very bored. And then I pressed PLAY, and everything changed.

****

When this magazine asked me to write about something I found fascinating on or about the Internet, you'd think I'd have been thoroughly chuffed. And I was, I *am*: what *scope*. The Internet is, after all, a glittering maze of rabbit-holes, conspiracy theories, sex, indulgence, idiocy, money-drains, furious accusations, eerie footage, vibrant icebergs, family archives, allusive algorithms, religious posturing, genuine artistic endeavour, love letters, forgotten comedy, televisual nostalgia, emails you don't want and no one will ever need, trex and more trex and yet more trex, thirst traps, reverse-pic-checks... It never ends.

And I could decide what I wanted to write about? *Really*? This is *the best assignment in the world*, I thought. What unbridled literary joy.

I considered a piece on bestgore.com, a now defunct site that used to host all the Islamic beheadings and much more... I must have watched dozens of snuff videos on there, from serial killers' Go Pro POV to cartel chainsaw beheadings to leaked police crime-scene walk-throughs to the aftermaths of religious massacres...

I understand why it was taken down, due to the fact that it had to luridly advertise itself to thrive, but it was, I felt, a necessary place to view such things. And I still consider such things important to view. Unless, of course, your internal pandemonium instructs you to do such things yourself, in which case you shouldn't be viewing any online content or even reading this...

I briefly considered a piece on the Mariana Web, a level of the Internet below the Deep Web and the Dark Web, a place where only Quantum Computers held true sway. But, for obvious reasons, I couldn't research that, alas.

So I decided to write about something that had intrigued me for well over a year: *Goncharov*. And here is my confession, dear reader: the film never existed. Everything I wrote above was a lie. If it read like my fiction, then good, it was just that, if overblown and rushed. But I didn't make up *Goncharov*, oh no.

The Internet made *that* up.

****

In 2000 or thereabouts, someone on Tumblr posted (together with a photo):

i got these knockoff boots online and instead of the brand name on the tag they have the name of an apparently nonexistent martin scorsese movie???
what the fuck

And, save for a solitary – and immediately brilliant response –

this idiot hasn't seen goncharov

that would have been that, had not some natty opportunist in 2020, presumably from boredom or frustration during one or other Covid-19 Lockdown, decided to run with it and create a film that never existed.

He/she/they began posting about having seen it, and soon others did too. At this juncture it's just a swing-door joke. Comment, disappear – no one cares. But, unbeknownst to us all, the Internet had lanced out its feelers... Up, down, sideways, even in dimensions unexpected... The photo of said boots showed that they did have that message stitched on the tag. The boots were most likely a sweatshop merchandising shoe-in for the 1972 film *Gomorrah*, which was endorsed by Scorsese, but none of that mattered. What mattered was *this idiot hasn't seen goncharov*... We instantly imagine the following: *if he* had *seen Goncharov*, then he wouldn't be such an idiot, now, would he?

Moral decisions, and here we genuflect, gratefully, and perhaps wonder if all or any of this had to do with Ivan Alexandrovich Goncharov – the novelist who began his career with *A Common Story* and concluded it with a memoir entitled *An Uncommon Story*. He worked, for a time, as a censor...

In 2020 someone made a poster for the film. I have it here. Not quite colluding to the Hollywood template, which arguably makes it more lovable, not less, the poster features Bobby De Niro, Tommy-gun in hand (a manipulated still from *The Godfather Part 2*) marching toward the viewer under the title in red. *Martin Scorsese Presents* appears *above* the title, which was clearly never going to happen in 1973, and above all of that is

AL PACINO   ROBERT DE NIRO   GENE HACKMAN
HARVEY KEITEL

Well, *I ask you.*

The tagline is WINTER COMES TO NAPLES. The Neapolitan skyline appears as a blood-red Photoshop rendering on the right and a silhouetted Kremlin appears as a blood-red Photoshop rendering on the left, over De Niro's shoulders. Beneath these red renderings are, on the left, Cybill Shepherd and Gene Hackman (in resplendent ushanka), and on the right, Harvey Keitel (eye-patched) and both Al Pacino and Joe Cazale in the background (nonchalantly, even defiantly, smoking cigarettes). It's a fine poster, even if it feels like it was designed by a reinstated employee who had been fired for pointing out sex abuse in the modern workplace – that frown of hope. It's okay, just, as a poster. And the Pacino and Cazale are clearly from *Godfather Part 2.*

There are rules as to what constitutes a meme:

1. an element of a culture passed from one individual or other non-genetic means

2. an image, video, piece of text etc typically humorous in nature, that is copied and spread rapidly online, with slight variations...

So *Goncharov* fits them exactly.

The film has a plot, a cast, a soundtrack, a trailer... It is, to my mind, simply what the Internet does best: vibrantly inventing no matter what. I am aware that people hate, or can't cope, or believe that such things shouldn't be allowed, etc., but *I* think that's where life thrives. Being uncomfortable is how we grow. *Goncharov* wasn't a quantity until it garnered belief, but now it has, it lives.

The plot, so far as I can muster is: Robert De Niro, the eponymous character, is a Russian gangster (and discotheque-owner) who has fled Moscow for undisclosed reasons – presumably to do with disco – for a new life in Naples of all places. But his fiancé Katya (Cybill Shepherd) is a spy and has inadvertently drawn heat from former love-interest Andrei (Harvey Keitel), who has only one eye due to an unspecified (and clearly unfortunate) accident... There's a one-legged Jewish refugee played by silver-screen siren Sofia Loren thrown into the mix and a subplot involving talking dogs. I could *buy* that. Who couldn't?

But there's a volatile hitman called Ice Pick Joe (John Cazale) on their tail. If that last one isn't a Tarantino-clue, then also included in the cast (and seen in the beautifully edited trailer) are Al Pacino, Gene Hackman and Daniela Bianchi.

As if things couldn't get even more confusing, Lynda Carter – the original *Wonder Woman* – produced a photo of herself and Henry Winkler (The Fonz in *Happy Days*) attending the premiere of *Goncharov* at Grauman's Chinese Theater off Hollywood Boulevard, back in '73. And with the recent re-emergence of the *Goncharov* legend, she, obviously realising that humour is paramount for stable mental health, last week got John Travolta in on the gig and they did a dance routine for *Goncharov*, raising $123,000 in twelve minutes. (Though what the money could possibly, or legally, be used for we shall never know.) I sensed sadness in them, a lifelong sadness that I'll wager stems from never being satisfied. Still, money is money. And even Scorsese himself got in on the joke. His daughter Deanna Martin publically tweeted him:

Dad, have you seen Goncharov?

And Martin Scorsese duly tweeted back:

Yes, that's one I directed years ago.

So there it is, a history as murky as a child's discarded Elastoplast, but no real history at all. And was it *all* made up?

****

A postscript: I feel this needs saying again. Joe Cazale appeared in only five films during a seven-year period. Every one of those films was nominated for the Best Film Academy Award, a record highly unlikely to ever be surpassed. Three of them won it. His films were (in order):

The Godfather
The Coversation
The Godfather Part II
Dog Day Afternoon
The Deerhunter

Joe Cazale died of lung cancer before the Oscars ceremony where Meryl Streep (his partner up till that point) called him, 'the love of my life.' Surely, if he hadn't died, he would have been an Academy six-er, for *Goncharov*.

****

Cybill Shepherd and De Niro did actually appear together in *Taxi Driver* (1976), as did Harvey Keitel, as Matt 'Sport' Higgins, the pimp of 13-year-old Jodie Foster's character Iris. Director Martin Scorsese has talked at length about both actors' involvement, as has Jodie Foster about hers, in separate interviews, so that has no place here.

Yet perhaps that's what this is: a reconciliation.

Daniela Bianchi, often overlooked, retired from acting, grew out of Bond-girl nonsense, opened a boutique in Milan, and was happier for that.

Gene Hackman retired from the acting life and began writing novels, and with his wife in Santa Fe, New Mexico, began raising horses, and was happier for that.

****

And that anxious feeling in my core – that fear of drowning, of going blind, and choking on tears in my sleep... It was surely all make-believe too, no? Was everything made up, with a sense of aesthetic bliss?

Nature Human Behaviour, 2019

On Sex

Should I get engaged to K.?
Not if she won't tell me the other letters in her name...

That's a Woody Allen joke, so perhaps not the best place to start, given his... Let's start again, from the top, people, shall we? Company, together now, *tutti*, from the top, yes, even you, Dav...

I had been asked to write about sex several times, most notably for a (now obsolete) men's magazine in 1998, when I was dating a famous woman... And I secretly coveted the challenge. In fiction, sex writes white. It's one of the things fiction can't do, along with dreams and belief, and, arguably, sincere happiness. But this piece isn't fiction. What worried me back then was that I wanted to write about sex humorously – it seemed the only logical way to tackle the subject – and that doing so would open me up to allegations of misogyny. How does one get *any of it done*, without laughter? After all, laughter is one of the best forms of birth control. Would the whole endeavour be worth the hassle? I sighed.

In 1998 I was a mildly successful model, and duly played the bad boy cum diarist part. Gosh, was I a dreamboat, and my outlook was – do it now, do it *all* now, or you'll regret having *not* done it for the rest of your life. I was entirely correct, and have never once since regretted being such a monumental slut. When word got out that I wasn't a story-seller, fame-hound, or ever likely to be knowingly indiscreet, I became for a time the go-to companion of girl-band pop starlets and rock-chicks... I squired D-list soap stars and B-list grunge and Emo actresses, humourless newsreaders and glistening sportswomen, scuzzy, jaded party girls, an elegant concert pianist famed for her sensual phrasing, a page 3 model, a ballerina (who had muscle-control in places one wouldn't presume) and even an American Feminist writer...

I enjoyed a week-long tryst with the young sister of a future Prime Minister: I was performing as part of a troupe of actors and singers in Fingask Castle in Perthshire, and she happened to be the caterer... we would rise from our four-poster bed and go blackberry picking among the prickly hoary hedgerows... Romance was never like this, or at least never this obvious.

Hell, there was even the occasional dalliance with another male model... this was showbiz, and theatrical types are notoriously unfussy about who they put their cocks up. In short, I was passed around like a dog-toy, and loved every second of it. It was suddenly *de rigueur* to do me.

A friend once delicately suggested that I was self-mythologizing all this, that it was all mere manifestation. I replied that if he'd been there, he would have *wept*. The sheer *amount* of pussy would have precipitated a weeping jag. Sometimes three couplings per day, there was so much pussy that I felt it followed me, like a fart-cloud or an aura. I could be walking down the street and passersby might stop me and ask: 'Did you drop that, sir?' And yes, *there* would be some pussy that had fallen out of my pocket onto the pavement. 'Thank you kindly, yes, that pussy *is* mine,' I would reply cavalierly, re-pocketing said pussy. I was a fervent alpinist and there were mountains of minge to scale.

But even before all this, way back in balmy '93 or thereabouts, I noticed a startling change... I'll wager that most people aren't sack artists from the get go – worthwhile endeavours take practise – and my sexual beginnings were no different. Tentative, somewhat un-invigorating and decidedly vanilla, it was only when I lost a great deal of weight, teenage acne mysteriously vanished, and I became muscularly defined due to a fleeting obsession with weight-training and rock-climbing, that suddenly I became happily irresistible to womenfolk. But that initial change wasn't the startling one, oh no – the startling change was when the *black* girls started wanting to fuck me. This, I felt, heralded a new era of prowess – like the feminine of *prow* – because black girls' standards of what constituted an attractive male form were markedly superior to white girls'...

At some point humankind is going to have to acknowledge that the 90s was our pinnacle as a species. That decade took me from 12 to 22. Brit Pop was all the rage, Tony Blair was the young charismatic PM we hadn't seen the likes of before, the economy was in fine fettle, British novels were blooming, prizes were flying this way and that, and we were proud... But one of the big differences then was pubic hair – back then everyone had some. The posher girls sculpted it, or maintained what was called a *landing strip*, but they weren't shaved à la mainstream porn. Now, in 2018, I haven't seen a resplendent bush in over seven years... I recently asked a friend, Dav – used to be David but someone stole his ID – a Sonographer and Radiographer – basically he looks at pussies all day – to corroborate this, my assumption being that not even Warren Beatty in his heyday could have possibly seen that many pussies per hour, despite the swinging studio doors. And my friend Dav cheerfully acquiesced to the verisimilitude of this pubic thatch lore. Apparently the *elderly* do it now. Imagine the *state* of those safety razors, oy vey... Is someone fetching Dav's ID? Is *any*one looking?

(To feint sideways for a moment: around that time – I'll scatter a guess at 1997 – I decided, for entirely non-sexual purposes, mind, to try out a prostitute, or, if you prefer, to have the prostitute experience. And it *was* non-sexual: I actually just wanted to know how it all went down, sorry, how it all *happened*... Call it research, if you like, that old chestnut; research, I suppose, for this.

In those days you made a call, they named their price and gave you an address, and you simply turned up and buzzed the bell, with, in my case, a complicated bag of feelings. Apprehension, exhilaration, a hot torpid hunger and an almost physically painful longing for tremendous stretches of bare female skin that you had *paid* to touch: here was the future... But no, it was a fiasco. Buzzed in, I ascended the stairs of the building in Kilburn – I was a student, and £40 was £40 – and was greeted at the door by a tiny fierce lady in the shape of a capital *O*. I had never seen so perfectly rotund a human before, but had little time to consider this, as I noticed, over her shoulder in the kitchen of the flat, a slobbering Rottweiler with demon-encrusted eyes under the linoleum-topped table.

Who puts linoleum on a table? I thought, as I entered, paid, and was directed to a room at the end of a corridor flanked floor-to-ceiling in red, burgundy and vermillion drapes. I noticed the carpet hadn't been cleaned, but the drapes were heavily scented. Yet as I approached my assigned room, all I could hear was the huge dog, panting as if in great lust in the kitchen behind, a constant beat in the ear. Any inkling of sexiness had unequivocally vanished. With a resigned shrug, I went in. There was no one there. I sat on the side of the (red) bed for a bit and imagined what getting an erection, let alone maintaining one, might be like. Then I looked around. There was ease in the décor, a beguiling simplicity – chest of drawers, tall cupboard and two pink bedside tables. Unsure of due etiquette, I didn't open any drawers. Perhaps that was a test, who knew? On a reclining chair in one corner, a beige cardigan, balding at the elbows, lay crumpled...

Then the assigned lady came in and introduced herself as 'Tony'. Tony was at least fifteen years older than me and looked like she was listening to something I couldn't hear – jaded, but not drug-addled, she carried herself with grace, like a dancer, yet when she stood still her feet were at ten-to-two, almost like a duck's. Well versed enough to read my deflated expression, she said: 'I'm going to get freshened up. Would you like to watch a video while you wait for me?' *Tony*, it struck me, wasn't the best hooker name of all time, but she seemed to be conscientious, so I duly agreed and pressed PLAY on the remote as she left the room. Nothing happened. I got up to take a look at the VCR. Something was clearly wrong, so I fiddled a couple of the leads and the TV screen suddenly flashed up static, and at ear-shattering volume... Yes, an utter fiasco. But Tony, as it happened, was fairly sweet, abrupt, honest and clear. One thing that I never forgot: she asked me if I had a girlfriend. I lied. And after we had finished, she ruffled my hair.)

But to return to racial matters, there are fascinating cultural quirks that reveal themselves in the bedroom and nowhere else. (These are necessarily sweeping remarks, mind, and I can of course only speak from my own experiences. 'Well that's just your opinion...' 'Who else's did you think it would be?' Alas, sadly, this needs to be pointed out.) For example, the salutary Japanese habit of mewling as if in pain when nearing orgasm (both yours *and* hers: happy days) took some adjusting to, or the American oddity of not considering oral sex to be sex at all. While not strictly penetrative, I suppose, although I am always unsure why a mouth should be of less importance than a vagina or an arse-crack, an American girl can honestly – in front of her god and parents – claim to be a virgin while doling out blowjobs willy-nilly. Yet in Britain, it's what girls happily do *after* full sex has taken place, some responsible intimacy having been established. Cultural quirks, hey ho.

Canadian girls have issues with cuddling at night because they overheat – this may not be an issue in Canada itself, but in the places I have consorted with them (Putney, Dublin, Reykjavik) they throw off the covers and sweat like boiler room stokers on the *Titanic* if one tries spooning... and I was always a talented spooner. When comparing Canada and the US in any way, it is always useful to remember Hitchbot. Hitchbot was a hitchhiking robot that made it all the way across Canada in 26 days with multiple drivers, and attempted to do the same in the US, but was instantly beaten to death in Philadelphia. Two weeks later the battered bot was found, thrown in an alley, its arms and one leg propped beside its crumpled form.

Black girls have more energy between the sheets than any other race, *catch up*, but Nordic girls like out-door shagging more than any others. They *insist*... something akin to grazing, I always felt. Eastern Europeans, excluding Russians, are the most genuinely enthusiastic. Perhaps it is connected to freedom from Communism – everything goes, you can do *everything* now. And they *do* do everything, and not just on your birthday. They do it on their own birthday as well. Double trouble. And all of them, Poles, Slovaks et al share the realistic French resignation to affairs... I could continue *ad nauseam*, and don't even get me started on the joys of Jewish girls and Alaskans...

A brief aside: a Czech partner told me about the films she watched with her family after the fall of Communism. Suddenly VHS tapes were available, but one person, wretchedly, dubbed all the films. She had me crying with laughter at her impersonations. Kyle Reese shoots the Terminator with a half-hearted '*Ow*'. Ripley blows the zenomorph out of the airlock – perhaps *blows* is ill-advised – with a languid: 'Yeah, that's it gone now', followed by the audible drag of a cigarette. And that's a little how they treat sex: with vim but not deep emotion.

****

It's going swimmingly – just keep the beat, people. Keep the beat steady... Did Dav just leave? Dash it all. Well, *Allegro*, people, aaaannnd...

...But what of looks? We have not touched on physical appearance... I must tread carefully here – that dog's head of misogyny rears up and barks a warning – alarum! – but I will say this. As an opera singer, I have often sung Puccini's aria *Recondita armonia*, from *Tosca*. Straight off the bat – the tenor has only sung for a minute – my character, Mario Cavaradossi, a painter, compares the dark beauty of his girlfriend Tosca, whom the audience has not yet met, with the blonde beauty of the woman he is painting (who turns out to be pertinent to the plot). Well... in my sexual experience, well over 90% of the women I have tangled with were dark... Save for one somewhat important one... But the dark wasn't just any dark: it was gypsy dark.

Gypsy, word-wise, has been cancelled: even the *Lymantria dispar* (colloquially Gypsy Moth) has had to be renamed Spongy Moth. This is because gypsy was a word coined to denigrate, to persecute. But look at *Carmen*. In Central Europe, the word gypsy, while still derogatory, denotes a feistiness of character, if not desirable availability. Probably from the bad side of the river, or a town over yonder that used to boast munition factories... And *those* were the girls *I* liked – the Musettas, not the Mimìs – a hint of mischief, something askance in the gaze or some unusual political stance. I abhorred boredom.

And dark-haired girls were more adventurous. They smoked: a sure sign of a better lay. It's true – girls who smoke are better in the sack. You don't need me to tell you why. Perhaps there were just more dark girls than fair, perhaps I was blinkered, or perhaps I settled into a niche and didn't try harder with the blondes. Yet it's true, not by want, or nature or nurture, I didn't seem to have diddled that many blondes – until the one I married and had children with. The mother of my children – she was all-out brutal full-on blonde (for maximum contrast gain), a top future tockbae, blonder than any blonde had a right to be...

There is also – and it's an endless topic – the question of having 'got to the end' of a partner sexually. I have had many chats with friends along such lines:

'Ez, mate, we need to talk. I split up with Melania last night...'

'How do you feel?'

'I'm in a world of pain.'

'*Ah*, then you haven't got to the end of her sexually.'

Because, if he had got to the end of her sexually, then there'd be no conversation, and little regret, and you wouldn't be reading this.

The relationship I was in for most of my twenties and early thirties – the Bush years – began at a then unknown, but now celebrated, author's party. On his balcony I was gleefully burning a book. Now, I don't condone burning books: idiocy and theism beckons. But the book was by Richard Littlejohn – an infamous xenophobe and appalling human, not to mention the *writing*... Yet there I was, burning a Littlejohn when a girl came out and vomited into the garden below while I held her hair back from the flow. That was H. She had an endearingly awkward quiver in her speech and laugh, as if she was observing life through a lense of mirth. Four years older than me, H. had nervous hands and appeared unglazed by cosmetics. Dressed nicely for the party, I remember asking her if she was going to a *ball*. Her smile was a phenomenal concentration of genetic blessings – plush lips, bowling-pin teeth – but her character was even finer than the diamond geometry of her figure. After the vomit and the book-burning we had a four hour chat about nude calendars and, as morning was drawing in, went home together to my flat in Notting Hill. And I knew she was *the one* (or at least the one for a while) when I awoke the following afternoon and she had cleaned my toilet... Raggedy head, slide-guitar inner ears, skin mottled as an Upper East Side New Yorker in June... I didn't even ask why she'd cleaned my toilet, simply pulled her back into bed. I never did quite get to the end of *her*, sexually. I didn't get bored of it: of not doing anything else. But to get to the end of someone sexually entails finding nothing to say, outside the bed, bedroom, or even shower. And there is *always* stuff to say in the shower.

You realise one day, smoking a casual yet bitter cigarette outside, that your sexuality needs to go somewhere else... I never got to the end of H. sexually, but alas, I wanted children and she didn't... Oddly, one can get to the end of someone sexually and then rekindle something years later and everything is new and doubly alluring because you know each other's bodies so well, and yet not at all. It's like cheating with yourself, or your history, and this makes it all the dirtier and less inhibited. Some of the best sex you'll ever have is with exes, in much the same way that some of the best drinks you'll ever imbibe are alone, in your study, writing an article like this, cock-in-hand.

In my late thirties I found that one's sex-life divides into before- and after- having children. I always wanted to be a father. The joke goes that even when I was a boy I wanted a girl. But truthfully I didn't care, so long as I could make that baby as happy as possible, or at least give him or her or them a more loving life than I had had. Secretly, as I believe many men do, I wanted to have a girl just to see how the other half lives – and that's a figure of speech. No need to get riled up for perceived discrimination. Besides, it reads better than *as the other percentage lives...*

My son came along in 2013, and while my relationship with his mother didn't endure, I found my sexual attitudes and appetites had subtly changed again... I began fancying decidedly older women... Why was this? I was thirty-seven, and had complicated mileage on the clock, but was relatively unscathed, looks-wise, by time. Yet suddenly the youngsters all looked even younger than they had before, and the older women had more to say, more humour, more understanding... Not to mention sack know-how and age-emboldened security of opinion. There was also something about the eyes – they didn't glow innocently, like the youngsters' – they glowed like wire filaments, harshly, but with full appreciation of the heat involved. The electric circuitry of the older woman, like jammed metal, and all the more alluring for that.

These seismic sexual changes have always felt rather abrupt to me, yet I cannot deny them. Colum McCann wrote, in *Let the Great World Spin*, 'the thing about love is that we come alive in bodies not our own', a line that I have seen more than once attributed to Milan Kundera. Now, Milan Kundera – *there* was a guy who could write about sex in fiction without it writing white – by inventing a unique language and way of dealing with it. Terse and glassy, his prose (particularly in *The Unbearable Lightness of Being*) perfectly reflects the mechanics of the act, while keeping readers at a convenient distance, via the use of short sentences and sparse metaphor. And of course he knew Czech girls and wrote about what I described earlier.

An alarmingly abrupt one of these changes happened around age forty. Not exactly at forty, that would have been too neat, although I would have preferred the pleasing symmetry. No, it happened at around forty-one and a half... I became invisible. Suddenly women didn't *see* me anymore... Until then I had almost always ended up in bed with any woman I wanted – and suddenly it wasn't like that anymore. An epoch had ended. There's much to be said for being settled down by that age, an age when you're still visible to women, some kind of a sexual threat: because what makes a man is not being *not* sexually threatening, it's learning how to *be* that – for evolutionary purposes – but controlably (and intelligently) so. As Pierre Teilhard de Chardin wrote: Growing old is like being penalized for a crime you didn't commit.

****

'Where's Dav? What was the matter? He definitely left? Okay. From bar 69 people, trumpets *on* my beat.'

Another one of these changes happened to me right at the beginning: when I was a child. Growing up in a household with a mother who professed herself celibate was hardly healthy. And this was in the days of the true meaning of the word celibate: unmarried, and nothing other than (or more than) unmarried. My mother was actually *chaste*. But the intervening years have interestingly remoulded that word, and now it has given rise to a whole toxic culture, of Incels, or 'involuntary celibates'. These guys – and some of them, like the murderous troglodyte Elliot Rodger, are surprisingly good-looking – believe that women *owe* them: sex, love, recognition, subservience... And there we are – a religious movement. Men invented religions and gods to control women: of course, what *else* was a logical step, when men fully grasped that they had no say over their offspring?

Inceldom, to me, is just another offshoot of theism. Males: I say it again – you don't have to even be *that* brilliant... Just a little spark will attract a mate, a tiny, flickering spark. Humour is a hearty evolutionary tool. Shake the tail feathers. Incels: you are slaves to your own inadequacies. And of course gods, the same gods who ought to have looked out for those you killed, but instead blessed you with coruscating entitlement...

But now we must momentarily move away from the flippant comic voice and shift into the realm of the raptor... the child abuser. It had to happen, I'm sorry that it cannot be ignored. This particular seismic shift happened when I was 11, nearly 12 and had to do with such a raptor. The etymology of paedophilia is literally [for the] 'love of children'. And I am certain that many of them would justify their actions this way: they believe they are loving children. An excuse, a get-out clause, like god. Certainly my abuser felt that way when he abused me, sometimes – in a flat in St John's Wood – where my mother was only four rooms and a short corridor away. Let's repeat that: only four rooms and a short corridor away. And what mind would it take, to think that acceptable, even as *loving children*? And what kind of astonishing presumption?

Four rooms and a short corridor away: this situation was complicated by the fact that my mother was in love with the man who was in residence to abuse her son, and not love her... He was her guest (and mine) and thus had his own bedroom, into which he took me. It was my dead brother's old room. Four rooms and a short corridor away, my mother was physically doing his dirty laundry. She was washing his underpants clean, by hand, because he didn't feel that our family washing machine was quite up to scratch. I still think that this was a humiliation tactic. And I think he abused her, at least in his mind, as much as he abused me. I have never written about this before, although I have discussed it in radio interviews and briefly on TV. I wonder why that is. I think it has something to do with the fact that I love language, and never wished to sully my pages with any trace of him. But I am old enough now, at 44, the advent of my twilight years, or more realistically, the beginning of the end, to write about him... So I will give him one sentence. The sentence is this: You are unworthy of my words and squalid in your beliefs; you are human, but only because you exist four rooms and a short corridor away from complete insignificance.

Stretto, people, *stretto*, and strings: *con il cantante*, yes?

So, after my son was born there was the aforementioned shift, the post-children sex-life. A sexless life is hugely unnatural, especially when endured for gods, and I have never gone more than a month without it. I always believed that it was only half a life without a woman, and so I rapidly availed myself of several after splitting up with my ex-wife. That may sound 'curt for cunt' (as a writer friend put it), but it was my life to live, and my choices to make. And now I am in it: the sexual twilight epoch. I am fairly solidly settled, with an Eastern European partner – cheer from the stalls – why settle for less than you deserve? – and three tortoises, Emily Hoffmann, Darth Murray and Jorja Horowitz. What pertains of the old life?

I occasionally play video games. And my user name is always female. My gaming profile picture is a female avatar, usually sporting green or pink hair and giving the finger or flashing a gang sign. Why? Because it is truly pleasurable to watch opponents cave, especially – particularly – the religious ones, to what they think is a *woman*. The horror. I taunt them in PlayChat and GoogleGamePlay: *how does it feel to lose to a girl?* And invariably they reply with the abuse I cheerfully expect. It's some kind of a victory – however tiny – and it makes me smile and nod to myself: yeah, that's how you do it. That's a good response to male dominance: just fucking with you all. Yes, that's how to do it. I just fuck with y'all.

I often think back over my ridiculous life and shake my head, sagely. Then I shake it again, with resolution. No, no regrets, none at all. Why *should* there be regrets?

You buttoned it, people, *con amore*, you made me proud: one little thing though – if you do find Dav's ID, please return it to the box-office...

****

It would be remiss of me, even irresponsible, to end without a word on love. In *The Only Story* Julian Barnes writes:

> But don't ever forget... Everyone has their love story. Everyone. It
> may have been a fiasco, it may have fizzled out, it may never even
> have got going, it may have been all in the mind, that doesn't make it
> any less real. Sometimes, it makes it more real. Sometimes, you see a
> couple, and they seem bored witless with one another, and you can't
> imagine them having anything in common, or why they're still living
> together. But it's not just habit or complacency or convention or
> anything like that. It's because once, they had their love story.
> Everyone does. It's the only story.

Julian Barnes has never published an ugly sentence, and the above passage is not even one of his best, but it captures love perfectly. Cave paintings were drawn on walls to attract a mate; the human voice was first raised in song to attract a mate. That's something I always remember when I stand up to sing in front of an audience, and subconsciously feel the line stretching back to the old Troubadours...

It's the only story. And we all have one.

Mumsnet, 2022

Readers' Questions

This Q & A was conducted online, as part of a blog (as opposed to a vlog – the visual equivalent), thus both the submissions and my answers were written, not spoken, hence their inclusion here. This immediately followed a radio interview I had just given – a whole hour to talk about one's own book, what bliss! – and the Blog was part of the radio station's website.

If a tree falls in a deep dark wood and there is no one there to see it fall, are you still a cunt?
  Leo Price, Birmingham

An excellent start, and one truly in the spirit of what the Internet's all about, or ought to be all about.

I admire your use of the cliché *deep dark wood* in this question, because it shows you have absorbed the fairytale elements of the book, which means you're either guessing, or have actually bought it. If the latter, well done, and I hope it improves your language skills, because while clichés are bad enough, I think the original metaphor is: *If a tree falls in a forest and no one around to* hear *it* [...] An interesting philosophical thought experiment designed to raise questions of observation and perception, if memory serves, the wording first appeared in a 1910 book entitled *Physics* by Charles Mann and George Twiss, although I can't claim to have read it. However, perhaps I ought to claim that I have read it, since I can't become any more of a cunt, surely?

I knew your mother in the mid-80s at Leeds University when we were both in Professor Zygmunt Bauman's class. What are your memories of that time, and of him?
  Christopher Powis, Edinburgh

I think you may have confused me with my older brother and overlooked the fact that I was born in 1978. But funnily, I do have some memories of him. My mother died in 2015, and I have talked about her extensively in print elsewhere, and so will not do that again here. But Prof Bauman occasionally babysat me in his first-floor office at Leeds Uni, and while he did whatever he was doing at his desk (correcting essays? writing his own stuff? simply doing admin?) used to make me gurgle with pleasure by making paper aeroplanes and sending them my way while gently shouting: "AIRMAIL" and making flying shapes with his arms. As a child I thought him a curious wonder of a grown-up human, and now I am a grown-up human I consider him a wonderful and curious man. And I was lucky to have known him, even if I didn't really make the most of it at the time. One related question I'm often asked is: Do you think your mother was a better writer than you are? The answer to that is: I consider everyone to be a better writer than I am. I think of myself as a musician. Having said that, my mother's stuff is very different from mine, so there's really nothing to compare.

Can we ask more than one question?
  Luba Direnzo, New York

Naturally, but in your case, I'm afraid not.

What do you consider your best book? I know you've done five but claim only two of them are any good... And what are you working on now?
  Sappho X, London

You're more up to date than I am! But yes, on social media I do claim that. The first three were poetry collections, and I don't count them, although it was nice to be in one anthology where I found myself next to my own mother in the index...

Right now I'm working on a memoir for my son as sole reader – an odd conceit – but also my big horror novel *Weltschmerz*. I'm really enjoying writing *that*. It's the first thing I've set outside Britain or the other European countries I know well, and it's a large-scale haunting... My favourite of my books will always be the next one. I can't recall who said that, but I *can* recall this lovely anecdote: When Joseph Heller was asked in interview why he'd never written a better book than his first, *Catch-22*, he would always reply: Well, who *has*?

On a related point, I actually read *Fairytales and Oddities* for the first time the other day. This may sound an odd, contrived or insincere thing to say, but writers cannot actually *read* their own books until a certain distance has been reached. It's curious. That distance takes nine months or so for me. When you do finally sit down (you never *curl up* with your own stuff) and read it as a reader, of course there are thorny corners you could have shaped better, and the false quantities you missed leap out at you in techno-punk colours ('How could I *possibly* have missed *that* one?') and, while each is a paper-cut to the soul, it is now a past production, so you don't care with your full heart.

Let it go. Farewell my child. Consciously you forget the material, but your trusty subconscious is there to make sure you don't reuse anything memorable. I'm already deep into writing two new books concurrently, but I don't give repeating myself a second's thought. It's the same with music. I was rummaging through the storage space under my sofa on Sunday and I came across a plush blue-bound opera score. Flipping it open I found the pages marked up in my own hand, and it slowly dawned that I had once performed the work, but my brain had filtered it out as being no-longer-needed information.

Where did you get the ideas [for Fairytales and Oddities] *from?*
Abbi Koldova, Czech Republic

I was sitting in the (empty) bar of the Ilmarine Hotel in Tallinn, Estonia, after a wonderful day exploring the city. It was late. Perhaps dusk. My then girlfriend was asleep upstairs. For some reason I needed to think. Or was it to drink? I required what is horribly called 'alone-time'. Thus, in that bar, the first lines were written. And the lines were the beginning of the third paragraph of The Town That Will Never Be Completed – *many boots have trampled this place...* And a spark formed.

But a spark can come from anything. A phrase overheard, an idea that excites the imagination, even just a single word.

I didn't set out to write a book of fairytales for adults – and only three of the 10 are based on real fairytales – it just happened that way. As a musician, I listen to what my ear tells me, and I trust in instinct to lead the prose.

What is your purpose as a writer?
Baz Brickshaw, Chiswick

Good question. I often feel a fraud in everything I do. How on earth did it come to this? While simultaneously not dismissing the ego, or placing too much *nous* on the id, I think I might drown in sentimentality at any given moment, but particularly upon waking up.

Still, I don't think any writer should wake and wonder if they have *a purpose*, or if their work has a *purpose*: I think that's a horrible concept. So I can't play along, alas.

In writing (and in music) I aim for aesthetic bliss – the Nabokovian idea of beauty of language transcending all, even morality. It's a musical thing, for me. If the sentence doesn't speak musically, then I recast it. The responsive verbal surface is everything – style over all.

Your question, I find, has somewhat discombobulated me.

I'm going to buy a copy of your book and ceremoniously burn it.
  George Williams, Glasgow

Why stop there? Why not buy ten copies of my book and burn them all? That'd really show me.

Of all your various careers, if you had to concentrate on one, which would you choose?
  Adrienne Walters, Hemel Hempstead

I'd rather be a writer in a warm climate than a musician in a cold one. Also, I can write anywhere, but to sing or play...

You have mentioned your mother [the poet Brenda Williams] *in your writing but never your father. How does he come into your story?*
  Don Weitz, Brighton

My father was a musician, but he gave up music before I was conceived, so I accept no blame. He was a composer and an opera singer with Welsh National Opera – a baritone – and for some reason, decided to destroy his legacy at twenty-five. I was born when he was twenty-eight. I have tried to research his musical history with the help of such wonderful old friends of his such as Martin Anderson (of Toccata Classics fame) and ex-girlfriends such as the actress Jane Asher (of *Alfie* and *The Masque of the Red Death* fame), violinist Sophie Langdon, and others, but no one has much to say about him. My dad seems to have been that oddest of things, an incredibly charismatic nobody. Or perhaps he blazed his streak so brightly that no one could keep up to remember, or he was so amazing that no one will now talk. Or perhaps he was simply a talentless nobody, and recognised it.

What *is* important is that I am deliberately leaving a legacy for *my* son. So that he will have me when I am gone. Unlike my own father, who is now... gone, in every way. There's nothing musical left of him. *Fizz.*

How do you prepare before you go on stage?
  Martina Court, London

I vocalise in my dressing room with the piano, but not too much. Five to ten minutes max. Never over-point the voice before you go on. You need to sound fresh, but also you need, I think, to feel (and sound) like it's the first time you've done it that day. For tenors it's a good idea to warm up with sharp exercises, not flat ones. Tenors 'read better' in flats, so exercises in sharps keep you on your toes.

And I never sing the same repertoire. For example, if I'm going on to do *Don Carlo*, I'll hum a little Kurt Weill in the wings, and if I'm going on to do Puccini's *Madama Butterfly*, then I'll hum a little Beatles. Also, lyric voices don't need anywhere near as long as dramatic ones to warm up, so it's easier for me than for some of my bigger-voiced colleagues.

As for reading my books in front of an audience, I just need more cigarettes afterwards.

What do you find most disappointing?
   Maddy Evans, Cornwall

The fact that my entire body cracks like a glowstick whenever I move, and yet steadfastly refuses to actually glow – that's highly disappointing. It would make the ageing process so much more entertaining.

Why are you still a cunt?
   Leo Price, Leeds

Ah, you've moved. That was quick.

Name a city that changed your life.
   Maria Ravel, London

Wuhan.

Your first book Losing Henry *includes several attempts to write women's characters. Nowadays such attempts by men are increasingly viewed as – at best – crass, dubious and misguided. You're not gay, so what made you think you could do it? Or is it that really, underneath it all, you silently agree with Jack Nicholson's character in* As Good As It Gets?
   Neil Formoy, Scotland
I do feel that your forthright assertion of my heterosexuality some-what underestimates me...

For those readers who don't know, Jack Nicholson's character in the multi-Oscar-winning film, Melvin Udall, is, in no order of importance, an obsessive-compulsive, racist, misanthropic, misogynistic, bigoted novelist who also happens to be a fine musician. So I'll take the musical compliment. But no, I don't hold Melvin Udall's views – and we should add that those views are necessarily fostered on him for the comedy to develop. The script has dated, of course it has, but why shouldn't it?

When you write from a female first-person perspective you feel much closer in... You feel involved in life in a way you don't when writing as a male. A fellow novelist described it as a *slow zoom* – the narrowing in on that which is often unavailable for male writers.

In *Fairytales and Oddities* I have three first-person narrators, a serial killer, a mythological creature from a lake, and – double trouble – a woman who finds herself in the middle of a global religious war. I like a challenge, what can I say?

Any plans to write about the composer William Byrd or any of his descendants?
Paul Featherstone, Norway

I didn't until you just mentioned it! Perhaps we should explain. The composer William Byrd (1539/40 – 1623) is my direct antecedent on the paternal side. I didn't do the research, my father did, and for a brief while I was the latest in the Byrd line of musicians. But then my son Eli came along and usurped my title. Not that I begrudge him it – also, at the time of writing, he's not yet eight, so may never become a musician. Which is completely fine, just so long as he's happy in whatever he finds what he wants to do that makes him happy.

And I write more than enough about myself already.

He is far more important.

Do you care what others think of you?
Michelle Riley, France

If I did we'd be here for a thousand years.

Alias Adora [the final story in Fairytales and Oddities*] feels like it should be a much longer work. What are your thoughts on this?*
Ben Foskett, Paris
Well, Ben, I'd say that's highly perceptive. And you're correct – it was intended as a longer work. In fact, what you read in *Alias Adora* was two different stories, the Milo Milkins one and the Lenny Plinth one. I always wanted to satirise a racist snooker star by heaping humiliation upon humiliation on him, and wrote a full story that ended with a

stowaway dying on a plane as it landed at Heathrow. Milo still lives in Hounslow, under the main flight-paths, but the rest was ditched. And Lenny Plinth was already a character in *Losing Henry*, and I found I liked him: he had some more life left to abuse on the page. But no one at all, in any of the book readings, radio interviews or other promotional events I have done for the book, has asked anything about the eponymous Adora. I always saw it as a three-hander, but readers clearly feel otherwise. I may have to resurrect her for something else. She deserves better, despite being a journalist.

The Town That Will Never Be Completed [the second story in Fairytales and Oddities] is a truly creepy story centred on a truly creepy character, outlining a series of truly creepy events. I can only imagine it could have only been cooked up by a truly creepy person. Am I right?
  Wilfred S, Canada

Unfortunately (or fortunately in my case), you'll have to ask the Estonian people, for it is one of theirs. Together with *The King of the Cats* and *Bluebeard*, it is one of only three actual traditional folk tales in the book. My retelling of it relies heavily on the plots of two operas: *Rigoletto* by Verdi, and *Die Meistersinger von Nürnberg* by Wagner. Both of these sources are highly creepy – the fascist overtones of the Meistersingers are personified in my Guildsmen – but Verdi's music of father/daughter relationships is always his best. Having lost both his daughters and subsequently his beloved wife, he went on to do what the artist does: he immortalised them in music. I can think of seven, but feel free to correct me, of his operas where father/daughter relationships form the backbone of the score. *Traviata* is my favourite, although *Aida* and *Boccanegra* follow close behind.

  I would say that it has to be creepy enough to make it readable.

  I would add that one ought not to confuse authorial voice with subject matter. The same book features a glitteringly abhorrent character that espouses racist views with vim.

  I am not him.

I hear you're writing a horror novel. What's it about?
  Callie Moorlake, London
Well, that would be telling, wouldn't it? What I can say is that the novel does exist, is called some variation on *Weltschmerz* and will take a while to resolve itself into a coherent book.

  But thanks for asking. It's heartening to know it might have an audience, even if it's just you and Leo Price.

I loved the illustrations [by Steve Poulacheris] *in* Fairytales and Oddities. *What is* [his] *background, and are you guys planning on working together again soon?*
　Betilda Morrison, Los Angeles

I can't speak on Steve's background – that's not mine to do – but his artwork certainly transformed the book, our book. It was the first time I'd ever worked with an illustrator, and the collaboration was transformative. Steve brought my characters to life in a way that I never imagined possible – now I can't see them any other way – and he was a fine critic during the process. His extraordinary eye, I felt, was proportionate to the degree of genius within.

Having said that, I'd never work with a visual artist again for one reason: control. Creatively, sharing is toxic: except for in Musical Theatre.

I hated that loss of control, and have vowed never to relinquish it again.

What's your favourite role as a singer?
　Kenneth Shaun Joynson, London

Without hesitation, *Andrea Chenier* – it's a role I haven't sung in full, although I have sung all the big bits: the three big arias, and one of the two huge duets. It's a tenor's dream – lots of high stuff (us tenors find that, oddly, easier), lots of loud stuff (it's easier to be loud) and lots of unmusical stuff to chomp on (it's easy to be unmusical in *Chenier*). It fits so perfectly in my voice that I almost imagine it was written for me – something that every singer ought to be allowed to say at least once in their life.

If I wasn't a tenor, I would love to sing *Billy Budd*. Those high As! What musical joy, and as a baritone, Scarpia and Jago.

Flipside, the most difficult role I ever sang was Mozart's *Idomeneo*. It's a dogged trudge of a role, a foul vocal beast, and with very few returns, although I have a fondness for it because my baby son heard me sing it.

What is your inner voice and what do you want to say or make people think? What type of journeys do you hope to take your readers on, and how do you hope they will be changed by your narratives?
　David Banbury, London

My 'inner voice' is inner for a reason. I don't want anyone going in there!

I take my readers, if they want to come with me, into a world of wonder and brilliance, of imagination and delight in language.

All writers want to change the world, but not *literally* – I would think it the height of bad manners to want to change any readers' opinions.

Still, as a musician, there's naturally a lot of music history in there, and a bit of education never hurt.

In Fairytales and Oddites, *you have a bit where your prose seems to veer off into reportage. What was the point of this, and is there more of it, or to it?*
Miles Rushton, London

I get asked this so often! I guess *Titbits With Williams*, the section you are referring to, touched a nerve in readers. The clue is in the title: no, not the titbits bit, the Williams bit. By putting myself in there, the reader knows something is happening. But what *is* happening? A classic American road trip, a narcissistic ego trip, something else entirely? I would gently ask for patience. *Titbits with Williams* hasn't run its course quite yet.

A last thing: watch that use of was and is. Stay in the tense.

How do you come up with all these unusual [character] *names?*
Carola Emrich Fisher, Germany

You have a pretty fine one yourself. There's a Saul Bellow novel with a cutthroat lawyer named Pinsker, an author surrogate with the surname Citrine. Herzog, Ravelstein, Sammler... Bellow is up there with Dickens for character names. I smile with unreluctant admiration at the multilingual puns of names in Nabokov's *Pnin* – check it out. It's really something. And Shakespeare doesn't need to be mentioned of course, since Shakespeare is always there, in every sense. I know I keep pretentiously going on about verbal surface, but a well-chosen name can excite the ear and keep the narrative zinging along.

There should be artifice in characters' names (hell, there should be artifice in everything one writes), but a bad name can totally alienate the reader. Clint Smoker in Amis's *Yellow Dog* is an obvious example, whereas Keith Talent (from his *London Fields*) is a genius name. *Cheers Keith! Keith, cheers!*

What would your superpower be?
   Lana Pretroyavitch, Krakow

To be allowed to speak, sing, or write, without fear of reprisals. Without fear of books, any books, or music being banned. Does that remind you of something, Lana from Krakow?

Do you have a motto?
   Mami Shikimori, Oxford

A question from the Proust Questionnaire! I don't, in all honesty, but there are two that I quite like, at least for right now:
Do what blows your hair back.
and
A boat is safe in the harbour, but that's not why we build boats.

Riverside Interviews, 2022

Beanie Baby Blues

Herein dwells something odd. A crazy tale, one of sadness and joyful frenzy, of clear sense and utter nonsense, of belief in, and the fall of, the gods of money. It's an American dream, perhaps *the* American Dream, writ large. Strap in, or on, it's quite the ride.

****

When Ty Warner – shapely boned, thinning black hair, horn-rimmed black glasses, and a primly cut smile – introduced a line of small fluffy animal toys called Beanie Babies to the world in 1993, his own brainchild, there was no indication that over the next decade – and beyond – the limp toys would be at the centre of one of the oddest economic bubbles ever recorded. An economic bubble that happened to coincide with the rise of the internet, or the Internet as it was then. No one could have imagined adults madly scrambling to collect as many of the toys as they possibly could – especially the rarer versions, like Peanut the Royal Blue Elephant, or the Princess Diana Memorial beanie baby – in the belief that their value would reach many thousands of dollars and potentially make their fortune... But then humans are strange obscure creatures. Let's take a moment, catch our collective breath, and examine the history.

By the end of the 1990s, Ty Warner owned a 370,000-square-foot warehouse, chockablock full of Beanie Babies. His merchandise in that one warehouse alone represented over $100 million worth of product. And he owned many more warehouses. But not one of those toys would ever be sold...

Tamed by deep sorrow, supply was starting to outstrip demand for Beanie Babies by 1998, and when the 'bubble' burst a few years later, many speculators and collectors were left with a huge stock of stuffed animal toys that, while undeniably cute, were as worthless as any other toy for a child to cuddle or play with. While Ty Warner became – and remains – a billionaire, and some of the earliest collectors were able to successfully cash in on the craze, many others lost their entire life savings. And this is all a mere smidgeon of the 90's Internet stock 'bubble'.

****

'Ty Warner was the worst boss in the world' – said Michele Quex – 'if we were one minute late he'd dock us a dollar for each minute.'

Briony Sozo added: 'He was smart, but an asshat. I guess you're gonna be hard-pressed to find anybody who liked him...'

'I would recommend not writing about this,' said Sam Mutrix, one of Warner's lawyers. 'He's still alive you know.'

'Yeah, but what can he do to me?' I laughingly asked, 'I'm just a writer.'

'You can write from me that he's a sociopath and a narcissist of the highest,' added Michele Quex, as the lawyer, reddening, noisily cleared his throat.

****

Most of those original toys are now not even worth the paltry amount they originally cost, but the Beanie Babies craze is a cautionary tale worth telling. What were the factors that led to the creepily adorable understuffed little animals becoming such a phenomenon?

Well, the idea of 'retiring' an available line of product was not, at first, a planned strategy, and was also one that looked doomed from conception. Yet in 1995, one of the Ty company's non-Beanie Baby toys, a stuffed lamb named Lovie, was discontinued because of issues with the company's distributor in China. The decision to discontinue the toy caused an angry uproar with Ty's customers, as Lovie was a big seller, especially in hospitals. Yes, Lovie was loved. And apparently Lovie had many excellent qualities. Excluding the oddly circular face (but not head), according to hospitals, having Lovie by their beside caused cancer patients to live, on average, a month longer than expected...

Having learned of a strategy used by an earlier toymaker who had told customers that discontinued toys had been 'retired', Warner and his sales force decided to use this strategy with Lovie. Soon, instead of being angry that the toy was no longer being made, buyers were excited at the idea that the Lovies they already had might be worth much more than they had paid for them. (Here I imagine Lovies being plucked from patients' hands, under the heavy silence of mass-medicated sleep.)

It was Lovie's success that led Ty to start deliberately 'retiring' various Beanie Babies. Death is money. By early 1996, 'retired' Beanie Babies that had originally sold for $5 were going for $15 or $20. The company used its website to make 'retirement' announcements and to wager which toy would be next. Some sellers would even change the price of various Beanie Babies throughout the day based on these hints. By the end of 1996, Ty's sales had reached $280 million, more than ten times what they had been the previous year.

According to Zac Bissonnette, author of *The Great Beanie Baby Bubble: Mass Delusion and the Dark Side of Cute*, at the height of the craze, Ty was shipping more than 15,000 orders per day to retailers. But the company limited each retailer to just 36 toys of each style or animal... [and] '...that's actually why they were able to work as a collectible: people just had no idea how many of them he was shipping...' said Charles Milkover, an employee of over twenty years.

In order to try and build the brand, Warner focused on working with independent retailers rather than large stores. There were several benefits to following this route. For one thing, because small shops needed to build up their inventories, Warner could ask them to pay for toys on delivery, while bigger retailers could afford to ask for an extended payment in which they might not pay until 60, or even 90 days after shipment. '...[Warner] did not want to take out debt within his business,' Bissonnette told the *Chicago Tribune*. 'He was adamant about that. He wanted to be as debt-free as possible.' By not taking on debt, Ty was able to sell Beanie Babies at lower prices than other similar toys. 'There was no one doing the quality he was doing at the price point he was doing it at...'

Another benefit to dealing with smaller independent businesses was that Warner and his sales force could speak directly with the shop owners and influence/manipulate them on things such as how the toys were displayed. Warner felt strongly that the value of Beanie Babies would be destroyed if they were jam-packed into plastic dip-bins.

'He wanted them displayed on shelves with their hair fluffed, looking pretty,' Bissonnette explained. And by dealing with a large number of smaller retailers, Ty's business wouldn't be as badly affected if a shop or two decided to stop selling the toys, as it would have been if a large retailer that accounted for 40-50% of the company's sales suddenly decided to stop stocking them.

I asked Michele Quex about this, and she said something very interesting. 'Ty was obsessed to an extraordinary degree. It was bordering on the *artistic*.'

'How so?' I gently asked.

'Well, he saw smaller businesses as somehow... *romantic*. Almost as if he was keeping a connection to the great toysellers of the past, like Meccano, or Monopoly. Or Rubik's Cube.

Briony Sozo added: 'Whatever you say about him, he was a genius. Such marketing strategies are fairly standard now, but he was the first. A visionary, if a troubled one.'

'They're all troubled,' added Charles Milkover, 'if they're worth a damn.'

'Too true,' confirmed Miss Quex. 'But they almost never are.'

We all nodded together at the obvious verisimilitude of this.

****

The first line of Beanie Babies was introduced at the 1993 World Toy Fair in New York City. But even though they were priced at just $5, the line was not an immediate success. In fact, sales were so poor that many retailers told Ty that they would only order six toys at a time – not the 12-packs the company was pushing. Undaunted, Warner had bigger dreams... Mid-way through a violent yawn, perhaps, it came to him. In a memo sent to employee R. Williams (no relation of mine), he stated that: 'Most retailers don't know what they're doing. When they're angry with you, it means you have a good product.' And with that we veer into the truly surreal.

Sales of Beanie Baby toys were still struggling when the company introduced a royal blue elephant named Peanut to the line in June 1995. Don't get me started on Peanut. Oh, Peanut. At first, this new Beanie Baby had little impact on the company's fortunes. But four months after it was introduced, Ty Warner decided to change Peanut's colour from royal blue to baby blue. Internationally, all hell broke loose.

Because only a few thousand orders of the royal blue version had been shipped to retailers, it became suddenly very hard for buyers to locate. When the early collectors noticed this, the value of Peanut the Royal Blue Elephant skyrocketed – one 1997 price guide listed its value as $2500 and predicted that by 2008 the royal blue version of Peanut would be worth almost $8000. Let's examine what happened.

Two pairs of women living in the Chicago suburbs are widely credited as being the first true serious collectors of Beanie Babies.

When Dr Paula Benchik-Abrinko noticed that the gift shop at the hospital where she worked sold Beanie Babies, she started buying them up. She expanded her collection by buying the Beanie Babies in every other hospital gift shop in her immediate area, and expanded outwards, like a bomb blast, from there. She was a doctor. Her sister, Peggy Gallagher, meanwhile, would buy through Ty's German distributor. This allowed her to buy Beanie Babies that were impossible to find in Chicago stores. When Bissonnette interviewed her for his book, Gallagher confessed that she had bought 'a bunch of Chilly the Polar Bear toys for $7' and sold them for 'more than $1800 each'. In total, Gallagher bought $2000 worth from the German distributor, and sold them for over $300,000...

Becky Philips and Becky Estenssoro were the other pair. An entirely different pair (and not sisters) but oddly also living in the Chicago area, they were avid Beanie Baby collectors. In her quest to find as many of them as she could, especially the rarer ones, Philips's long-distance phone bill often exceeded $1000 every three months. She once called a gift shop only to be informed that the store had already sold their stock to another collector from the Chicago area, Dr Paula Benchik-Abrinko. It would be amiss of me, as a writer, not to notice the Nabokovian doubles here – the doctor and her sister, and then the two Beckys... I wish I'd made it up, but while it's perfect fiction fodder, I assure you this is all true.

In early 1996, Gallagher wrote an article about Beanie Babies for a collectibles magazine called *Rosie's Collectors' Bulletin*, in which she emphasised the rising value of the rarer toys – including the aforementioned royal blue version of Peanut the Elephant. She also touted the price guide she had put together for collectors (even though she made up many of the values) as a true market for the toys had yet to be established. But it wasn't long before the actual value of some of the toys was close to the prices she had invented. So...

****

Warner launched the Ty company out of his home in 1986. When he went to that Atlanta toy fair and sold $30,000 worth of his full-sized plush toy cats in one hour, he knew he was onto something, but it would be several years before he introduced Beanie Babies to the toy market. A huge key to the eventual phenomenon that Beanie Babies became was in how they were designed – they were *under*stuffed with PVC pellets.

'At first everyone told me I was cheap,' Warner told *People* magazine in 1999. 'They didn't get it. The whole idea was that [the Beanie Baby] looked real because it moved.'

I think he meant that they *felt* real, or more real than other fully stuffed toys on the market. In addition, each one was given its own name, birth-date, and accompanying poem, with the idea of making them seem more like a real pet to a child. Remember, this was the 90s, before the advent of 'realistic representation' toys. And what of those poems? As one would expect, they are just cute, gentle doggerel, but some go in unexpected directions. Here are a couple of my favourites – Ewey (possibly the late Lovie's offspring), a constipated-looking sheep, has

> Needles and yarn, Ewey loves to knit
> Making sweaters with perfect fit
> Happy to make one for you and me
> Showing off hers, for all to see!

Ahem. And Valentino, who resembles a starving polar bear with pleading eyes, has

> His heart is red and full of love
> He cares for you so give him a hug
> Keep him close when feeling blue
> Feel the love he has for you!

****

Bissonnette claimed that Ty Warner... *was obsessed with every single detail of every product they ever released – sitting late into the night poring over eye samples, spending eight hours on a photo shoot of a single stuffed cat...* In an interview with *Book Page*, Bissonnette stated that Warner would ask random people to give their opinions about the designs. One Ty employee told me about the time he spotted Warner wandering the corridors holding artist renderings of some upcoming toys. As they passed, horribly, Warner said:

'Do you think the ass on this one is too big?'

'Ty, I'm an accountant,' the employee replied.

Bissonnette suggested that the constant changing of the designs of Beanie Babies was driven by Warner's insatiable quest for perfection and his need to make the cutest stuffed animals of them all, bar none. And of course when this drive led Warner to halt production on Beanie Babies that had already been released, the value of the discontinued toy went stratospheric... Until...

A computer programmer named Pierre Omidyar introduced his e-commerce site – originally called AuctionWeb but now universally known as eBay – in September 1995. Reportedly, eBay was only a hobby for Omidyar until his internet provider informed him that he had to upgrade to a business account because of the high amount of traffic on the website. In 1997 a public relations manager made up a story about how Omidyar had founded the online store in order to help his fiancée trade Pez candy dispensers. Although baseless, the story resulted in a great amount of publicity for the site and fuelled major growth among toy collectors.

And this is where Beanie Babies enter the eBay story, or should that be the other way round? Either way, this is a hugely important juncture in our story. Ty had set up its own secondary-market online site as a way to try and help collectors trade the toys, but it wasn't able to handle the overwhelming demand and it didn't allow listings to be sorted. When collectors went looking for a more efficient user-friendly online trading site, they found eBay. By April 1997, Beanie Babies dominated eBay (then still called AuctionWeb) listings, with around 2500 separate auctions. It reached the point where the site had to give the toy its own separate category. In May 1997, the e-commerce site sold $500,000 worth of them, accounting for approximately 6.6% of its total volume.

****

In the 1840s, something happened that has historically become known as the British Railway Mania. This was an instance of a stock market bubble. It adhered to the common curve: as railway shares increased in price, speculators invested more and more money, which further increased the price of the railway shares, until finally the share price could do no more and gave up on itself. Or collapsed, in financial jargon. In his study of this event, a mathematician named Andrew Odlyzko proposed his theory that attributed what happened at least in part to 'collective hallucination' – which he described as an extreme form of groupthink in which a significant percentage of people excitedly buy into a shared idea or dream, completely ignoring what sceptics or opponents might have to say about it. This theory of 'collective hallucination' can be used as one method of trying to explain the Beanie Babies craze, although it doesn't explain why they in particular had this allure while dozens of other trends that popped up during the 1990s did not. With Beanie Babies, the earliest collectors can be seen as some sort of an in-group who shared this amazing secret of the toys' value, and as more people learned about the toy, they wanted to know what the secret was so that they could also cash in on the market for them. Within a couple of years, millions of people were caught up in the idea that they had discovered an easy way to accumulate great personal wealth. The problem was, thanks to this 'collective hallucination', many of these people failed to understand that the only thing driving the market for Beanie Babies was their own conviction that the toys were valuable. Once that collective conviction faded, the 'bubble' surrounding Beanie Babies popped.

An economist named Charles Kindleberger – and could there be a more perfect name in this tale? – proposed a now well-known theory about economic bubbles. According to him, every 'bubble' has 4 stages.

1. a big new development that shocks the market
2. euphoria over that development
3. a sudden boom in sales and speculation
4. panic [when the 'bubble' finally bursts]

Economics professors David Tuckett and Richard Taffler added a Coda to Kindleberger's theory – *revulsion*, which describes the collective feeling society gets when it realizes it has invested in junk. They also built on this theory by positing that a person can view new products or creations as 'phantastic objects', a thought process that can skew a person's sense of reason. Phantastic differs from fantastic in several ways, but the important one here is that *fantastic* is merely *imaginative or fanciful*, whereas *phantastic* implies definitively *created in the mind; illusory.*

In 1997 – and here we should acknowledge another collective human hysteria that was building for the turn of the millennium, even though 2000 wasn't the actual millennium anyway. That came a year later, at midnight, 31 December 2000, because we went from B.C. to A.D. without a year nought, but hey ho – a story began to circulate about a secretive invention only known as IT. IT was billed as an invention that would change the world as we knew it. Jeff Bezos said IT was one of the 'most anticipated product introductions' [of all time], and Steve Jobs predicted IT would become 'easily as big as the PC'. Well, IT turned out to be the Segway. Yes, the affordable personal transportation vehicle that it was 'impossible to fall off of' [sic] – duly, the President of the United States, George W Bush was quickly photographed falling off one, or falling off of one. It was said to be able to go up stairs – it couldn't; it was said to be the 'next step' of transportation: it wasn't, and so on. The hype had been enough to immediately scupper the Segway, but there are parallels with the 'collective hallucination' and hysteria of the Beanie Baby craze.

The result of such a collective hallucination is that a person will begin to think that by obtaining these phantastic, 'magical' objects, they will achieve some profound level of satisfaction. The thrill of chasing after such objects muffles the person's ability to rationally evaluate the actual worth of said objects.

Applied to the Beanie Babies craze, it's easy to see how a small group of people, who were the first to jump on the idea of collecting the toys in the hope of seeing their value increase, spread the idea of how Beanie Babies brought some sort of almost translucent joy to people.

Eventually, of course, realisation set in that owning these toys didn't result in some sort of nirvana, and the craze began to combust. While some collectors were able to cash in on the frenzy, many others ended up losing everything and found themselves stuck with a surplus of essentially worthless crap. Many were left reeling and sick at having been caught up in the Beanie Babies craze to begin with. Still others, such as myself, wondered what all the bother was about to begin with, if one didn't want to be noticed...

So what does this tell us, about humans as a species, about you, and about me? Well, from sheer sympathy with failure, it tells us that herd thought is endemic, tribal, and that independent minds are rare. It sheds a light on consumer sensibility – find the happy patterns, but never be in their thrall.

Always the lawyer, Sam Mutrix had the final word. 'I don't know why you're pushing this,' he said, 'what's in it for you?'

'The story,' I replied, 'I just want to write it.'

'You said you weren't a journalist.'

'I'm not.'

'So what are you going to write?'

'Whatever takes me...'

And we shared a chuckle.

Financial Times – 2013

A Divertimento On Words

I'm potty about words. I truly love them – the feel of them, under the tongue and on the page, the way they manipulate feelings and can bring shivers to one's spine – the way they play with perception, and can be utilised as weapons... I think of it as a love affair with the English language: *my* love affair, the only affair that really matters. Words are bloody awesome, I love them, and some new ones have recently entered our everyday lexicon...

But before I address those, let me also formally admit my love of lists of words, of obscure words, forgotten words, words that are due a comeback, et al. In Edward Abbey's *The Fool's Progress: An Honest Novel* he describes the word *prairie* as being so feminine that he'd always adored it. The book is a sprawling American road trip, and highly recommended, but of course masculine and feminine are no longer favoured, perhaps not even in Virginia Woolf's feminine usage, as masculine words having sharp edges (and letter combinations) and female words those with softer connotations (more close vowels). No cutting (masculine) the mustard (both, but debatable) there. Now: knife versus pillow; table versus song. The opening pages of Woolf's *The Lighthouse* provides several good lists of them, although personally I can never bring myself to forgive her for dismissing Joyce on grounds of *class*. Of all the things one could conceivably dislike Joyce for – the reflexive inherited Irish racist impulses, the provincial squalidness, the skewering of the language (could any novel written now give the form as violent and evolutionary a lurch as *Ulysses* did back in 1920?) – to pick on *class* shows Woolf up as a proud, inherent snob. And also as someone who never had the talent to write a line such as: *...the heaventree of stars hung with humid nightblue fruit.* Born in Kensington? Died in Lewes? Educated at King's? Ooo, such privilege – now there's a word that has become corrupted.

So what am *I* doing here, a Yorkshireman for vocal coaching? The horror.

****

A recent list that gave me pleasurable pause was of things that are now known by their marketing names but were never intended to be – Velcro, Thermos, Hoover, Kleenex, Taser (Tom A. Swift Electric Rifle), Jacuzzi, Rollerblades, Q-Tips (and that Q stands for Quality), Aspirin and Dumpster – the Dempster brothers started their waste collection company in 1936. The APA (American Psychological Association) suggested in 2010 that people stop capitalizing the word Dumpster so that it could officially become generic. It's so symmetrically arousing to see them arranged like that. Dumpster, Dempster and dumpster.

But let's take a word such as ultracrepidarian. Roll it around your mouth like expensive cigar smoke. A splendid construction, it dates from the 19th Century and means someone who regularly spouts opinions on subjects they know nothing about. And exhale. Push all that smoke out. Make a cloud, but not The Cloud, mind.

Even the blob of toothpaste hardening on a toothbrush has a name. According to Reuters, a nurdle is a wave-like gob of toothpaste applied to the toothbrush. Wonderfully, GlaxoSmithKline, the owner of the Aquafresh brand, liked it enough to create Nurdle World, an endeavour to reclaim plastic from the sea, thus helping the environment. No, of course, it wasn't that to begin with, but that's what it's become... And the punctuation mark *!?* is called an interrobang. Can you believe it!? In a dictionary of Victorian slang I recently came across this beauty:

Got the morbs (soc., 1880). Temporary melancholia.
Abstract noun coined from adjective morbid.

Other recent favourites – and that *recent* is more important than you know, because my favourites change sometimes three times a day (chores depending) and thus some inevitably get forgotten, sieved out by my word-heavy brain. Prospection (pro·spe·kshen), the art of looking forward in time or considering the future; in Japan we find *kuchisabishii* which literally translates as when you're not hungry, but your mouth is lonely.

I could, if so inclined, describe American President Donald Trump as a throttlebottom: an inept and futile person in public office. But that wouldn't be quite far enough for him, now would it?

And what about *these* linguistic wonders?

Anagapesis – an absence of feelings for someone who you once loved

Blatteroon – a babbler or boaster, usually without justification

Potvaliant – to be brave or recklessly so as a result of being inebriated

Satisdiction – to say all that is needed or ever required

The etymology. Look at them! Pepsis, roon, pot and satisdiction, are all so...

I have a personal love of *scurryfunge*: a hasty tidying of the house when a last-minute guest is coming to visit. In 19th Century England one might say: I scurryfunge every time that old hag says she's coming round... or, in the 21st Century, The EU tightens its pantstrings as Boris Johnson [British Prime Minister] scurryfunges his way around the European issue... *Bitchcraft*, the art of pissing people off by telling them the truth, preferably in an ironic manner.

And what of those *new* words, or at least words we were not familiar with before? What of them?

During the Covid-19 pandemic (the global equivalent of burning down a mansion to kill a single rat) we have become familiar with (and inured to): furlough, and Zoom and the acronym WFH (work-from-home). We have begun to recognise Rule-of-Six as an actual quantity, *maskless* as a common verb, *Covidiot* as a common noun, and *doomscrolling* as an everyday activity upon waking.

Social Distancing is not new (being found as far back as 1920), but has achieved much further reach, as has *self-isolation* – a negative term now infused with righteous wonder, and the perfect excuse to get out of any social interaction. It began life in Harriet Martineau's autobiographical *Life in the Sick-room: Essays by an Invalid* (published 1844). Yes, I did subject myself to the torture of reading the book in its entirety, and it is not without its merits. But Martineau had domestic staff, so her (seemingly self-imposed) seclusion is pertinent to few of us, I'd wager.

Quarantini was good: a bracingly strong beverage enjoyed alone in one's living room during quarantine... The *Before Times* had their day in the sun in several illiterate newspapers, and don't get me started on *contact tracing*... I enjoyed the following exchange in my local pub sometime in 2021:

– I got Astro-Zeneca-ed this morning.
– You cheap fucking peasant, I got Pfizer-ed last Tuesday.
– You're both inbred. *I* got Moderna. And I'm wearing ladies' underwear.

For many weeks there was a nationwide clap for the NHS. After many of these I became so used to them that I began clapping when I saw a nurse in a porn flick, before even considering the reflexive and obligatory wank... Puts one off one's stroke, alas.

One of the things 9/11 did was introduce boredom into everyday things. Look at those huge queues for the metal detectors... The Covid-19 pandemic changed the pace of London. I noticed how no one walked up tube escalators anymore, or observed the 'stand on the right' rule. Everyone just stood, as if getting to the top would not bring better days, just more of the same.

The Rona quickly became slang for every illness, oddly, other than Covid 19, and *Coronasomnia* became a recognised Mental Health Ailment, and I was publically dubbed a *Covidiot* because I appeared online (alone) without wearing a mask... in my home, in a video from my own kitchen... Oh, never mind, you find yourself thinking. Why bother anyway, with humans? Stupidity is a mere default position.

Let's just revel in words. Let's conjure something from the ruins...

In Spanish, French and Italian, decisions are something you *take*, like a train that leads you somewhere new, whereas in English you *make* them, like little pieces of your own creation. In German you *meet* decisions, as you would a friend.

If you say *fuck off* backwards, it's still fuck off but in an Irish accent. Beer-can is bacon in a Jamaican accent. And try saying leaf, leaf, leaf repeatedly while tickling your hair... *Space Ghetto* in an American accent is also Spice Girl in a Glaswegian one. *In Detroit* with a Scottish accent sounds like an Irishman saying *ain't that right*?

Have you never wondered why your ear accepts tick-tock and not tock-tick? (If you insert a cotton bud far enough into your ear, you can re-set yourself to factory settings...) It is because *ablaut reduplication* dictates the order of vowels and consonants in repeated words. This is why *zag-zig*, or *cross-criss* sounds alien to us, and the flipside pleases... It is believed hip-hop, flip-flop, dilly-dally and other constructions are related to the movement of the tongue from the ancient Caucasus languages. Having said that, *Kong King* does have a certain ring to it...

Freshly fallen snow absorbs sound, and lowers ambient noise over a landscape because the trapped air between snowflakes attenuates vibration. That's why it gets so quiet when it snows. So next time it does, open your window, if one is *privileged* enough to have a window, and yowl, if one is *privileged* enough to have a voice, the following, into the dark: BACKSLANG RULES! Because backslang is extra-ordinary! Let's start with the obvious – yob is boy, but that's old school, and basic. In next level backslang, good becomes doog, drunk becomes kennurd, hot becomes totch...but my favourite by far – embargo: O, grab me.

Now, aren't we having fun, boys and girls and others?

Peri, tele, micro, endo, horo, stereo, I believe there is a scope for us all.

Every time I make a typo, the errorists win.

The opposite of assassin is dickdickout.

'Do you think I reference dinosaurs too often, when I write?' I asked her.

She was silent, like the p in pterodactyl, but her silence spoke volumes...

This may all strike you as whimsy, and it is – a mere divertimento, a diversion. Hell, I have been known to do live theatre gigs with poets. The horror!

Spuddle (17th Century) to work ineffectively; to be extremely busy whilst [sic] achieving absolutely nothing: that's what I'm doing here. A Yorkshireman waist-deep in words.

****

But I can't be relentlessly positive – there have been some constructions (seen in waveringly respectable publications such as *The Independent* and *The Times*) that have irked my very soul. *Towing the line* (instead of toeing the line) has become almost everyday, if not exactly trendy. If you type this, you're in a lose-lose situation. Either you think everything is a nautical instruction, or the only reading you do is limited to Internet threads where correct grammar is a highly elastic concept. Either way, you are a 'looser'. The same, broadly, goes for *I could care less*. An obvious and lazy Americanism, it makes far less sense than the English *I couldn't care less*... Only use if you are the kind of person who notes in their diary: Went to Tesco's to pick up some groceries, but there were no cheese and onion chips, goddamn, and my ass felt cold... I also hate misuse of the word *gaslighting*. A sterling word, from the play *Gas Light* (by Patrick Hamilton, but perhaps more associated with its cinematic adaptation of 1940), it is now used as a genteelism, or a pretentious way of saying *lying*. For example, Prime Minister Boris Johnson isn't gaslighting you, he's just a brazen liar, who would claim to have fucked your wife to check if the bed was comfy enough for your uncle (who had never even planned to stay). Also widely misused now is *Socialist*. While boasting a variety of legitimate meanings, US right-wingers are attempting to recast it as a purely pejorative term, and this will not do at all.

****

Let's riff rapidly through some common oxymorons: uninvited guest, partial cease-fire, plastic glass, original copy, new tradition, assistant supervisor, true replica, standard options, etc. I don't include in this list items such as dry lake, which boasts a specific meaning.

From there it's no leap to neologisms, such as coffee (n.), the person upon whom one coughs; willy-nilly (adj.), impotent; Negligent (adj.), a condition in which you absentmindedly open the door in your nightgown; abdicate (v.), to give up all hope of every having a flat stomach. There is a huge amount of fun to be had with such word games, and I encourage you, dear reader, to try some yourself at home. But before I go, contronyms are wonderful, obscure beasts, often hiding in plain logic. A contronym is a single word that has two contradictory meanings, as in their own opposites. Here are my ten; how many more can you locate?

- Apology – a statement of contrition for an action, or a defence of one
- Bolt –   to secure, or to flee
- Bound –   heading to a destination, or restrained from movement
- Cleave – to adhere, or to separate
- Dust –   to add fine particles, or to remove them
- Fast –   quick, or stuck or made stable
- Left –   remained, or departed
- Peer –   a person of the nobility, or an equal
- Sanction – to approve, or to boycott
- Weather – to withstand, or to wear away

I could continue in this vein – it's so joyful – but as I am primarily a purveyor of fiction, I give you this gloriously funny, yet poignant and salutary glossary of terms found in book blurbs. Many of these could also double as what reviewers really mean when reviewing prose:

Enchanting	there's a dog in it
Heart-warming	there's a dog and a child in it
Moving	the child dies
Heart-rending	the dog dies
Thoughtful	numbingly tedious and undoubtedly pretentious
Haunting	set in the past
Exotic	set abroad
Audacious	set in the future
Award-winning	set in India
Perceptive	set in north London
Provocative	infuriating

Epic	reviewer cowed by author's reputation
From the pen of a master	the same old shit, year after year
In the tradition of	shamelessly derivative, if not baldly plagiarized
Spare and taut	under-researched
Richly detailed	over-researched
Disturbing	the author is insane, or at least suffering addiction issues
Stellar	author young, photogenic and possibly sexually available
Classic	author just about hanging in there
Vintage	author definitely past it, if not already diagnosed senile.

****

One last thing before I go. It would be selfish, even perhaps churlish, of me not to let you in on a little game I've been playing recently: finding puns that work in different languages. I would encourage readers to write in – oh, please do! – with suggestions of their own, but I'll leave you with a mighty one, the pun heard 'round the world.

Q. Where do cats go when they die?
A. *Purr*gatory.

It works in Italian (and gains an entendre) – Q. *Dove vanno I gatti quando muoiono?* A. *Nel* pur-gatto-*rio*…, French – *Où vont les chats quand ils meurent? Au purchattoire*, Spanish – *¿De dónde van los gatos cuando mueren? Purgatorio*, and Portuguese – *Para onde os gatos vão quando morrem? Para o purgatorio*.
Peak pun right there, people.

Language For All – 2020

On Testicular Cancer

Let's begin with the most important part: how to self-check for testicular cancer. It's four simple steps, but they're important ones, because not only do we know that men are notoriously reticent about getting their gonads professionally checked, but even if they do, as in my case, they are often misdiagnosed as merely having cysts. So, if you know how to self-check, you can cancel doubt and immediately ask your GP for an ultrasound referral. They can't refuse, but why would you ask if you merely thought you had harmless cysts? So:

1. Cup one testicle at a time using both hands – this is best performed during or after a warm bath or shower.

2. Examine by rolling each testicle in turn between thumb and fingers – use slight but not uncomfortable pressure.

3. Familiarise yourself with the spermatic cord and epididymis – tube-like structures that connect on the back side of each testicle.

4. Feel for hard lumps, smooth or rounded bumps, any change in size or any other irregularities – it is perfectly normal for one testis to be larger than the other.

****

My first collection of short stories, *Losing Henry*, appeared in 2007 – it was my first solo effort, after the splutter of anthologies and poetry collections – and shortly after its publication, and just in time for my birthday, I was diagnosed with testicular cancer. Fine times. In the room with me, other than the consultant, was my then partner, the long-suffering H., the dedicatee of that first solo collection. With pear-shaped tears tottering on the lower lids of her eyes, she sat to my left, in a chair under-slung with taut rubber straps and upholstered in dull orange, as the consultant, a man noticeably younger than myself (and I was a mere, insolent 29), began his rehearsed talk... *The test results are back and we* [always plural, for maximum diffusion] *regretfully have to inform you that...*

I was not surprised, or alarmed, and neither was H., really, because I had already shared with her what I am about to share with you: your body knows. It just *knows*. There's no sense to be had, other than certainty and resignation, and perhaps a wry smile as if to acknowledge *Ha, I told you so,* which would be infantile and inappropriate. As I was born, in 1978, the *Nostromo* walk-through set for *Alien* was being constructed in Shepperton... Still, it is a shock to be diagnosed with cancer, even when you're expecting it. So I sat there, slaked of feeling and asked, as H. took my hand comfortingly in hers,

'So will I still be able to sing?'

This was apparently an unexpected question. The consultant's eyebrows steepled and his mouth took on a quizzical slant. 'That's not a question we've ever been asked before, I don't think...'

'So what do people usually ask? And please just say *I* and not *we*. It's needlessly vexing.'

'To be honest, most men ask us... oh, sorry, ask first about their continued ability to have sexual intercourse.'

'And second?'

'Er... well, they ask us...'

'*Christ...*'

'I meant we, I, they ask if they, you, will be able to have children.'

'I see.'

H. shifted in her chair – a shift that somehow entailed moving her handbag from one side of her body to the other, while simultaneously retrieving a pack of mints from her inside coat pocket and slotting one into her purple mouth. It was a hugely weathered pack of mints. The pack had been in there for some time. That was clear. Untangling her arms, H. looked to me and daintily coughed. I asked again:

'So will I be able to sing again or not?'

'We, I, have to be honest,' replied the consultant, 'I genuinely have no idea. There is no study about this that I, sorry, we, have ever heard of. *Ah*, sorry, I'm not used to just using the singular. Please give us, *shit*, a second. My bad. *I* can call a colleague and ask. Do excuse me...'

While the consultant dialled his help, I leaned back and regarded H. At that point we had been a couple for six years, but in truth I'd always felt like an imposter, a jaded joker she'd deigned to spend time with. H. looked like the greatest film star in the world to me then: tucking that coarse dyed-black hair nervously behind her ears, and sighing obstinately under her breath to signal that office work was waiting. However, I was suffering from a world-class hangover, a frankly legendary and wall-eyed one, so I just gazed at her like a needful baby bird until the consultant replaced his handset and said: 'Good news, er, well, news. Sorry, bad, actually. I meant good for me, in that I was correct: there has been no study of it. None exists. Bad in that I can't tell you if you'll be able to sing or not, but as a medical professionals we, *I*, should say you'll be fine. Singing.'

It was my turn to sigh, although I was physically aware that no work was waiting for me. It was all going to be surrender from here – the work was all going to be done *to* me.

Casting a glance over the room, I was overawed at how dowdy it was – fitted nylon carpet, brown plastic-tiled walls – no medical equipment in it at all: one salutary filing cabinet in a corner; a water dispenser alongside. All somehow reassuring for such diagnoses, I felt, as if, look, it doesn't get worse than this, only better. I said: 'So basically, there's nothing?'

'I'm afraid not,' replied the consultant, wearing a bewildered expression, that rendered him flustered and clammy, but also obscurely relieved. Under the strip lights his skin held a churchy sheen.

H. cleared her throat untidily and asked, eyes now dry: 'What's the prognosis, doctor? For *him*, I mean? Health-wise?'

The consultant looked instantly non-plussed, but then realisation dawned, and he looked stricken. 'Oh my god, I *am so* sorry... this has never happened before...'

So over the next nine minutes he explained it all. They – and this time it would certainly be a team – would be amputating one of my testicles (the right one) in an operation called an orchidectomy. This is where an incision is made in your abdomen above the pubic area and the testicle is pulled up and through the opening, and then chopped free, and all the once-connected and needful tubes soldered or sutured shut.

'Mmm hmm,' I nodded, wondering half-heartedly how a procedure so invasive could sport such a beautiful name, before remembering that John Lindley had introduced the term orchid for testicle in the 3rd edition of *School Botany* in 1845, so as to avoid using the term castration... Ah, sweet dreams... But suddenly H. was scratching my arm and the consultant was asking me something. 'What was that?' I asked, rousing myself. 'I'm sorry?'

'Would you care to consider a prosthetic?' the consultant asked, with hopeful eyes and an eager smile, mouth upturned at the very corners, but straighter than a dead man's electrocardiogram in the centre. I noticed his lips were tobacco-stained. Perhaps he hadn't had time to shower. The fucker.

There was a beat, during which London ticked, and I felt unfathomable, un-locatable sadness, my soul full of clean-cut shadows. I realised I was looking round the room again, letting my gaze dwell on each object in turn and imagining what it would be like to see them, or indeed any familiar object again, after the ordeal, and then recall what it had been like to perceive them through the prism of its expectation. The water dispenser, filing cabinet, the consultant's frail small feet and the brazen stretch of bare shin where his trousers had ridden up, my own self, miscast in a tawdry TV film – would any of it be recognisably the same again, or would everything be seen slightly differently, and forever seen that new way? H. scratched me again and I rejoined with:

'What are the pros and cons of a prosthetic?'

'Call me Gary. Well…' he replied, delicately glancing at H. with the tiniest of shrugs, 'no woman will ever be able to tell the difference…'

'I don't think any woman has *ever* been *that* interested in my testicles…' I interjected, as H. flushed mauve and hastily swallowed another mint, coughed, and asked, with full female need-to-know:

'What are the cons?'

Her handbag was now shouldered, ready for departure.

'Well…' Gary haltingly continued: 'it's very rare, but they can rupture at high altitudes…'

It was my turn to cough. 'Anything else?'

'Occasionally they may have to be changed…'

'I wasn't planning on climbing Everest.'

'He doesn't mean that,'

I was in surgery the next morning *sans* implant. A flatbag, let alone oneball, was preferable to anyone having to go in *there* again for merely cosmetic reasons…

****

There were many bizarre conversations during my treatment, and as I have always maintained that there're not many things to be said for being sane, but knowing what's funny is definitely the best of them, I resolved to laugh at the whole process as much as I was able.

But first, let's quickly go back and refresh the history…

I went to my GP in 2003 or 4, when I was living in Notting Hill, because I had noticed some changes to the right testis. My family jewels had been of alarmingly different size – the right over twice as big as the left – since as far back as I could remember: nothing new. But it seemed to me that there was something *different* about the tubes I could feel. And, at that time, I was not given to self-checking at all. But I duly rocked up at the Pembridge Villas Surgery (my GPs) twice, and was hastily told I merely had *cysts*.

Forward three or four years and, overnight, my right testis went from its usual large size to almost triple that: it was bigger than a tennis ball, and more densely furred. Men wince when they hear this, but actually there was no pain, which was why H. and I had a jolly fine laugh about it that morning. Without pain, we naively postured, it couldn't be *that* serious – probably an inflammation of some kind. But once the GP had seen it (and felt it, to be sure), I was dispatched forthwith to St Mary's Hospital, Paddington, to procure an ultrasound and see the earliest available urologist.

I am sure readers will assume I am exaggerating what happened next, as it is pure slapstick, but this is it, verbatim. The ultrasound chap oiled up my scrotum, scrutinised the screen, said: 'Just hold tight there Mr Williams, I'll be right back...' and vanished from the room, leaving me on a gurney with my trousers around my ankles, my penis (which had shrunk to the size of a peanut) pressed upwards to my chest and covered with both hands 'for better access', and lubricant spread luxuriously over the large alien nut. I was considering the absurdity of this predicament when the door sprang open and the chap reappeared, closely followed by another chap, in full scrubs and still wearing surgical gloves. Without a glance at my prone form, they began pointing at the screen with pencils, nodding and muttering to each other. The new chap removed his surgical gloves, dropped them in a bin and then announced: 'Wait here, I'll be right back.' I should add that this chap said this to the original chap, and not to me, whose penis had now shrivelled to the size of an introverted toadstool. A few moments later Chap 2 returned, with Chaps 3 and 4 and Chicks 1 and 2 in tow, and they all crowded round the monitor and marvelled at my right bollock in black and white reproduction. Is the word 'crowded' even necessary? And should the word 'reproduction' even appear in this paragraph? Interestingly, I thought, not one of them actually regarded my prone body. The black and white little screen was their sole focus.

Eventually I was told that I had three tumours in Kathryn. My cock was Kevin, my left testicle was Konnichiwa (because H. had lived in Japan for some years) but Kathryn was the one with the issues. My nether regions were suddenly the Kardashians, and on multiple screens, to boot, go figure...

I was told to make any necessary calls and to head upstairs.

I called H. and, grudgingly, with many a moan and curse, she said she'd leave work and head over to the hospital. I went outside for a cigarette, an indulgence that I guessed I wouldn't be enjoying any time again in my near future. Breathe in, breathe out: some kind of an accomplishment all on its own.

And that *was* a *great* cigarette. I had chance to think – and I thought: who is going to be with me, in life terms? Nicotine is exemplary for this. Should I get out now? I don't want to bring you down. Nicotine doesn't want to be bringing anyone down. Yet. I finished the fag while watching birds swarming over the canal, and then headed upstairs for the formal diagnosis...

****

I was out for five hours. Surfacing, I found I had been assigned a carer. *How lovely*, I thought, *proper cushty NHS love*. This is the life. But no, it turned out, alas, that I had had a very bad reaction to the anaesthetic I'd been administered and had missed out on so much time that H. wasn't there to 'meet on the other side', as we'd agreed, and the 'carer' was there to make sure I didn't wake up and become suddenly and uncontrollably psychotic. In short, H. had long since fucked off home and I could have come round mental.

But, adjusting, I wasn't concerned about carers or bollocks or even my future as a singer. I just wanted the human touch – more specifically a woman's touch. H. would have done. My throat felt blasphemous and pornographic. Eerily, I didn't seem able to draw a full breath. Yet my 'carer' was acting with unashamed delight. Like a children's TV presenter, full of false cheer, he was nodding and delivering a hideous pep talk from a chair two feet from my face: '...it's as maybe that you are perhaps suffering some dryness of the throat, a tad of shortness of breath, well that's what I'm here for! I'm all yours until you recover, get back on your feet, so to say, you feel better, then *I'm* your man...'

I batted my arm for him to stop.

'What's your name?' I croaked. 'And may I have some water?'

'I'm Bartholomew,' he said, flashing up a jug of water and a Styrofoam cup from beneath the bed. 'Call me Bart, anytime, anywhere, for you, and just for you, only for you, I'm Bart. Here, have another.'

I took the second cup of water greedily, splashing my shaved chest, and wordlessly held it out for a refill. After the fourth, I relaxed a little, although breathing was still painful and my legs didn't seem to be obeying cerebral impulses. I glanced down and noticed the huge felt-tip arrows drawn up my right leg toward the groin. I vaguely wondered why they needed such visual clues when one testicle (Kathryn) looked like a hairy hand grenade and the other (hello!) was just trying to get by. Not to mention Kevin, who seemed to have retired into misanthropy...

Bart had started wittering on again in a light lyric baritone. '...Anything you need I'm here for you... another? Yes, certainly. *Another?*'

He was, despite the fake brightness, an elegant man, with an oval face, diffident posture, and something in the shoulders that implied cold. Solid brow: a hairline hinting at strong parentage; glitterous irises. Something dependable in the thorax, as if capable of sports but not wishing to play – perhaps his ancestors had been cricketers or economists. I liked him.

Distracted by a commotion at the end of the row – and we were all in a row, coming out of our surgeries – Bart suddenly dropped the paper cup, which made no noise as it hit the floor, craned back and said: 'Oh, gosh, sorry, I must just help my colleagues here...'

****

Two hours later I was ploughing down Bishops' Bridge Road. Several phone calls had been made on my behalf. H. was on her way, but there, just right there, my old friend and neighbour Lenny went by, waving, from the top deck of a bus. I was early, or he was late, but I couldn't stop, and wouldn't. And *ploughing* was right – slow progress was being made, but everything looked better for it. Stopping would surely have been a gross miscalculation of subdued and partly drugged energy. Lenny caught up with me, took my arm – careful not to hug as we would usually have done, because of the scar and my bent-over posture – and asked:

'So, how was it? What happened?'

And I was suddenly vibrating with emotion – body thrumming with fierce rhythms – and I didn't feel like a man anymore. It was immediate, all of a sudden. But I needed a friend there to let it out. Figuring my chance at ever having a child was shot, gone, I sank to my knees and began to shake, or shudder. Lenny picked me up, dusted me off, and we began to stagger back together toward my flat. Slowly, him supporting me 75%, a third-crying, a third-coughing, a third-laughing, step-by-step we wound our way toward Porchester Hall. If I could make it there, my flat was just a breath away. If I could make it there I'd make it anywhere... A glitterous breath away.

The thing about friends is that they never judge. Lenny didn't expect an answer to his question. All he wanted was to get me home. And he deserves a word. Lenny was my oldest friend and sometime neighbour – a man who always seemed (longsufferingly) to be, in fictional form, hotfooting it into my prose...

The day was helping itself to light as we dragged ourselves in. The light left was all prickly and disorganised, not fully ready for the day to end or indeed to come. [I later found out that this was the morphine wearing off, as were the unusual glitter exploits.]

He plopped me on the futon – helpfully extended and ready to receive a guest – and called H. who was *on her way*, but still had *a little bit of stuff to finish* at work. We bore with her, and Lenny didn't leave until she arrived seven hours later. The mattress smelled good. I was happy. Nothing could harm or touch. I would stay there for two weeks.

****

I had to wear a linen girdle for a month. It had a slice at the back through which I could shit, and it had the recognisable front opening as of regular boxer shorts. One could shower with it and even have baths, but I couldn't wait to get rid of the beast. H. had apologised for not being there, and she was always trying to make a second chance into a good impression, and had broad ambitions for a sympathetic imagination. She generously went out and got food – with my bankcard – and we'd cook it together. Girlfriends have always loved me most when I was vulnerable, and those were happy, verdant days.

After a week I could piss entirely unaided and no one had had to come and inject me with anything.

After two, sarcasm had returned – humour had returned. But, alarmingly, it had brought back something with it, all gnarled and jaded... My body was no longer my own, and my humour had changed along with the sense of self... I no longer found my own thoughts funny. It was a cataclysmic shift. Everything had to be rewritten.

After three the jockstrap came off, but I found I was oddly attached to it, in an emotional way, so rather than hurl it in the bin, I put it in a cupboard, in a drawer not used for anything else.

After a month I began tentatively singing again... The abdomen – where singers expand to support the voice – was still sore, but I was making a passable sound. One day I leaned back without groaning.

And one day H. wasn't there anymore, but love had always been complicated to me, and perhaps I never knew how to love anyway. One day I realised that it wasn't my fault, but cancer's. I wished H. well. But it took time to realise that cancer does not just attack the body – it attacks one's belief in oneself. As a man, I was expensively compromised.

Lenny checked on me, oftentimes bringing drinks and food. But, stagnating, my personality became sour and cursory, I pushed everyone away: in truth, I was rudderless, but then, I was *invited*... In February 2008 I sang my 'comeback recital'.

But it wasn't a comeback. I was a new (and better) singer. Everything had changed: my outlook, my body, my music.

As pointed out earlier, there have been no medical studies done on this. There simply haven't been enough classical singers who are also testicular cancer survivors. But I *can* tell you this: I did not gain any extra high notes. The voice does not get higher. But what happens, or what happened to me, is that you stop worrying about the high notes and merely think: *they'll be there.* For a tenor, particularly, this is hugely important. I listen to the recordings I made before 2008 now and they're painful to me – the voice is pushed, deliberate, indelicate, and musically ugly. But, unmanned, suddenly I could actually sing!

Of course, my hormone levels were scattered and had yet to be medically resolved, but my body didn't correspond to my voice. So, by 2012, I had the body of a dramatic tenor and the voice of a lyric tenor, and, at 6'1", all the sopranos were queuing up to sing with me because they didn't have to bend down to sing love duets with me – I was taller than them!

Now, some years later, my body is settled, and I have also had a child, conceived naturally, I feel uncomfortably forced to add, but not with H.... The relationship with H. didn't last, although I still count her as a friend, and we very occasionally laugh together about our strange tribulations back then... And my son, the beautiful boy, turned out to look exactly like me! Double trouble.

****

A final word or two: guys: check yourselves. Hell, check each other. Ladies: you can get involved too, particularly if you're in the shower with your guys. Just follow the four steps at the top of this essay. I'll print them again at the end, so no excuses. And love one another, and love the world. No one has much time on this planet and we are all just a heartbeat away from death.

And that 'comeback' recital wasn't any good anyway – all my big online recordings have been done *post* then – but it was important to me for two reasons. To prove to myself that cancer doesn't define you anymore than being a onebagger or a full flatbagger does (and is 'full flatbagger' an oxymoron?). I dragged out the old recordings yesterday and took a listen. The dusty tracks weren't unforgivably excreable, but my mother actually came to that gig in 2006, so it meant a great deal to me. By 2009, she didn't go to anything. She didn't leave the house. But she came to that. And like the phantom pains of the missing testicle – just like a limb, it cannot be scratched – I miss her all the time. And, like the phantom itches that persist to this day in my groin – that cannot be dulled by any amount of scratching – I miss Kathryn. So:

1. Cup one testicle at a time using both hands – this is best performed during or after a warm bath or shower.

2. Examine by rolling each testicle in turn between thumb and fingers – use slight but not uncomfortable pressure.

3. Familiarise yourself with the spermatic cord and epididymis – tube-like structures that connect on the back side of each testicle.

4. Feel for hard lumps, smooth or rounded bumps, any change in size or any other irregularities – it is perfectly normal for one testis to be larger than the other.

Everyman Newsletter, 2011

Book Reviews (Part 2)

Ben Golomstock – *Dreams From Hell*, Kali Discorporation

From the Introduction:

> The author of this book was arrogant, rancorous, infuriating, abrasive, contrary, condescending, supercilious and perverse. He was also loyal, perceptive, resourceful, charismatic [...] and one of the finest people you could possibly ever meet...

He died in 2018, but I concur: Ben Golomstock was all of those things and more. Oft called the 'Bard of Stoke Newington' and the 'sarky sage of old Stokie', he was a card. A writer, club evening presenter, musician, seer and general irritator, he defied the injustice of repetition by sheer force of character. I sometimes wonder what his character really meant. Was it to persevere in the struggle that left him frightened? Or was he a misunderstood genius, let down by us all?

A smidgeon of both, perhaps, and why not mix the drinks? I see you admire that cheap Kandinsky print on the wall. It's counterfeit, sure, but there is much to be said for the fake – sometimes the fake is more real than the original. Sometimes it's all that's left, emotionally. Perhaps the worry about doubles, or copies, or not-being-true resides in our own insecurities. Why do we admire the original? *Should* we admire it so? I'll tell you this: no one cares how you respond to that print on the wall. It isn't Kandinsky, and this is just a below-average hotel room. The window on the left doesn't shut correctly, so pull on a sweater, and hunker down...

I got to know Ben in the late 90s, when he was still somewhat sprightly in body – his spirit remained so till the end – but I never really got to *know* him. And when I finally received this book and spread it out under the dual lamps over the desk in my study, I felt a spiritual itch. And I already had a waiting feeling...

It's a physically beautiful thing, *Dreams From Hell*: gorgeously produced with full-page colour artwork on every other page. Fifty-two artists contributed, and this is salutary to Ben's talent. The whole endeavour is a posthumous act of love by his friends (one of whom is Steve Poulacheris, who provided the artwork for my 2021 book *Fairytales and Oddities*). Of course even the act of composition, of putting those words, or that artwork, onto a page, is also an act of love, and his friends have done him proud.

Ben (aka Ben Hell, aka Johnny Rocket) was the son of the art historian Igor Golomstock (1929 – 2017) who published books on Picasso, Bosch, Cézanne, and others. Born in Russia, Igor argued that totalitarian art looked much the same regardless under which regime it was created. Understandably not well received, his later books went largely ignored by the art community, but this is not about him. It's about his son, and *Dreams From Hell* is a sensation, an illusion or an experience. Perhaps even a scent... the scent of pine-trees, disused medication, regret, old coats, forgotten tobacco pouches, and the spirits of girls.

Gazing more than reading, I found the experience one of liberation, relief from the gravity of commitment to a narrative, or of simply having no idea what to expect. This levity allows one to move sideways, into whatever one wants the book to be, while giving the reader the unicorn fist and challenging them to run the great gamut of fashionable hatreds.

There are people who like getting ill and getting old. Ben was not one of them. In the hundred or so hours I spent in his company he always left me feeling slightly drugged. Stoned: strange to the earth. This was pure, and apt. I don't think I've ever met anyone so exactly sure of who he was. So reading this book was like the odd sensation of waking up happy – obscure yet welcome. Ben usually looked scrawny and famished, and oftentimes tremblingly brandished a cigarette. We once went to a kebab shop together, and left together, and before I'd even taken a bite, half of his kebab was already strewn across the street. Passing cars' tyres crunched the lettuce and a sliver of onion adhered to my trousers. I was about to ask, 'What the hell happened?', but then remembered there was no need. Ben Hell was himself and there was no point in discussing it. For example, I once said during an evening when he had been bemoaning his impoverished state: 'If you cut down on the cigarettes, you'd save shit loads of money...' Without missing a beat he replied: 'No, I wouldn't, because then I'd live longer...'

What of the book? *Dreams From Hell* is a cornucopia of the absurd, the wonderfully grotesque, and the charmingly offensive. I am known for hating dreams in fiction, but what of an entire book of nothing but them? Oddly, it works. There is no great literary writing here, no turn of phrase that makes the reader pause and go back, but that's not the point at all. There *are* moments of linguistic glory:

I still reckon that The Apocalypse has already happened. This is all you're gonna [sic] get. Most people were just too dumb and screwed up to notice.

And this:

Dreamed that I met a beautiful girl and we fell in love... [I] said: 'You know, sod it, this is all a dream! We can do whatever the hell we like! No conventions, no constraints, no morality... Let's just have a great time while we can!' And we did.

And I'll bet that his dreams are more vivid than yours. The recurring themes of the book are talking animals, *The Rochester Castle* (in Stoke Newington), obviously booze and fags, gates – both to and from a place – religious guilt, a phobia of marine creatures, sexual insecurity, and a gentle loneliness:

There was a man sitting on a chair in the middle of a bare white room. He had been told that everything was going to end, so he was calmly waiting. But nothing ended. He kept waiting.

He also has the ability, as do I (is this a musician thing?) of waking himself from a dream and then allowing himself to re-enter it. What I don't have is his ability to then... [give up] *on the dream. It was rubbish.* I dearly covet that ability.

****

Ben asked me to sing at 'Club Hell' in 2007 and again in 2010. I sang the first one with an insouciant disregard for anyone's feelings. I brought along a troupe of singers and we performed a set of Gothic opera, with an American soprano, a Canterbury-based baritone and a mezzo who was high on cocaine. I'll never forget the faces – implacable yet resigned. And Ben to the side of the tiny stage, laughing his intentines out and gesturing us all for a fag in the venue foyer. In 2010 I was supposed to sing Club Hell but, at the final moment, decided not to. Ben had asked me to perform (in an ironic manner) a Nazi hymn... It was all for effect, of course, he wasn't a racist, and neither was I, but nonetheless I had to refuse. That was the last time I ever saw him, and that was also the time of the kebab incident.

There are people who hate happy ends. They feel cheated. Ben was not one of those. It surprises me to remember how fond I was of him. He used the word 'disgraceful' too often, but hadn't been comfortable in the early years, so could be forgiven for that. 'Why on earth,' he once asked me, 'did you invite that dolt to this party?' I replied that I'd missed the bus on doltage... And he roared with laughter: a default position for him, as was, oddly, the melancholy. In him, there often seemed no clear line between the two states.

Two years after his death I met his 'beautiful girl', Estelle Riviere, one of the artists featured in the book. And Ben was correct: he had, finally, met the one. But he never lived to fully enjoy their time together, the ultimate unfairness. On the cover of the book is her picture of him, with a huge moth in place of his heart.

Dreams From Hell is a numinous book, full of beauty from unexpected corners, and an un-reluctant laugh on every page, if the twelve-bar blues of your thoughts don't lead to that angry question: why couldn't Ben have lived longer? And: Why were we robbed in the night by that gigantic green octopus? And: did I fully close the gate, because that's how the light gets in...?

Overall, I love my dreams. They're better than real life.

****

I stayed in the very same hotel room last week, for a different tour entirely. The cheap print was still there, as was my deep regard for Ben. If it had been a real Kandinsky, perhaps I would have reacted with surprise, or reverence, or examined what my expectations were. Perhaps I would have been honest; perhaps I would have been cruel, who knows? But one begins to wonder – reading Ben's dreams – if there's something to be said for never waking up again, and simply enjoying oneself, while one has the time, in the subterranean depths of unconscious imagination.

The Memoirist, 2021

****

CN Lester – *Trans Like Me (a journey for all of us)*, Virago

A camera shine: *zaa*. Blinded, and plying from the glare (and all the attention), I turn to this empty page. I'll confess to being nervous about penning this review – will I get death threats, or be irreversibly cancelled? I am twitching with fright. Of course, facetiousness aside, as a cis heterosexual male, not to mention a white one – all that teeming, bleeding privilege – I almost turned down doing it. But one rises to meet a challenge... And I am used to death threats from religious groups. So bring on more hate, I say, I can take it. But then I don't think the world should change to accommodate what I want: call me old-fashioned, but I like different opinions.

The trans conversation has arguably become the most toxic of all current conversations, more toxic than climate change, more toxic than politics, more toxic than religion (Islam always excepted, naturally, being the only major monofaith yet to undergo a Reformation), more toxic than veganism and the Israel/Palestine debate. I foresee many writers and comedians being vilified over the coming years, and I predict that *belief* will win. Belief, the most overrated of virtues. Belief, that barely matters anyway.

Of course there is no such thing as 'cancel culture'. The idea of a cabal pontificating on things cultural is amusingly ridiculous. What and who attracts the ire of the mob is arbitrary, and the parameters are in constant flux. And never forget – the mob comes dressed up as those who care about you, and everything you love. That's the point of it, and partly, the point of them – gorgeous to look at (or at least glorious), but with no substance except vitriol or violence. And we love them the more for it. It's the mob in us, the subliminal tribal chant. We cry from the pram for basics. We crave basics.

My colleagues all told me I was insane to even consider reviewing this book. But a book review is not a think-piece about how trans rights may or may not have affected women's rights, or how to approach trans athletes in sport, or 'deadnaming' (where one uses a trans person's original name, or birth name – innocent words are already proving hard to find), or whether the B in the ever-evolving acronym LGBTQGI+ is transphobic or not. 'Transphobic' itself is meaningless, as one is obliged to fear what one has a phobia about, and I suspect that the trans community poses no serious threat to anyone, save through rhetoric and destruction of character... A student (teenage, arguably lesbian: although of course, it's none of my business) gave a postscript to their homework some months back that read:

> LGB walked blindly into an arranged marriage with T.
> It was a forced marriage and now it's an abusive one.
> We want out. It's time for a divorce.
> And you don't get the kids.

Watch that last line, I thought. Watch that last line. And promptly gave them an A.

****

The author CN Lester and I have history... We have 'previous' as they say. Who says? We say? I say? Who they? Sorry, that *they* is a figure of speech, not... Anyway. They is/are a/an social media acquaintance, although I believe we have only met personally once. And so let's briskly deal with that before progressing to the book itself.

In 2015 or thereabouts, CN Lester, who or whom, like myself, or themselves, is a musician as well as a writer, auditioned for the rôle of Alfreda [sic] Germont in a production called *The Trousered Traviata*, presented by the London Opera Players. I was the Music Director and the show was conceived (not by myself, but by the company) as an all-female version of Verdi's *La Traviata*. So, in a church in Fulham, on an afternoon the colour of a healing bruise – the sky was jaundice-bleached and full of misangled clouds – and while the strong of the city strode purposefully by outside – CN Lester came in and sang the Act 2 Aria and Cabaletta, *De' miei bollenti spiriti* and *O mio rimorso*. And they sang exceptionally well. While accompanying them from the piano I glanced at the director and producer in the second pew, and not only were *they* leaning forward on their elbows, but their eyes were kaleidoscopically transformed. After a rough day of auditions, this was a wonderful turn-up. I felt sure it would end wonderfully...

But alas, in those days I was not fully woke-d up [woke: culturally appropriated from the black community...] and unfortunately addressed CN Lester incorrectly in my – we're-very-pleased-to-be-able-to-offer-you – email. I shan't sully this page with the title I used, but at the time it seemed like the most innocent and inoffensive. Just to add, it was advertised as an ALL FEMALE TRAVIATA... I received back an email with various attachments that looked forbiddingly complicated and mysterious. Feeling scrawny, I opened them with apprehension... Click. Ah. Click. *Ah*. They had declined the part in the opera and had, horribly, attached multiple pages educating my ignorant cis ass on my abject linguistic failure. I learned a great deal from the experience, and vowed to be a better man, but I also realised what alienates many people from the trans conversation: the self-righteousness, and the understandable need to control the language of those around you. I also instantly realised that I didn't want to become so preoccupied with things that didn't matter that I missed all the things in life that actually did matter. My bad, they're(ir) bad, you(re) bad.

I have no truck with religion, unless you shove it down my throat. And I have no truck with calling anyone by their preferred pronouns, of course not, what kind of a douchecopter would? (Although I do object to vilification if one forgets and accidentally or momentarily gets a pronoun wrong...) But one thing that almost no one has addressed is how such changes affect the poetry of language. It's a minor change, true, but only if one accepts not rewriting history to get there. In *1984* George Orwell wrote:

> Every record has been destroyed or falsified, every book rewritten, every picture has been repainted, every statue and street building has been renamed, every date had been altered. And the process is continuing day by day and minute by minute. History has stopped. Nothing exists except an endless present in which the Party is always right.

The statues are being ripped down as I type these words, and streets are being busily renamed. I don't particularly care, if I'm honest. But I do care about language, and even a simple *they* can create a train-wreck of a sentence, in literary terms, if one is talking about an individual. Which then throws up the further possibility of making trans people an artistic laughingstock, which would not only be a further indignity but would also have the opposite effect of setting themselves back in time... And 50 years is no time at all...

Every worthwhile movement has had a difficult birth, and in some ways CN Lester's book is like the amplified beating of an unborn child's heart. It's a courageous sound, a necessary sound, and almost abnormally alive. The trans movement is an admirable one, even with its teething difficulties, and in CN Lester it has found a truly resplendent spokesperson/spokesthey. See what I mean about linguistic decimation? Recast all your favourite literature – poems work best – with appropriate pronouns. The literature dies. One could argue that this is after the fact, but if not now, when?

> Macbeth: Wherefore was that cry?
> Seyton: The queen, my lord, is dead.
> Macbeth: They should have died hereafter...

But there isn't any time for such a word. Hell, if you want, let's do the prayers.

Our father/mother who art in heaven... etc

And my favourite destruction of rhythm :

...the father/mother son/daughter and the holy ghost...

This is easy to continue. An endless joke, as is religion itself. But my current favourite joke on the subject remains:

A man has a heart attack and falls down in a crowd.
The man's friend: Is anyone a doctor here?
A person: Hi, I'm a Doctor, what's happening here?
TMF: It's a fucking heart attack!
AP: I'm a Doctor in gender studies...
TMF: Please help, he's going to die!
AP: Did you say *he*?

There is also the question of how much one takes offense at things and whether that should mean anything at all to anyone else. This is delicately subjective. As a writer of fiction I have long goaded the reader, with due caution, to think for themselves on a subject, but I have also challenged them to make their own minds up, via the tools of my trade: words. Being challenged is how we grow. But saying one is offended by something or someone, and having it taken as important, is a modern luxury and deserves no time at all. It's just a whine, and far less than an opinion. If you don't like CN Lester's arguments you can put the book down. If you don't like mine, you don't have to continue reading this. But, as I pointed out earlier, the malignancy of the trans conversation means that literally everyone is having a pop. And what is shocking about *Trans Like Me* is, sadly, its almost inevitable humourlessness.

I once asked the great Christopher Hitchens, in the back of a taxicab in Washington DC, if he'd rather religion had never been invented. He took a prolonged drag on his cigarette and replied, with a garnish of patience: 'But then there'd be nothing to argue about.' I loved him for that, and I love CN Lester for their brilliant book *Trans Like Me*. Wait a moment... my chest fills and my eyes freshen, sensing the promise of confectionary on the air... *trans like me* appears on the title page – and I considered the lack of capitals to be important, and not merely a design feature. I thought it inclusive, or in some way universal, given the subtitle *a journey for all of us*. This pampered to my artistic senses, as did the actual design – a beautiful yellow cover with lettering in two shades of maroon. On the spine was the bitten apple emblem that I had always associated with Alan Turing, famously persecuted for homosexuality, although I received no answer on either score when I asked the publisher if these were the intended impulses.

****

What of the writing itself? Of course, nothing's safe, and it is not an insult to call CN Lester's prose necessarily pedestrian. As stated, I had expected more humour, but of course humour hasn't any place in the trans conversation: the conversation hasn't evolved that far yet, and the prose reflects this. The movement cannot take any joshing yet, and the author seems highly taken with the publisher's name: Virago.

In the first chapter, The Production of Ignorance, CN Lester rightly points out the abhorrent treatment of trans people in the media – but it's an easy target. Every independently thinking human knows not to put any credence in media-speak. My old maxim – 'if it sounds like journalism, then it's unlikely to be true' – chimes here. Still, CN Lester makes some pertinent points about the media story on trans rights not being their own.

In 2014, American scholar Jamie Colette Capuzza published a study analysing sourcing patterns of trans stories in the US media. Looking at data from the preceding four years, Capuzza found evidence to support what has long been noted within our trans communities: trans people are far more likely to be written about as an 'issue' than we are to be recording our experiences and insights as equal participants. Just as often as not, the cis journalists writing an article or putting together a news segment would fail to include even a single quote from a trans person. Of the trans people who were quoted, the vast majority were white, the vast majority were trans women, and trans people who don't fit into the gender binary were hardly present at all.

Beyond that, Capuzza found a distinct skewering of focus: trans people were far more likely to be written and talked about in the entertainment, beauty and lifestyle sections of the media than in the 'hard news' categories of political, legal, economic and medical reporting.

How has the trans conversation allied itself to the racist conversation? What on earth should trans issues have to do with skin colour? Yet here we are – and I use that *we* inclusively, and not in an 'othering' way. At the end of the chapter...

> [there are] serious lists on Cracked and BuzzFeed, and a host of well-informed, well-researched bloggers and academics... [who speak for the trans community]

I wonder if 'academics' should have come last. And BuzzFeed? I felt like an adolescent wanking in the changing room, armpits burning with shame upon being discovered.

Of course Caitlyn Jenner gets a dressing down – and that is the correct cliché:

> It's strange that a trans woman who, so far, hasn't done any work in the trans community has been crowned our queen. It's strange that a trans woman who is famous, rich, white, etc...

It's obvious – unless every high-profile trans person, by their very nature, is obligated to speak for all. And then there's the 'white' thing again... It smacks of resentment, and resentment never writes well. Indeed CN Lester misuses, in the same chapter, the either/or, neither/nor rule, and the that/which rule, but I'll cut them some slack for that, because they do bring up Christine Jorgensen, who is an important figure well worth Googling. By the end of essay two, it seems that, if a trans figure is 'privileged' then they have no business speaking, even if they are cleverer or more eloquent than others. An interesting point: the 2010 killing of Sonia Burgess is given less prose space than the effect it had on history: the founding of the UK charity All About Trans. And in the following paragraph CN Lester goes on to write about Sonia Burgess's killer, conveniently without pointing out that the person who killed her was a client, had been born a she, was a he at the time of the murder, and later went back to she in prison, where she was later found dead under mysterious circumstances. The papers used *he* in the subsequent follow-ups, which shows a lack of awareness – an alarming lack of awareness – but, hey, it's the *press*. At this point I shook the book to see what might fall out of it.

Let's look at these six examples from essay 3, Finding My Voice: some are made up, some are CN Lester's:

1 ...[I am]... not someone who wants to subvert gender norms...

2 ...Every time I was referred to with the wrong pronoun, a fundamental part of me was spoken away...

3 ...I would be scattered into pieces if I let other people decide me in their own words...

4 ... I discovered Kate Bornstein, and ordered a copy of *My Gender Workbook* from America...

5 ... I had a breakdown when I was thirteen years old, and have been in and out of treatment ever since...

6 ... Every time I heard that pronoun, it reminded me of the abuse I had suffered...

So, could you tell which were real and which were not? I am a writer of fiction, and the world currently swelling around me increasingly seems to be fictional, a place of sudden hatreds and herd hysteria, wild dreams and inexplicable manners. So it's no surprise that I lied here. Only number 6 is by me, the others are CN Lester's, rendered verbatim. What does it show us?

****

A book review is not a think-piece, as I pointed out above. I'm not required to be there when the howling begins – and there will be howling. Psychoanalysis, as its very founders pointed out, doesn't work on, or for, artists. No sincere artist wants anyone going in the subconscious, where all that *stuff* comes from. But I am not sure 'working things out' or 'being understood' were ever part of the agenda here. The searching for *othering* leeches off the page, and victimizing oneself is powerful, if you are what your imagination says you are. Obedience is strength; bravery is dangerous. Reality has had a little too much to drink. But surely emotional intelligence is partly steeped in realising that you can change your own assumptions? Is that not so?

Between a written sentence and your feelings about that sentence, lies your interpretation of the writer's intention. It's a stimulus/response. Which is where the book falters. And also, alas, where the whole trans movement falters, in spite of salutary intentions. Because how can one's face be turned to the sun yet still be shielded? Well, very easily it seems: because of shadows. The shadow of progress... Progress in our world will be progress toward more pain, it's inevitable, but who are *we*? I watched with detached and ironic amusement some years ago as the Black Lives Matter movement was met with wails of All Lives Matter – because I knew something none of them did: no lives matter, no not one.

I could write about the myriad wonders of *trans like me* for weeks, but I am vaguely aware of a word-count to adhere to. *Sex and gender are totally separate: gender is a lie, sex is real: sex is gendered and also a lie...* writes CN Lester in the essay on sex, without specifying if they are being ironic, or paraphrasing some cis fool... But to me, that's a *rather unique* way of putting it. Later in the book, Lester falls for the simple and baseless idea that natural is 'good' and unnatural is 'bad'. Well, I would argue: racism is a natural thing, and occurs often in the animal world (look how deftly I dodged the word *king*dom), but humans should always strive to rise above it. We're not the only animal to be racist: we're the only animal to meaningfully question why we should be so, and subsequently how we could rise above such discrimination.

There are some unfortunate clangers, such as ...*our sexed bodies at seventy are not the same as our sexed bodies at seven*... which seems alarming, but just leaves one scratching one's forehead. And don't get me started on ...*two thousand and twelve research at the University of Washington*... Was that intended to be 2012? I reread the sentence five times before futilely concluding that, although it must be, I didn't want to read the sentence five times. Mistakes like that – and that's clearly not a typo – are what a writer must at all costs avoid. You must want the reader to love you, as much as you love the reader.

But, while I do seriously recognise CN Lester's *trans like me* to be an important book, I cannot finish without adoring some of the sources they quote. No novelist could have made them up, Karl Popper, T Kuhn, P Feyerabend and K Ringrose, among others. Humour is vastly important, and can help a growing movement more than anything. And you really ought to read this book.

I'll leave you with Lester (inadvertently, I think – there's nothing to suggest otherwise) paraphrasing the old warmonger Donald Rumsfeld:

...We do not know it all yet. We do not even know how little we know... [but that is]... not a trump card to deny the existence of trans lives.

Cascando, 2018

Postscript. Reading this now, I feel a little mean-spirited. Not because I like the book, but because I like CN Lester, who, I happily note, has recently joined the ranks of us fiction writers with their book *Furies*, that I look forward to reading, if just to see if the Virago fixation has followed through...

Sadly though, I was correct about the vilification of writers, comedians, feminists and others. And as 'sextortion' victims grow, I clearly see a school shooting due to pronouns. Indeed this 'regular reviewing' of language has, as I write this, seen Roald Dahl censored – words such as *white* become pale, the Oompa-Loompas are gender neutral (!), *fat* has been entirely excised, etc., and this for a writer who has been selling well for decades. I heard a transgender popstar, in full seriousness, talk about wanting to become a fisherthem. Not a fisherperson, like a policeperson or fireperson, but a fisherthem. What hope is there for language now: what nextly? Thus I await *Furies* with hope and dread.

As Tomiwa Owolade wrote last month [January 2023]:

If you want to show what a wonderfully tolerant person you are in today's febrile political climate, there are two things you must do. The first is to accuse anyone who disagrees with you on a sensitive subject as being on the wrong side of history. The second is to accuse them of stoking a culture war.

Nat King Cole
and eden ahbez

"In the late 1940s there was a rumour that there was a hermit, disenchanted and disillusioned with the world, supposedly out-of-sync with society, living in California, in a cave under one of the Ls in the Hollywood sign, who gifted Nat King Cole his first big hit."

I read that cumbersome sentence a little over a month ago and it sparked something in the part of my brain that can't be sated or quenched and which never goes to sleep. Firstly, let's look at it: *gift* as a verb – always linguistically lazy, if not downright offensive – the false quantity of dis-(enchanted) and dis-(illusioned), 'out-of-sync' being very, er... well, out-of-sync with the 1940s, two uses of there, etc. Yet...

...In the time between me reading that sentence and you reading this one, Natalie Cole, Nat King Cole's daughter, and a famous musician in her own right, died. And so, while not directly honouring her, I felt it time to write the story of one of her father's earliest hits, a story that also happens to be a thoroughly (and healthily) bizarre one, full of passionate intrigue, the collision of societal movements and, of course, talent. So let's recast:

One night in 1947, a man wearing a discoloured white robe, sandals and sporting long hair and a refulgent beard, turned up at the stage-door of the Lincoln Theatre in Los Angeles and, while not demanding entry, asked to speak to Nat King Cole, who was performing there that evening, as he had something to give him.

Now *that's* a better sentence. It sets up suspense, gives hints of a cult and immediately introduces a famous name... And it was specifically the left L in the Hollywood sign as you're looking at it. So, stage right.

****

The man who was at the stage door that night was eden ahbez (always lower case). His Wikipedia entry reads:

George Alexander Aberle (April 15, 1908 – March 4, 1995)...was an American songwriter and recording artist of the 1940s to 1960s, whose lifestyle in California was influential in the hippie [sic] movement.

And that night (imagine rain abruptly lashing down on usually sunny LA if it helps), where we join him: that was his genesis. His career hadn't begun. Oddly, Nat King Cole's had hardly begun either – he wasn't yet a star. One can amusedly imagine the (white) stagehands' consternation when eden showed up. Wanting to keep their jobs, they hastily located Cole's manager – there is no record of whether it was Mort Ruby or not – who came down to the stage door and accepted, on his client's behalf, what the strange sandal-clad man had to offer. 'What the fuck is this?' What eden ahbez was offering was a song-sheet of his own composition. Why it wasn't immediately discarded we'll never know (there is a literary agent in Brooklyn who routinely labels unsolicited submissions WPB – waste paper basket – for his assistant to dispose of), but it found its way into the hands of the great Nat King Cole, who, recognising an arching melody with no definitive cadences, used those hands, being a pianist as well as a singer, to create *Nature Boy*.

But before that happened, Cole had to locate the man who wrote it, which was no easy endeavour back then, before Smart phones or Internet search engines, and with a Mafia unwilling to help black folk. Still, after months of searching, Cole located eden in New York City. Here the dusk lightens, and we settle in for the story proper. When Cole asked him where he was staying, the strange man – whose strange name was as yet still strangely unknown – declared that he was staying at the best strangest hotel in New York: outside in strange Central Park. The song he gave Cole was *Nature Boy*. It became Cole's first huge hit. It stayed at No. 1 in the charts for eight weeks in 1948, the year my mother was born.

It brought in over $3,400,000 during that time. In *1948*. I'll leave you, dear reader, to do the math[s] on *that*.

If you watch Cole's performance of it (on YouTube) today, you'll notice how uncomfortable he looks. Almost apologetic, wearing a Gioconda smile and sounding like a shadow of himself, he croons as if a democracy of ghosts was in his ear, dictating every note. Even the guitarist looks bashful and only the bass player at the back goes for it, because he knows no one ever watches him, so he can do whatever the hell he likes.

The song *Nature Boy* has since been covered by Frank Sinatra and Sarah Vaughan, and in the current era by Tony Bennett and Lady Gaga, not to mention others: it lives, it is a *song*. It is repertoire. It is catalogue.

Of course the media went crazy about the mysterious man who handed Nat King Cole one of the biggest hits during that time. They went all-out to try and find out more about him, but what little they found was that he was an orphan, who never stayed in one place very long, living in multiple foster homes. He just never fitted in and was always searching, searching, for something. No one wanted him. He wanted a name, as we all do.

They say he wandered very far...
Very far over land and sea...

They found out he would hop freight trains – classic hobo – and walked across the entire USA several times, a half-arsed-Forrest Gump, subsisting solely on raw fruit and vegetables, until one day he completely vanished.

A little shy and sad of eye...
But very wise was he...

When he finally showed up again in the Hollywood hills and police stopped him, ahbez apparently said: 'I look crazy but I'm not. And the funny thing is that other people don't look crazy but they are.' Classic.

And then one day...
One magic day he passed my way...

And next he showed up backstage at Nat King Cole's concert in LA to present him with the song *Nature Boy*. No one seems to know why he selected Cole, but there were rumours that it had to do as much with the name King as his musical prowess. Combined, they created a perfect example of brilliance from nothing. Or, depending on who you choose to believe, he came out of hiding when he began to hear about some big racism going down and trouble throughout the world, and he thought 'King' was the best person at that time to pass his message along. We will never know.

While we spoke of many things...
Fools and Kings...

When asked about the big racism, eden ahbez replied, 'Some white people hate black people, and some white people love black people, some black people hate white people, and some black people love white people, so you see it's not an issue of black and white, it's an issue of Lovers and Haters.' Not as good a talker then, as a lyricist. To be fair, Nabokov said: 'I think like a genius, I write like a distinguished author, and I talk like a child.'

It was that theme of love that eden ahbez continued to talk about, what was missing in the world, and what would be needed in the future if humankind were to survive. ahbez *would* eventually get his message out, especially after the counter-culture finally caught up with him and the hippy movement began, when other artists such as Donovan, Grace Slick and The Beach Boys' Brian Wilson sought him out. He wrote songs for Eartha Kitt, Frankie Laine and penned many novelty 'rock'n'roll' songs. In 1957, during a period when he claimed to be living on $3-a-week and eating only fruit, nuts and vegetables, his song *Lonely Island* was recorded by Sam Cooke. It was to be the second of ahbez's songs to reach the Top 40, and the last.

In 2009, Congressman Bill Aswad recited the lyrics of *Nature Boy* before the Vermont House of Representatives at the passing of his state's same-sex marriage bill.

Somewhat unusually, the song has no middle-8, or bridge passage. It is just three verses with an extra instrumental one, at least in Nat King Cole's version, and perhaps that's the point. It has no ending. It continues rolling, like the rail cars eden used to ride. A middle-8 is therapy. It's where a new chord is introduced. Verse: my girl has left me, oh how bad. Repeat verse: my girl is still horrible... Middle-8 (new chord): but what if there is someone else even better for me? Verse: combine the two.

Nature Boy is intended as a song to just keep on going and going, because it's an engine. Author Raymond Knapp described the track as a 'mystically charged vagabond song' whose verses evoked an intense sense of 'loss and haplessness', with the final line delivering a universal truth, described by Knapp as 'indestructible' and 'salvaged somehow from the perilous journey of life.'

This he said to me...
The greatest thing you'll ever learn...
Is just to love and be loved in return.

New York, 2016

Postscript. Last night I went on a date with an oddly aggressive lady to the stage production of *Moulin Rouge*, at London's Piccadilly Theatre. I had once seen the film, but other than being impressed with Ewan McGregor's singing and the band arrangements, it made little impression on me. So I was happily surprised to find *Nature Boy* is basically Toulouse Lautrec's signature song, and occurs several times throughout the show, most notably at the end of Act 1. So, having that afternoon greenlit the inclusion of this piece, I found myself hearing the song live...

The Murder of Mary Rogers

It's quite common now for real-life crimes to spur writers to create their own version of events using certain facts and making others up as they go, but Edgar Allan Poe's *The Mystery of Marie Rogêt* was one of the first. (Indeed, one hundred and twenty-three years before Truman Capote's *In Cold Blood*, the book often hailed as beginning the genre.)

The story behind Poe's inspiration, that of Mary Rogers, begins with the beautiful young woman working in a tobacco shop, where something sunny in her shyness attracted customers to sample her employer's wares. Not much is recorded about Mary's early life, but it is said she was born in New York in 1820, although others have claimed her birthplace as Lyme, Connecticut, in 1818. What is true is that after her father passed in 1825, her mother ran a boarding house in Manhattan, and little Mary assisted until she received a job offer from John Anderson, owner of the aforementioned shop, in 1838. The young beauty was hired as an attraction for the distinguished patrons of the tobacconist's, who included the writers James Fenimore Cooper and Washington Irving.

Although many men flirted with Rogers, she only smiled and sold them tobacco, fulfilling her role as eye candy for the customers. Rogers was friendly but never took any of the men up on their offers of dates – apparently even her boss John Anderson was turned down. She built a solid reputation as 'the beautiful cigar girl' and was something of a local celebrity in New York City.

Her first disappearance of a few days has many different reports giving different dates. Whether it occurred in 1838 or early in the year 1841, Rogers certainly disappeared for several days, and her mother claimed a suicide note was left behind. Somewhere between six days and two weeks later, she reappeared, and the public concluded that John Anderson, possibly in collaboration with the newspaper *The Sun* – not the British redtop – orchestrated the whole thing as a publicity stunt for his shop.

If it was a stunt, it worked, and Rogers's admirers soon overwhelmed her at her job, at one point sending her back to assist her mother with the boarding house. Rumours also spread, claiming Rogers met up with a handsome naval officer in New York – the discoloured and diamond city – instead of visiting family that either resided in Brooklyn or the countryside, depending on the source.

At this point, what is true is that Mary accepted a proposal from cork cutter Daniel Payne, a boarder in her mother's home. Although some sources claim the two were no longer engaged at the time, others report that Rogers told her fiancé and mother that she planned to visit an aunt on July 25th, 1841. She set off for New Jersey, and a heavy storm in the area made it reasonable for the young woman to delay her return by a day to avoid travelling in such inclement and unseasonal weather.

However, Rogers didn't return the next day either, sending her mother and Payne into a frenzy of worry. The two contacted the relative Rogers intended to visit and found that the pair had no plans together and that she had never arrived at her supposed destination. A few days after her departure, two men found her body floating in the Hudson River and contacted authorities. A former fiancé of Rogers's, Arthur Crommelian, identified her body.

After Rogers was pulled from the water, the coroner's examination found a cord around her waist with a heavy rock tied to the other end. Her face was swollen and her body showed signs of a struggle and a severe beating. Her dress was torn, and a piece of it was tied tightly enough around her neck to suffocate her. Some reports claim she was also sexually assaulted.

The coroner specifically noted she was not pregnant at the time of her death. Foul play was concluded, and the search for Mary's killer began.

Arthur Crommelian, the former beau who identified Mary's body at the scene of the crime, was cleared of any wrongdoing. Newspapers and individuals began airing out their own theories and rumours concerning what happened to Rogers near Sybil's Cave in Hoboken. Some believed Daniel Payne and Rogers had fought and he had killed her in a rage, but police quickly ruled that her fiancé's alibi was airtight. Others suspected that one of her customers at the cigar shop may have killed her after being snubbed. Still more theories included a visit to an abortionist gone wrong, gang violence, or a random act of brutality.

Fredrica Loss ran the Nick Moore House pub in the area around Sybil's Cave. She told police that Mary Rogers left the establishment with a dark-skinned man. Loss later heard screams from the nearby woods where the pair had headed, but she paid it no mind given the reputation of the area. Another witness in Hoboken claimed he saw Rogers travel by boat with six 'rough-looking' men and dock near Elysian Fields before willingly walking into the woods with them. Later, three well-dressed men mentioned by the anonymous witness came forward to corroborate the narrative. A carriage driver later came forward and claimed he saw Rogers with the mystery dark-skinned man on Sunday as well, and saw the pair go into Loss's pub.

Two months after the discovery of Mary Rogers's body, Fredrica Loss's two young sons came across some of the late girl's clothing in the woods. They allegedly found a soiled white petticoat, parasol, silk scarf, and a handkerchief embroidered with the initials M.R. in a pile. These items were in a thicket close enough to Sybil's Cave, where the crime supposedly took place, to connect directly to it. The boys also claimed the underbrush was torn up as if a struggle had taken place, and there was a path created by something being dragged through the area.

Emotionally wrung out over the untimely death of his betrothed, Daniel Payne fell deeply into alcoholism. In October 1841, Payne began binge drinking his way to Hoboken over the course of several days and nights. He eventually purchased laudanum from a pharmacy and used it to end his life outside of Sybil's Cave, where Mary Rogers was said to have died. The note he left behind read:

> To the World here I am on the very spot.
> May God forgive me for my misspent life.

The sensational story caught the eye of famed author Edgar Allen Poe almost immediately, and he based his sequel to the well-received *Murders at Rue Morgue* on it. He set the crime in Paris, changed the victim's name to Marie Rogêt and had her working in a perfume store, but kept most of the other specifics as they were. Not only that, but Poe also claimed to have solved the real-life crime during his time writing out the fictionalized version. He wrote to his publishers:

> Under the pretence of showing how Dupin unravelled the mystery of Marie's assassination, I, in fact, enter into a very rigorous analysis of the real tragedy in New York.

In reality, Poe never named a killer in his short story, ironically mirroring the real crime perfectly.

In October or November 1842, one of Fredrica Loss's young boys accidentally shot her, sending her into multiple days of suffering and slow death. During one spat of babbling, Loss claimed that Rogers had died after a failed abortion. She also claimed that Rogers's spirit was haunting her to make the truth known, so her confession was questionable. Loss claimed that the man she saw with Rogers was the doctor who attempted to perform the procedure. Others believed that

Loss actually worked as an intermediary for the illegal abortionist Madame Restell, who took her own life in 1878.

Police arrested and tried Loss's oldest son for the murder of Rogers, but charges were quickly dropped and the crime remains unsolved.

So there are the facts. What do I make of them? Everyone's a suspect: John Anderson, both boyfriends, any lodger at the mother's boarding house... Loss and her sons, the unnamed doctor, hell, even the aunt in the country, or a random person in Hoboken... All could have done it.

And the names are better than any fiction: Loss, Payne, not to mention Elysian Fields – Elysium in Greek mythology – the final place of heroic souls. I can see why Poe was taken with the story, as am I.

And of course Sybil, tenth prophetess, and an Oracle. She is depicted on the ceiling of the Sistine Chapel. Every time you look up there, remember Mary Rogers – she deserves a voice, even if it's merely a whisper.

Riposte, 2015

On Dreaming

I had been told about ageing but not prepared for the reality. It's impossible to comprehend except in hindsight. In my late thirties I was expecting a change, and nothing happened. I hit forty, and – wonder of wonders! – nothing happened. I was clear, free, I felt invincible. None of the horror stories would apply here, not to me, it was all exaggerated; I was a stone, a tank, tortoise-like, invulnerable.

Then I reached forty-one and it all came at once: the alarming rapidity of decline. I knew that one's brain is already rotting from twenty-five onward, but I cannot overstate the frankly staggering acceleration of every discomfort in every corner of your frame. You might be the sky and everything else just weather, but you can't get out of bed without four alarms. And, disconcertingly, things kept falling off, or falling out of, my body, and they were things I missed, things that had served me well up till then, and were taken for granted. Back pain that casually (and habitually) incapacitated a weekend developed into a fortnight; headaches of a Tuesday became so long that one found oneself confusedly arguing with oneself, while the brain itself was seemingly made of ever-hardening putty. Eyes so stinging and streaming that one could no longer lie for long periods on one's back. Toothache became skullache and coruscating heartburn began to spoil even the most meagre meal, although by then one's tastebuds had become so insensitive that food was mere texture and not pleasure... And we haven't even touched on the nightsweats that leave you waking to a lagoon of a mattress, the tropical tundra regions of rest, where every gasp sounds like a wad of tissues being ripped in half. O, what a poet of suffering am I! You couldn't even enjoy a stretch anymore – formerly one of life's lone pleasures – without lower back spasms, like an emotional tax: a tax on pleasure, a tax on every previous good thing.

Age is an accusation and the process of punishment in one. Much as the death of the family pet readies the child for the long walk to the grandparent's bedroom, we are supposed to become disappointed in people: it readies us for discernment. I have been mesmerizingly distressed this past week by revisiting childhood classics. They don't stand up. Nesbit, Tolkein... *Where the Wild Things Are* stands up (let the wild rumpus begin) but then there aren't many words.

Yet there were areas that were going in the opposite direction: my mind, for one. In fact, as you age you become the person you ought to have been all along. So, while physically falling apart, you appreciate things more fully, and become more fluent and assured in creative and emotional parts of your life. Ah, the palpable injustice. Hindsight is an extraordinary thing. Another plus is that you stop worrying about financial things, because you realise that there is nothing any debts can do to you that life has not already done, so fuck it. Don't play their game.

Sometimes, after an immense trauma, life seems like an act, something 'put on', with everyone watching to see how you fare...

And, perhaps unsurprisingly, another thing that becomes more focussed or assured, is dreams, or more specifically, dream*ing*. I had long been able to exert a degree of control over my dreaming: I could go in and out of certain ones, re-enter pleasant ones after briefly waking, and (at times) decide to leave particularly harsh ones. And I had always adhered to the maxim: you can't smoke or drink in dreams (something verified by, among others, a famously confessional novelist friend), until, at forty-one, I found I suddenly could. It was disconcerting to indulge to satiation, yet wake up as refreshed as one can believably be in one's forties.

A mid-life crisis, one might claim, and it undoubtedly was. Everyone has a mid-life crisis, *everyone* – if you don't have a mid-life crisis, then *that's* your mid-life crisis – but I wasn't bulk-buying silk underpants just so I could fart in them, or arriving at work preceeded by tumbleweeds of prostitutes, or taking enough cocaine to routinely guarantee a halo. So what *had* changed? I had become a father.

When you see your own baby for the first time, after those initial thoughts of almost hysterical joy and overwhelming, unbridled emotion (where did all these tears and all this laughter *come* from?), one of the things that happens is: you forgive your parents everything. When I was a boy, my mother knew that the harshest punishment she could inflict was *sending me to bed*. I would cry for hours in the dark with my soft toys, some of which I still have at the very back of the cupboard in the very backest of my backrooms. The curtains being drawn, at age five or six, seemed like life being banished with no recourse back – as the curtains squeaked when opened, I couldn't touch them. Doing so would have precipitated a furious whirlwind... It seemed that I would sit there for hours, unable to sleep, indeed not trying to sleep. And over my youth I developed almost an aversion to sleep. It frightened me, until I learned to do something about it.

In my late twenties I found I could set a scene and go into it to dream there, in that place. I had no go-to place – those all came later – but if I pictured a SF (only amateurs say sci-fi) palace, say, floating above a volcanic stew, I could enter it and enjoy that place until, I presume, REM took over, where memory would stop. This would also, interestingly, be where bed partners would have to wake me up, because I began *wailing*. The wailing, for a subsequent girlfriend, became *crying*, and for another *screaming*. By that point I knew something had to give, so I introduced the go-to places.

The go-to places began as two then blossomed into four.

The first two were a dungeon and an ampitheatre. The dungeon, briefly, was an unsophisticated place to put all my hatreds, and always dimly-lit: even in dreams you don't want to fully see what you'd do to those who'd wronged your family. However, the ampitheatre was fully lit and boasted cottages in the grounds for all my friends. There was never anything beyond the walls, however, only full darkness. Nothing. Sometimes the ampitheatre was built into a cliff, and the dungeon was inside the cliff, and accessed through a secret door in the lighting booth. A lighting booth in which, oddly, only I was allowed, despite never having been a lighting director. Also, no performances ever took place in the ampitheatre, but in each dream there, at some point, I would patrol the upper wall like a sentry or unarmed guard, gazing into the aforementioned darkness. It always felt as if a performance had ended and I had seen the last audience members out.

Sometimes, in the ampitheatre, I would sit on the top of the descending steps and smoke – again, new – and a dog would come and join me and we would snuggle and never mind the smoke. (Later I learned, in bad dreams, to unlock a door into this place and thus escape whatever was following me.) Although I felt the presence of several friends there, I don't think anyone ever joined me in those cottages built into the walls. It was always solitary.

Before I address the other go-to places, let the authorial voice interject: I called Professor Revelle Dalton, from Harvard University, who had studied sleep patterns and ways of dreaming for over twenty years, about all this... We discussed childhood trauma and she confessed that she had never come across a case 'quite so unique' as mine. That annoyed me for the obvious reason – there is no such thing as *quite unique* – but also because her voice was a tad cloying, or was it just me? She said that a client of hers had gone to a clinic to help with lucid sleep, one based on shamic teachings. This sounded wonderful, but apparently they were all raised by a gong clang at 3.30 a.m., before being told to go back to sleep again, as this would aid better sleep.

Now, I don't think shamans are general hate figures, but at 3.30 a.m. I would have murdered them/him/her. Dalton's client wrote: 'I went [there] to talk about the history of lucid dreaming (ancient

Roman sleep temples etc!)... and then I also went to a "lucid dreaming sleepover" at a café/community centre type place... where I really enjoyed the meditation/gongs etc before bed, but had a terrible nights [sic] sleep cos [sic] there were so many people and very loud pipes.'

The other go-to places: well let's do them, if we have to.

One, a glorious house overlooking a city – no human or earthly city – I even drew up ground plans in my sleep. I could walk you through it now, although, to be fair, it largely featured one or other of my old school buildings.

Two was fixed – for some reason I could never leave – the back garden of my mum's old flat where, alarmingly (and repeatedly) I had buried a corpse. And the corpse, strangely, was almost always that of an unnamed child – perhaps myself, a psychologist might have said, or more probably the 'me' that had suffered abuse in that flat (although not at my mother's hand). I must have buried that child thousands of times, in thousands of ways...

You think you know guilt? You have no idea, until you wake up screaming every night about it. In other dreams, I once dreamed a whole Sibelius piano concerto that doesn't exist. It was as good as Schumann's cello concerto that Clara destroyed, citing her husband's mental health.

Henry James said, *tell a dream, lose a reader*. And, in fiction, dreams write white – they will never show up on the page. But he also means they are a distraction from the plot, or a luxurious authorial interjection.

While chatting with Professor Revelle Dalton I became aware that she was similarly disposed, but with one gaping schism: *belief*: that most overrated of virtues. Revelle, the doctor, was a slave. If you need to be told how to behave, you don't need a master.

So as you sleep tonight, unfettered by gods, let your mind roam through the corridors of your past. Flash old footage of yourself, crackling as newsreel, of schooldays, of happiness, of when we were good, and the centre of everything. Then settle back, as your body wastes away, and enjoy what dreams you have left before you're too old to care.

Dream at your peril, peeps. I'll be listening for the pipes and a gong.

Safe Sleep, 2021
On the book tour for *Fairytales and Oddities* (published June 2021) I was quizzed in interviews – many of which can be viewed or listened to online – about *Titbits with Williams*, a part of the book where fiction

appears to veer into reportage or, as I prefer, a travelogue of the classic American road trip. Was there more to it? Was *Titbits With Williams* just a taster of something more expansive?

As I suggested in the Foreword to this volume, is there any such thing as truth anymore? And does journalism still exist? Salman Rushdie reminded me recently of the idea that *the opposite of history is love... [that is] ...worth hanging on to, like a lifebelt, like a raft.* I admire this very much, even if it isn't prescient. And what *is* history? Rushdie disappeared into the front page – he knew what history was if anyone ever did – he became it. And he will always be looking over his shoulder. [As this book goes to press Salman has been stabbed in New York...]

Sadly, the repudiation of our past condemns us to the acidic cycle of repetition and ignorance. It's no surprise the Holocaust happened: it's surprising it doesn't happen more often.

I am constantly amazed by how short memory is; I am constantly amazed by how stupid people are. Stupid isn't even a quantity, to my mind: it's a default setting. Hell, not even a setting, that's letting people off lightly. No. It's: be what you *say you are*, a reclaimed insult, but one with no profit. Everyday we hear as Londoners... *Welcome to London Underground – all lines are operating without delays – and we are running an excellent service...* No. You aren't running an *excellent service*. It's what you advertised the trains to do. Run as they were advertised to do. The bar is set so low that no one even recognises a lowest common denominator any more. No commuter even considers it. You can't *always* be experiencing a higher volume of calls than average. That's not how averages work. We blindly blunder on, full of lit purpose, every light signalling some hope or ambition, but with implausibly heavy hearts.

In those aforementioned radio and YouTube interviews I casually batted the questions away, saying: 'Well, you never know'... But there was in fact more, and here is the best of what didn't make it into *Fairytales and Oddities*. And why didn't they make the grade, you may ask? I answer: for reasons of artifice and balance, sure, but mainly just because I wanted it that way. And perhaps because I lost heart somewhere along the way.

Titbits with Williams: Extra

Churchill, Manitoba, has the odd distinction of being the polar bear capital of the world. Every spring and summer, the icy bay near Churchill melts, depriving the polar bears of their primary hunting grounds. Unable to stalk seals, about 1000 hungry bears come into town looking for food. And these bears aren't picky. They'll eat anything, from garbage to dogs.

Despite the danger, the people of Churchill have managed to adapt to the annual bear invasion. For example, it's customary for people to keep their homes and more importantly, cars, unlocked so if someone is being pursued by a polar bear, they'll have somewhere to shelter.

To prevent bears from following, or investigating the smell of something cooking in the kitchen, doors are protected by special Welcome Mats made from nail-studded plywood. Curious bears quickly get the point. During Halloween, trick-and-treating kids are escorted by armed adults, and no one is allowed to dress up as ghosts for fear of being mistaken for a... well, you catch the drift... Too. Many. Puns. There's even a special polar bear hotline (675-BEAR, in case you ever need it). If you call that number, a group of conservation officers will show up, armed with firecrackers and rubber bullets (with a backup of real ones), to drive the unwelcome visitors toward town limits.

But if a bear doesn't take the hint and keeps wandering back into Churchill, then it might spend a few months in the Polar Bear Jail. Repeat offenders are tranquilized and taken to the prison, which was once an aircraft hangar. When the bear wakes up from its nap, it finds itself in one of 28 cells with only around two meters (six feet) to move around in. The polar bear jail is a pretty rough clink. The bears are deprived of food and they are given only snow to drink. The idea is to make their stay in Churchill so unpleasant that they'll never come back. It may sound harsh, but authorities believe it's a better alternative to killing them (or being killed *by* them for that matter). When the bay freezes over again in the colder months, the bears are released, having hopefully learned a valuable lesson about Manitoba justice.

While many people think of the polar bear as cute and cuddly, the Inuit people give it a little more respect. They consider the Nanuk (polar bear) to be a mystical, almost human creature, which deserves reverence even after death. After a successful kill, an Inuit hunter would honour the Nanuk by hanging its skin in his home for several days. Along with the hide, the hunter would also hang up tools as an offering to the bear's spirit. For male bears, the Inuit would give knives and bow-drills, and for females he would offer gifts such as skin-scrapers and needle-cases. It was believed that the Nanuk needed the souls of these tools in the next life, and if the hunter treated the bear with respect, the Nanuk would tell other bears about the hunter's kindness. Then other bears would offer themselves to the hunter to be killed in exchange for tools. Everybody wins.

However, if a hunter mistreated the Nanuk's soul, he would never be able to kill another polar bear. The same goes for the hunter's wife. If she disrespected the bear, her husband would never again be a great hunter. This was especially problematic for women if their husbands died. Chances were pretty good that they'd remain single because no Inuit hunter wanted to marry into the Nanuk's curse...

Naturally, belief has kept the crime rate low. But then Canada has always dealt with white problems better than other places...

****

Las Vegas is close enough to California that when I met my online social media pal M – why I'm not using their full name will become clear asap – on the Strip at 9.30pm, outside BJ's bijou Bar and Grill, it seemed entirely natural that we should spontaneously burst into a verse of *California Dreamin'* – *All the leaves are brown / And our dreams are grey* – as we hugged, gathered our bags, and went in search of adventure.

What kind of adventure? Well...

The Adventures of Huckleberry Finn, *The Adventures of Augie March*: adventures seemed to me such an admirably American term – Europeans are more accustomed to picnics, or day-trips – but I was defo up for an *adventure*. And I should add that 'close enough' in American terms is heroically meaningless... America, where ones nearest neighbour can seem utterly obscure, and distances are elastic concepts... America, the only place on the planet with all five active climate zones: tropical, dry, temperate, continental and polar. America, where freedom is minted in race, guns and healthcare; America, where it seemed entirely natural to embrace a stranger and begin singing: *'You know the preacher liked the cold/ He knows I'm gonna stay/ California dreamin''...*

After alluringly brief introductions, during which M flicked their (still smouldering) cigar into a trashcan and I began rolling a cigarette, they said: 'You ready for the adventure to begin?'

I laughed, licked, and rolled. Lighting, 'bring it on,' I said.

'Oh, *oh*, I *shall*,' they nodded to our shared British heritage.

'Just before we do,' I ventured, 'what's with the scar?'

'This?' M fanned both hands out, as if one side were stronger than the other, cupping their whole head. They added: 'Nothing. Ah, this was a long time ago.'

'Mm.'

I won't attempt to render M's accent in prose (not because it's crude and arguably racist to do so) but because their accent was seriously fucked. Idling somewhere between Birmingham (England) and the iceberg that sank the *Titanic*, it was harsh, unrelenting and cloying, a quality that wasn't helped by the enormous 'snitch' scar down their right cheek. M had availed me of their pronouns during our email honeymoon – what barmy, balmy weeks – and I am always faithful on the page. While I greedily sucked on my roll-up – it had been a gruelling flight – M loaded our bags into the car and explained, in their alarming voice, our itinerary...

We would register into a local motel, the Whole Year Inn. I was too tired to argue. Then we would go and *do* Liberace the following day. Fine. The flies seemed attuned to my fresh un-American meat and began to feast, first forearms then neck but this was dusk and I hadn't readied myself. On the way to the hotel, M said: 'It is terrible here, just awful and brilliant. You can do things you'd never dream of anywhere else.' Then, almost as an afterthought: 'I got married yesterday.'

'Mm. And where is your spouse now?'

The room was sparse: two startlingly bouncy single beds in between which I happily ditched my luggage. Three chairs, an oddly-angled cupboard in one corner and laptop-desk in the other, and broadly orange, it seemed adequate, until... the bathroom shower didn't work. I called Reception.

'Mista Willa? Vroom 13?'

'I guess.'

After some tense minutes punctuated by faint clanging, Reception came back on the line: '...Try thee shower if pleaze.'

Cupping the phone between my shoulder and right cheek, I gently turned the shower nozzle, and a wall of scalding water flew out. Violently recoiling while attempting to keep hold of the phone, I slipped and came a cropper across the lino floor, hit my chin on the toilet and momentarily lost full consciousness.

'Mista Willa? Mista Willa? All is good. Now.'

I came to.

'No people dere. He dead I sink.'

'No,' I rejoined, 'I'm fine thanks. Good night.'

'Welcome to Vegas Mista Willa we wash you a present stay.'

M was braying at the door at 6am. The fucker. I could have put a fork through his eye at that moment, but of course I didn't say so.

'Duuuude! Get up! Let's go!'

'I'm *English*. I'm jetlagged. Fuck off.'

'Duuuuuuude!'

'If you don't stop I'll put a fork through your eye.'

Americans are persistent. I'll give them that.

'Ya*hu*llo! Wo*wo*wow! Rise and shiiiine!'

I opened the door and attempted to plunge a teaspoon into M's eye – it was all that was available, and it was plastic – but he caught my arm and said, 'Let's *not* do that. There's an old cinderbones.'

'Does this have purpose?'

'Of course my friend, buckle up. We'll grab breakfast, and then on into the *quest*. Great deeds a*wait* us. Us Knights of the...'

'Christ.' I stopped listening and shelved latent homicidal inclinations.

I had become acquainted with M through their YouTube videos that I mildly admired, given M's enthusiasm, knowledge of their subject – urban exploration of famous dead people's houses – and willingness to gain entry to places without fear of legal retribution. Perhaps this was because they never showed their face – hence my surprise at the highly identifiable scar. We had had an email exchange, then a telephone chat (what archaic beasts!), and arranged to meet on my forthcoming roadtrip.

Thus after breakfast, we broke into Liberace's house, three minutes by car off the strip. To be fair, Las Vegas was suffering terrible economic depression, and most of the houses were dilapidated and easy to enter, so it didn't feel like burglary – besides, we weren't there to steal – although I doubt the LVMPD would have seen it similarly. Refuse sacks, chipped cinder-block chunks, used needles, and discarded skips lined the houses. Apart from the gates (which featured the ornate iron *L* of Liberace), this one was no different from the next.

Set on a corner, Liberace's was smaller than I had imagined, but then he had bigger places in Palm Springs and elsewhere. Our plan was to stay there for a night or two, drink, party, and then move on to the Hearst Castle, the one Orson Welles recreated for *Citizen Kane*, which boasted three estate cottages, each one big enough to be an average British ancestral home. But right now we were in Liberace's house, and my first impression as we turned on our wraparound head torches and boarded up the small alcove through which we'd gained entry was of sadness. No one cared about Liberace anymore. And, despite whatever else you might think about him, Liberace was a great pianist. He didn't always play or behave like one, but nonetheless he was one.

Born Wladziu Valentino Liberace, yes, really, that was his name, in 1919, in Wisconsin, from Polish and Italian parentage, from the late 50s to the early 70s he was one of the highest paid entertainers in the world. Also known as The Glitter Man, Mr Showmanship and Walter Busterkeys (as he started out), he began playing at four and later studied with the legendary pianist Paderewski. His father was a former orchestral horn player and his mother had played piano professionally before her marriage. He later said: 'My father's love and respect for music created in him a deep determination to give as his legacy to the world, a family of musicians dedicated to the advancement of the art.' Two brothers followed him into music, one sister did not, but today he is all I remember of the family, save for that his younger brother was literally called Rudolph Valentino (sharing the same sibling middle name) Liberace, in deference to their mother's showbiz longings.

So as I advanced into the house, I expected to see some evidence of music. But there was little, although I recognised the inner workings of a 'player piano' – that which plays itself on a circular studded cylinder – which M, busily vlogging ahead of me – had missed. Discarded in a corner, the mechanism appeared intact, but ironically there was no piano to put it in, and Liberace famously boasted at least one piano in every room of all his houses save the bathrooms.

There was one huge open space with what appeared to be the remnants of a bar in one corner, then, turning, I saw it: through an arch, the famous inlaid bathub that featured in the titles of the The Liberace Show (52 – 69). At its peak, in 1956, the non-network half-hour TV show was viewable on over 225 television stations and had as many as 35,000,000 viewers. Thirty-five million. Almost all dead now, and I was standing in front of the iconic bathtub. I caught my breath. To the left, past showers and wash stations, was his old bedroom, in an L shape with the master bathroom making a square.

I sat crosslegged in the corner of the room for a brief while. To pay respects? Well, perhaps, but more to feel the atmosphere thrumming. *His* rhythm was here, and I embraced it. Having had to deny his sexuality for his entire performing career, this was one of the bedrooms where he had surely been happy with his longterm boyfriend Scott Thorson. Emotionally, I illuminated the faded, cracked, flaked mural that covered the walls. A deliberately overblown rendering of the Sistine Chapel on the ceiling where spraycans couldn't reach, and the outline of L's upright against the right wall, this room was viewable in the TV show too. The grand piano was almost where I was sitting. The shadow of the upright was an afterthought on the wall on the only way out, as if L couldn't even wait to play something, anything, before leaving the room.

M had finished their downstairs vlog and called out to me.

'In here,' I shouted.

'*Wow*,' they exclaimed, 'missed this. What the actual fuck?'

'Amazing, isn't it?'

'Mm. *Mm*.'

By the (unopened) front door(s) there was a staircase that, according to Google, Liberace had seen somewhere in Europe and, upon returning, had commissioned a replica to be built. M and I trod carefully, and each step groaned, happy to be used, but unhappy at being so long lovingly ignored. Upon reaching the top there were two offices to the left, but to the right was the crown jewel. It was what we'd come to see, to be honest. And I can't explain the emotion that came over me upon first seeing the Morocco Room.

In the old days of Hollywood, Ginger Rogers had hobnobbed with Dolly Parton here. Barry Manilow famously came up with Copacabana on this very spot, at the bar at the far end from the door where I now stood: he said it in interview. Michael Jackson and Barbra Streisand both partied here in the late 70s and 80s, not to mention Lucille Ball and Elizabeth Montgomery and other comedic legends such as Bob Hope and Dean Martin before them. For an Englishman new to Vegas, it was overwhelming. I needed a cigarette.

'You can smoke here,' said M, but I just couldn't.

'I'll smoke in there when I'm ready, thanks,' I replied, and lit up on the landing. M was vlogging the room, doing close-ups on tiles and the bar. I was just trying to exhale without coughing or crying. This was my childhood: Judy Garland had had a drink here while observing the views to the strip from the glass-domed top.

We set out sleeping bags that night. Mine was green. Just a little sweeping of areas and plugging of windows was all it took.

'Did you really get married?' I asked M, as we smoked and the little radio between us played *Don't Bogart That Joint , My Friend*, a song made immortal by the film *Easy Rider*, but also perfectly timed for the passing of a spliff.

'Oh yeah, we did.' M coughed, softly.

'And… I'm sorry, but where is, I mean where are…'

'Don't be. He left.'

'Mm.'

'I don't know you.'

'True. Still, I know about short-term things like that…'

'That's why I have a therapist.'

'Of course.'

'Are you happy?'

'I'm English.'

'*Man…*'

'Mm.'

My head resting on the cold Turkish tiles, I thought of asking one last thing. Columbo, aka Peter Falk, had owned a house only a street away. Minutely runnelled, like corduroy, the tiles made imprints on my skin. Like the pretty patterns of streets in London, curving and flowing, the life of the city, the opposite of grid life here, where streets know they all conform and suffer rejection issues for that.

As for M, I'm sorry I left them there.

An adventure it was, but I resolved to go back to California in the morning and not continue on with M. Why? I'm not sure, but I suddenly felt a huge pull in that direction, as of rusted rolling stock being pulled along condemned railway tracks. M was a drag, no need for more innocent words,

Perhaps it was the girl I'd left there. Perhaps because I had got all I wanted. Perhaps it was irritation at M, whose character had effloresced into boredom and pronouns. Perhaps it was American smoke, unused to it as I was; perhaps disappointment at how Liberace was treated. Perhaps it was a man escaping his past, or even his present. Who knew?

****

By now, everyone knows that 'Reality' shows are fake, in the sense that they use creative editing and staged scenes to make their 'reality' more interesting than it would be if they just let a bunch of spoiled people screech at each other for half an hour. Although, as the comedian Stewart Lee pointed out: watching 'twats in a place' is exactly what we're doing. But the scam that was pulled off by *P.I. Moms* took it to a whole new level.

You may not have heard of it, but *P.I. Moms* became a minor pop culture phenomenon in 2010 when it was proposed as a reality show on Lifetime, a network primarily known for showing movies like *Sleeping With the Enemy* (and I mean movies *exactly* like it. *Killing Your Husband: the Theequel* and *No Adverts Just Murder the Wife*). The show would focus on middle-class suburban mothers who, instead of the usual mom stuff, picked up work as licensed private investigators. They'd track witnesses, spy on suspicious individuals, gain intel on narcotics rings and trick paedophiles into chatting with them online.

The whole thing was the brainchild of Chris Butler, a former SWAT officer, who decided to start Bosleying around soccer moms because he'd rather not get shot himself. *Lifetime* reviewed his exploits and offered him fat basic cable dollars to bring *P.I. Moms* to fruition. So what was the problem? What could possibly go wrong? Well...

A journalist named Peter Crooks went for a ride-along with Butler and his P.I. Moms to see them in action, but was suspicious from the start. Crooks had been contacted to do the ride-along by Butler himself – clue one. Butler tried to bring Crooks in on a cheating-husband-sting, which actually turned out to be a cheating-husband-entrapment. When Crooks said he wasn't interested in tricking people and would be more interested to do a story on Butler and his Moms if they blew the lid off an affair that was already in progress, Butler called him back the next day with a case he'd *just been offered* that happened to fit the exact criteria.

The 'sting' involved trailing a guy and his mystery date all over Napa Valley, spying on them over a lunch that Crooks thought felt oddly scripted – virtually every single sentence between the two involved an oblique reference to sex, as if they wanted it to be perfectly obvious to any eavesdropping moms and/or journalists that they were going to be having some sex later:

Man: I hear your huband's out of town...
Woman: He's not only out of town, he's out of my life. At least my bed.
Man: That's good to hear. Would you like another drink? A cocktail?
Woman: Sex-on-the-beach? Don't mind if I do...

and

Man: Hey, remember when you took your swimsuit off earlier?
Woman: How could I forget? You wanted to ravish me...

Man: That I did, but I cannot until my wife is dead...
Woman: Dead to me? Or dead in your marital bed?

Crooks and the P.I.s eventually tracked the suspected cheater to a Holiday Inn, where they *stole his car*, evidently confusing *inconspicuous* with every single word in the English language that meant the exact opposite.

This seemed fake as hell to Crooks, and shortly after that he received an email from an anonymous source confirming his suspicions: not only was everyone involved in the 'sting' an actor on Butler's payroll, but every single media piece the *P.I Moms* had been featured in was scripted. The source turned out to be an actor named Carl Marino, who had worked on Crooks's ride-along as one of the investigators in Butler's employ.

But here's the best part: Marino also revealed that Butler was reselling drugs confiscated from busts done by an actual narcotics team he had contact with. This was the same task force that helped the Moms entrap a supposedly drug-selling kid using the totally plausible promise of chicken, bowling, and group sex with lingerie models. Only in America, eh?

Eventually, Crooks got Marino in touch with some less corrupt officials, who used him in a legitimate drug sting (one that involved much less sexy dialogue and car theft) that landed Butler and his partner at the narcotics task force in federal prison. Needless to say, *Lifetime* cancelled the show, although it seems to me that they killed it right when it was getting good.

2017/18

Postscript. In the years since I was there, happily the Liberace house has found a new lease of life. Bought by British businessman Martyn James Ravenhill, who cleverly cashed in on the housing crisis, on March 2nd 2016 it became the first residential property to become a Historic Landmark in Clark County, Nevada, after undergoing extensive renovation. He had just bought the derelict shell when I crashed there. The 14,393-square-foot property at 4982 Shirley Street boasts a fully restored Morrocco Room – apparently Ravenhill is such a fan that he commissioned replacement tiles from the same place in Turkey that had made the original ones, and a new hall which serves as a rental venue for weddings and other events. You can tour it, and I recommend you do. That player piano (probably boasting a different mechanism) is now fully operational, and once again there is a piano in every major room, including where I sat in the bedroom. I haven't yet been back, but I surely will.

What Is Stammering About?

I was a strange bescarved boy: confused, pudgy, insecure, obscurely needy, acne-scarred, shuffling and speechless: quite literally speechless. And all the afflictions were connected.

They say, 'Oh, you'll grow out of it.' and to a certain extent you do, because you gain confidence and decide that your mind is yours alone to abuse. No dryout or decoking yet. At eight-years-old the plethora of life-threatening debaucharies were yet to be enjoyed. But puberty didn't change anything either. 'You'll grow out of it.' But who are you to say?

Stammering, or stuttering as it is often maddeningly described by doctors – ts and ds being personal enemies – is not a physical ailment. There has been research done into whether stammering is hereditary, or a psychological condition, without definite conclusions. But I can tell you this. It has a lot to do with confidence. If there is no malformation of the soft palate, it is mostly indicative of a traumatic childhood – particularly one of religious observance. Acne-scars: god certainly gave me *those* to teach a harsh lesson. It's a psychological one. There can be of course a physical side: the aforementioned malformation of the soft palate, but I'm an opera singer and have never had any trouble singing. Now, if the soft palate (basically that bit at the top of your mouth that extends back past the tonsils), where one 'places' the notes, or pitches them, much as where the violinist knows to touch the string, or trombonist knows to place their slide, is 'malformed' as certain doctors assert it is for stammerers, then I wouldn't be able to sing. Doctors also love 'stutterers' and not stammerers. It's maddening because the consonants – and it's almost always consonants – I find, apart from ts and ds – what is/are hard are the ss, the ms and combinations of them. Words such as *society* and *mnemonic* and *station* and *totally* and (shudder, because it contains both) *stutter* never appear in my everyday speech. All stammerers become used to avoiding certain words or phrases – it's how we live. But I have been asked to share my story with you, so here it is, with many tangents and interlopings and jokegrabs (but not gropejags).

I was around seven when I first consciously noticed it, or at least internally recognised – the ability to not be able to *talk*. In fact *that's* not quite right. I could talk, but I couldn't communicate. What came out was a series of gasps and clicks, and my mother understood me, but no one else did. Her insistence that I wasn't any different from any other child wasn't helpful for my development, although I'm sure it came from a belief of doing the correct thing at her end.

Naturally, there was trauma behind all this that is probably helpful for personal understandings, but which is unnecessary here. When I was nine, at St Michael's School in Oxford, I began to sing, rather than talk. It became an exaggerated part of my character – so my actual character had to go with it, or move, or shift, to catch up. Luckily this was before the days of labelling everyone with a diagnosis: innocent times, when innocent words were becoming harder and harder to find. As a nine-year-old I'd swagger down the halls of St Michael's singing my arrival to a classroom, to the lockers, and finally, to the stage. They put me on the stage playing the king in a big school play. Now, I don't remember what the play was, but I remember very clearly that I didn't stammer. The girl playing the queen was named Kelly (who has probably forgotten it ever happened), but it will forever be the time I realised I *had* to be on the stage, because *there* was more comfortable than *here*, in real life. I still have the (blurry, 80's) photos of us on our dual thrones, Kelly and me. I hope she went on to become someone well adjusted and secure.

Many famous actors including Bruce Willis and Samuel L. Jackson suffer from stammers. But it doesn't affect their work. And over the years, I began to realise why. Singing and speaking come from different sides of the brain.

The right-hand side is where creative thoughts come from: we produce melody and rhythm from there. It is the fount of creativity. Now, if you're a stammerer, and you're playing a part – that is, playing someone other than you – it comes from that side of the brain, and you don't stammer. It was the same for me with singing. The opposite side, the left hemisphere, is for everyday speech – that of the everyday that I didn't want to be much a part of – often labelled the *dominant* hemisphere, it also interprets visual information and spatial processing. So, apart from allowing you to speak – and make word formations resulting in sentence stuctures – it makes you see, and judge what will cause harm. It is why we don't walk into traffic, and why we do appreciate a rainbow. But it is not what what allows us to invent a rainbow for a book of fiction. So perhaps us stammerers are the keepers of something special.

But if I could offer any young person advice on stammering, it would be this: pitch your speaking voice slightly lower. Take the time to get used to it, and breathe more often. Practise breathing in front of a candle at mouth height, but without leaning forward or looking down – the candle must be exactly, and *safely*, positioned. Then, inhale to a count of five (or three if this is new to you) and draw the flame 75% your way, then exhale to a longer count and make the flame go almost 90% away from you, but always without going out. The flame must never be extinguished.

Build up yourself till you think you're the centre of the universe and never let anyone tell you otherwise, or talk you out of it. You won't 'grow out of' stammering. It's there for life. But it can be manageable. And you can be wonderful and, as I do, actually look forward to speaking in public. Although it still helps to have a plan of what you're going to say. Learn to speak in paragraphs. By which I mean, plan: the last line of a paragraph ought to be its apotheosis, and lead on to the next paragraph. Imagine you have a permanent audience and all this 'living' is merely acting. Then, if anyone makes fun of you, it won't matter, because you're the burning still centre of everything.

O Write, 2017

Outpost 31

The second thing that struck me upon arriving in Antarctica was that I was South. *Literally*, I was South. Couldn't be more South. Everywhere I turned was North. If I turned here, at right angles, still North, if I turned here, another right angle, North, if I turned here, 270°, North. If I turned *South*, still North... Very odd, but it didn't *feel* different. There was no perceptible moral shift. No compass gauge had been magnetized, or hunted deer shot. And I almost believed it: the fact that, when one is a sticking point, the world revolves around *you*. You are here, South, and literally the centre of everything. Antarctica is the dream of narcissists. Shakespeare, as usual, is the linguistic template. You do look, my son, in a moved sort, / As if you were dismay'd. Be cheerful, sir. / Our revels now are ended...

The third thing that struck me was: there weren't any animals, or anything else, flora or fauna, birdsong or plane-noise. Expecting penguins and seals – I got nothing, no place for anything delicate, or what was before. It was entirely *other*, and I had travelled some largely unexplored areas of Iceland (where the opening landscapes of *Prometheus* had been filmed, as that haunting horn theme unspooled – no, those weren't CGI, excluding the enormous spaceship of course).

But the first thing: it was exceedingly, and unexpectedly, noisy. Nightclub-loud, the sailors communicated many things by gesture. Sheets of ice constantly grated against each other, horizontally and vertically, and they were all unhappy about our ship rutting its way through them. They *screamed* against the hull.

I had been on it for over a week, but I cannot disclose the ship's name because Antarctica is still contested waters for those who have bases there, Russia, the USA and Great Britain, Finland, Norway, Sweden, Iceland (ironically, I thought), and some more, less important ones: the crappy countries, those less able to afford it. The Southern Continent is peppered with specks of humanity from everywhere. There is even a tourist centre that is currently unmanned, on an island called Bovet... The ships all monitor each other, and have clear knowledge of each other, but I am not allowed to share that information in print, despite the fact that I could wave at some of them from a porthole.

Of course, I was just along for the ride. I am not a scientist, nor would or could I ever credibly claim to be one. My passage had been paid for by a magazine, to write this piece – I was here for *this*... Christ. Hence the friendly but dubious scepticism that greeted me every time

I came up top. And I couldn't argue. Why would I? This lot were keeping me alive.

The quietest member of the crew, so far as I could tell, was a young kitchen-hand named Klaus, who, a week into the voyage, asked what I was reading while I ate the food he served me in a deserted canteen. I guess I had had my nose in a book – *Moby Dick* – for most of the time. Partly, I felt obsolete, and after initial, gentle, snubs to join the sailors proper, I had made my bed and had to lie in it. I didn't want to be anti-social, I just wanted to get there and then see what there was to write about. I was in a disillusioned phase of my life, and sick of everything. Precisely why I was on the bloody ship. But when he approached me, I wasn't reading Melville, and he seemed to be an outsider also.

'How was the food?' he asked.

'Good today, thanks.' Then, seeing his deflated expression, I added, 'It's always great. You know that. Particularly good today. Don't worry, I'll put my plates up there.'

'Actually, if you don't mind...'

'Of course not, what is it?'

'I wanted to ask, if I may, what you are reading.'

'Oh, of course, I'm reading this...' and showed him the lurid cover of a thriller by someone with a middle initial, Jasper M. Throwcher, say, or Daniel P. Exeter.

'Why do you read that?' he asked, 'they say you meant to be a clever writer? No? That's what they say that why you're here.'

Stifling a wince, I replied: 'I read this shit because it relaxes me. What's your name?'

'Klaus.'

'Ok, Klaus, I'll be here reading trash if you want to chat.'

'Okay, I have to clean kitchen though. It is long.'

'So is this procedural.'

I didn't of course, read. I was thinking about writing about him. A (very) young – and, to my mind, inarguably gay – man serving in hospitality for a mostly inhospitable audience in one of the most inhospitable places on earth. Klaus never rejoined.

On Day 12, the crew called us up on top deck. And on pulleys, lifted a helicopter out of the body of the ship – belly? – and announced that some of us would be continuing our journey in it. It looked like a dilapidated flamingo, or a stun-gunned kangaroo to me, propellers all folded and floppy. But soon it was all defrosted, hot liquid in its pipes. Then, inelegantly, almost gangly, we nosed down into a headwind to push through.

By Day 13 I was at the base, and sharing a cabin with Verter.

No, my job was to write about it in a novel, and to be fair, the journey to even get this far had been extraordinary, crossing time-boundaries where yesterday became today via an announcement on an intercom, and watching different coloured rivers within the sea meet but mysteriously refuse to join... And where were my qualifications? I was with people who had trained their whole lives for this, yet I was the one given the position of writing it up. That hardly seemed fair, and it wasn't fair. But friendships developed, indeed flourished.

They say the first night is the worst, and it's true. Acclimatising isn't quite right: one's brain and body have to seismically adjust. I was bunking with a geologist named Verter. I made some *Werther* jokes early on, but they went down like the *Titanic*, so I stopped doing that... On my replenishment expedition drop-off were biologists, mechanics, doctors, meteorologists, cooks, IT and radio personnel (in case that was the only mode of communication), geologists (like Verter) and me, a writer: most were simple replacements – the staff at Amundsen-Scott base was necessarily rotated due to the conditions and the effects it could have on one's psyche. But this was clearly not a tourist jaunt – no one was entertaining any whimsy, and no one was treating me with deference. For about three minutes I smarted like a divo in the cold until I remembered that an old friend, Sir Peter Maxwell Davies, composer and for a time Keeper of the Queen's Music (a sort of Music Laureate), had undertaken a similar trip some decades before, and he told me that he had received no special treatment, and confessed to being minutely disappointed but sturdily unsurprised. Max's trip was to undertake work on a new piece, to rival, say, Ralph Vaughan Williams's (no relation of mine) *Sinfonia Antarctica*... Incidentally, Vaughan Williams's piece had been mentioned in the novelisation of John Carpenter's *The Thing*, itself based on a novella called *Who Goes There?* by John W. Campbell (published 1938). Max had taught me a great deal about music, but I was here to write prose. I thought that odd. He said: they made me use a leaf-blower to see what supplies we still had. 'It's pretty much all I could do. Or was allowed to do.'

Still, *The Thing* had been an infamous flop on its release in 1984, but has since come to be regarded as a classic of several genres: the paranoid Cold War 80s, the body dysmorphic terror of *Alien* (1979) and its ilk, a groundbreaking beast for practical special effects (courtesy of the cocaine-crazed Rob Bottin; pronounced Bot*teen*), a 12-tone score courtesy of Ennio Morricone, who used the Second Viennese School to full creepy effect, and sweeping cinematography by Dean Cundey, who went on to work with Robert Zemeckis on the *Back to the Future* franchise and Spielberg's *Jurassic Park*, Ron Howard's *Apollo 13*, and was Oscar-nominated and BAFTA-nominated... and indeed it was on my mind when I accepted the challenge, well, job, to write what you're reading. I did geek-ily insist on calling it Outpost 31... But then, with good pedigree – every Christmas Eve on the base the scientists have a tradition of settling in to watch all three. Carpenter's film, the original (1951), and the prequel (2012), in one evening.

We landed at Amundsen-Scott base at 9 a.m. But it could have been any time really. The helipad was the only dark space in the area, save the landing beacons. As we disembarked I felt an acoustic change. Sound somehow widened-out and filled. But we were all wearing helmets, so I think I was hallucinating.

It turned out that I actually was hallucinating, due to altitude and dehydration, and I continued to suffer spasms and moments of stringent clarity for a couple of hours.

****

Verter and I got along well, if fairly wordlessly, and I settled into the Amundsen-Scott base like a pro.

A large white and grey slab on stilts, it was surrounded by cladded outhouses for the scientific experiments which, so far as I could glean, were all about weather, or more precisely predicting how weather would behave. This is hugely important work, as being able to outthink weather cannot only save thousands of lives, but also impacts how governments are formed. It can affect the aviation sector, land transport (food for cities), flood and storm damage avoidance (which alone can add billions to an economy), and also allows farmers to grow better crops. To understand the weather gives a better yield, which can lead to a happier populace, with more revenue to invest, which in turn enriches the country and pays for people like me to travel here and tell you about it in careful measured prose... But there wasn't any booze.

On the third day bunking I offered Verter a cigarette. He took it, while simultaneously somehow scoffing at the idea of having one. I warmed to him, despite his comically aggressive mutterings. He had been 'trained in submarines', which I took to mean he had once been a submariner, and he was certainly short, and I could see how the build might fit...

We smoked in the cabin. Outside, a lighter wouldn't light. And you wouldn't enjoy it anyway. There would be no taste. There were unconfirmed tales of average conversations being overheard over four miles away across the ice. Astonishing bouncing acoustics.

After two days Verter asked: 'what did you mean about my name?'

'Sorry? I, don't...'

'You made fun of my name.'

'Oh, you mean Werther! I do aplologise. It's not *your* name! It's a name that sounds like yours. A pun. Like... er... how many singers does it take to change a lightbulb? None. Because none of them are watching. Wait. Sorry, that wasn't a pun. I meant...'

'I was kidding,' he laughed. 'Kept you going as long as I could.'

'Wa da fa?'

'Yeah, sorry. I pegged you for a twat, but you've actually been okay.'

We locked eyes, and I understood the impulse. It's like on a flight when they announce they've lost all flaps, brakes, hydraulics, spoilers, reverse thrust. You never believe it will happen, and hopefully it never does, but you instantly recognise it – panic. Panic for acceptance. He recognised a kindred soul. We were both imposters here.

'Ah, fuck,' I exclaimed.

'You're the Wir, though, aren't, no?'

He didn't say double-U-eye-are, he pronounced it *weer*, like the start of the word weird.

'It's an acronym,' I replied, 'writer-in-residence. Like, where else is there to stay around here?'

'Yeah, I'm not an idiot. Try one of these,' said Verter, beautifully flourishing a slimline pack of mini-cigars.

We talked for hours. I explained that I was going to be Writer In Residence at the Amundsen-Scott Station for three months, he told me how he wasn't allowed to be head chef because he'd been born female (which had to be precisely declared on military forms: and we were military, apparently, but news to me...), I told him about how I was planning on calling the article Outpost 31 and explained why, he told me to tell his story, I promised I would.

Very drunk, around what we reckoned to be nighttime, although how to be sure? Verter said: 'You'd fucking adore Lydia.'

****

Also on the base was Lydia, a marine biologist, who was out to study tiny organisms and bacterium recovered from the ice. She was dark-eyed, soft-spoken and showed great promise for mild sexual perversity. And this proved true, during the voyage. Unable to legally fraternise with her cohorts, she looked to the WIR, and I happily fulfilled her needs. We met for the first time on the evening of the fifth day, in the corridor on the way to the canteen to have dinner. 'After you,' I said. And she replied: 'You're the WIR, aren't you?'

She didn't say double-U-eye-are, she said *weer*, like the beginning of the word weird.

'Oh, *for fuck's...*'

'Lydia.'

'Tiny organisms?'

The ice is alive. All around it, light dances. Normally, after one of its many tantrums, the groaning ones, the splintering ones, the ripping ones, the iron-busting ones, it settles, but not this time. She flung herself on me with the passion of a blood-deprived leech. Fair enough.

Over the course of dinner we wound together and I said: 'I've read you're not allowed to die here. Due to... Oh, that sounds a bit...'

'Totes fine. So, you're the double-U-eye-are.'

'What would you like?' I asked, glancing at the meagre bar.

'That,' she indicated with a slender incline of the head. I looked. There wasn't much to be had. I looked back. With flicked glances we went our separate ways out of the dining area, left, right.

I went back to my cabin.

And I wrote this, before I began the job proper.

Private diary, 2018

My Generation

The breakdown goes:
The Greatest Generation: born 1901 – 24
The Silent Generation: 25 – 45
The Baby Boomers: 46 – 64
Generation X: 65 – 79
Millennials: 80 – 94
Generation Z: 95 – 2012
Gen Alpha: ?

I'm talking about GENERATION X.

We had Indiana Bones, the cat who prowled around The Museum of Osteology while you lot were asleep. We were reading about the silent film era and thinking about how stupid the word *talkie* was while you... wait... *Movie*, no? Give me the luminous ceiling stars and the He-Man duvets, the first kisses in doorways at country houses, and farting on my balls and using my ears like a steering wheel, while playing football barefoot, like everyone young, we were kings.

You guys were asleep for Belushi, Lennon and Heller.

You guys missed how they put us down.

We had Bernard Herrmann's *Wuthering Heights* as repertoire and didn't feel the need to have to explain ourselves. Heathcliff, make everything stop right here and never move again, let the moors never change and you and I never change. Vicious of tongue because it was required: Hitchens was proper journalism,

We had Blair, *The Guardian* was a literate newspaper (I know – *un*believable), the BBC didn't ban anything, papa didn't preach, and I smacked ma bitch up in song and on stage with impunity. Royalty didn't matter, or wasn't an obsession, I was pretty, Racism still held its sting of disapproval and wasn't yet diluted by belief. Cathy was still my queen, we didn't need to justify why *Rain* became *Oasis* or why Will Self took heroin on John Major's private jet and... what did we do? *Laugh*. We didn't have to justify. Because it wasn't like that then. Ha ha and *ha*. Shame of the naked human body had not yet crept back in: we thought it fine. We enjoyed sex – and we had it left, right, and up there. We clawed our way to the middle and fucked our way down again.

I'm talking about my generation. Rage against the dying of the light.

There's a full moon this Easter. You know what that means? Werewolf Jesus? *Defo* werewolf Jesus. I'll get my shotgun. All 8-shots-full. Of course God is a woman, that's why all the holy books are loads of men making up rules to obey her. But she's ours, she's all ours, arriving with no message or talent or even longevity, but I'll watch her over and over again because at least she wasn't Kardashian (famous for a murder trial), and she didn't intrude. Tolerance will reach such a level that intelligent people will be stopped from thinking so as not to offend imbeciles. *Alien* has been bought by Disney, *Star Wars* too: I do not want to father a flock, to be the fetish of fools and fanatics, or the founder of a faith whose followers are content to echo my opinions. I want each man to cut his own way through the jungle.

I'm talking about my generation.

We had disrespect, we enjoyed being annoying, Hell, we gave back Ireland, cheers, and Hong Kong. We appreciated cunts because we *were* them, hence all the silly hair styles. We knew that the key to happiness was insensitivity, and Serge and Charlotte Gainsbourg weren't a couple and TV wasn't real, *The Terminator* wasn't inexorably coming, we were all along for the ride. Hell, fuck, we knew who we were.

I'm talking about my generation.

You lot were asleep when we merely sneezed. You missed the first openly gay character on screens, you missed men and women enrolling in universities in equal numbers for the first time, you missed the diversity of *Sesame Street* and the use of typewriters, you missed a call. Yes, when you missed a call you had to find out who had called and then call them back, while parents watched and tapped their wrists: You have five minutes left. You had life before me, you had life before us, you had life before you, and you had life before the Internet. Do not go gentle.

There were children then, just. Barely. But there was also greenery and happiness and peripheral vision. Distant shrubbery. Due to grasping environmental sustainability at a young age, we considered planetary health long before needing teenagers to shout at us about it. We cared. There was focus.

I'm talking about my generation.

We saw the Challenger Space Shuttle explode, and the Exxon Valdez oil tanker spill, we saw Yeltsin on a tank and the fall of the Berlin Wall (technically the end of World War 2), we saw Europe as more than just the birthmark on Gorbachev's forehead, and grew up under the spectre of the Yorkshire Ripper, Watergate, Vietnam, the Iranian hostage crisis, Jonestown and the Three Mile Island meltdown, which nearly killed us all. And what did we do? Laugh. And we keep on laughing: Ha and Ha and *Hahaha*. Don't go softly.

I'm talking about my generation.

Everybody wants to rule the world, and be a firestarter, but do you remember when we were in the crosshairs of Operation Desert Storm? I do. I remember exactly where I was. And we never got a single word of thanks for that, from the religious that we saved. Not one whisper.

We saw free speech fully championed in the guise of the Rushdie Affair, during which even sensible people were cowtowing to Islam, we saw our parents' financial situation as a burden not a boon, and wages stagnate while inflation skyrocketed.

I'm talking about my ge-ge-ge-generation.

We got raped and murdered too: it wasn't just you. We had Trickle Down Economics before you, and we had the Miami Circle – just a glorious pile of shit – there was the first official email sent and the Attenborough turtles died. We didn't light the fire, but it burns on and on and the Millenium, so goodbye, don't cry, we both know that we had Europe and saw the fall of Communism just as our parents saw the fall of fascism – although that's making a big comeback with the youngsters. We hated Nazis. We continue to hate them, my generation. We made loads of films about how much we hated them. We had Pavarotti – when he opened his mouth the whole world was suddenly in sunlight – and I was there when he did Hyde Park and met Princess Di – '*donna non vidi mai*' – that was my generation, in cagoules to hear the sun sing. And no regrets, except one: my son wasn't there to hear and feel that. Rage, rage against the dying of the light.

We had BeJams and RadioRentals, we had Blockbusters and English pubs with firesides, we could smoke there, indoors, we had *see you later* and *fuck right off*, and both were endearing, without offence. We had parents. We had tabards coming out of our eyeballs because we wanted to help: and why?

Because we weren't who you think we were; and because you are you. If you weren't you then I wouldn't have been me. If you hadn't been you then I wouldn't have ever loved.

All I needed was a pen, a piece of paper, a pot of glue to keep me there, and you, dear girl, come what may. Where were words when you needed them? Besides... It couldn't have been me, because I was a busy boy, bizzying *la* into *a*, and wondering about my generation.

If you can hear trumpets, *Freiheit*, listen harder. If you can't you're not here. We had dads, even if our mothers hated them: but they still didn't do it to *you*. We'd see them on bicycles, hemi-demi-semi-quavers coming spilling from the helmet... we saw the Noughties come in. Despite the lovely innuendo-laden name, they seemed to be going down a well-maintained drain, *Freiheit,* until... September 11th, which changed everything.

I'm talking about my generation.

For you, my son.

My Actual.

Never give up.

And never believe.

Selected Pieces, today

Acknowledgements

A big thank you to all the publications and websites where much of this work originally appeared, but particularly to Anne Samson and everyone at TSL Books for peerless dedication and admirable commitment to the industry of writing as an art form. Without such people, literature would be poorer. Thanks to the twinkly Mike Wells for designing the cover of this collection, to Helen Capper, as usual a most perceptive editor (congratulations on baby Victoria), Topsy for lighting the flame and MA for sustaining it, Will Wiles ('your blind idealism will get us all killed!'), the Cullen family, proprietors of my local, *North Nineteen*, the Klojdová family for half-heartedly adopting me as one of their clan, the elusive Joynson – erstwhile partner in creative crime, the mercurial Rosalind Nashashibi and Pietro Manacorda – and all my colleagues at Harrow Opera, Instant Opera, the Royal College of Music, Purcell School and Koru Kids. Also, thanks to Milla Jovovich for her remembrances of Anno Birkin, even if I couldn't use them in this volume: I won't forget your care.

In the last 15 years I have often passed my old flat at 17 Westbourne Park Road, and I always pause for a moment by the steps to grasp the crooked black railings and smile quietly, with due respect for those indelible times, with love for the people I knew – many of whom are no longer alive – and because so little looks to have changed, and yet everything has: the whole world transfigured. Eli, my son, you visited that flat with me a few times (and sat on the pool table), but you were too small to possibly remember. Still, everything I do is yours, and will continue to be: you are my Actual, and Daddy loves you so much.

And now for the 'bonus track' – here is a sneak preview of my forthcoming novel *Weltschmerz*, the jewel in the crown. I hope you enjoy.

X
X   Ezra Williams   X
X

Weltschmerz Inc: A Ghost Story

PRELUDE

The saddest sound in the world – and we have to start somewhere – is a solitary woodwind instrument being practised from behind closed doors when one walks down a street at early evening. Or at least, it's the saddest sound in the world for me. It happens only a few times every decade, but each time it fills me with glittering horror. It's usually a saxophone, occasionally a clarinet, and this only happens with woodwind – a trumpet, say, would not work. In fact a trumpet had had the opposite effect of filling me with joy, when I heard a young person playing one as I passed through a neglected part of town many years ago, Lewisham, say, or Kidbrooke, or Lee Green. Perhaps it was a cornet, played by an old person. I wasn't close enough to tell.

Sound has been my life, you see, or at least the largest part of it. The emotional part, if you will. While I am heterosexual – how quaint is that term? – women, sadly, don't feature prominently in my story. There are a few, as you will see, but they are mostly spectral beings now, memories in newsprint that haunt my name. So I've only ever had half a life – marriage and offspring never came, despite my deep longing for them.

But again, it could be that *deep longing* was something else entirely, as you will see. It comes late, swooping in with the shadow of the retreating sun, and chases out the music that dwells in my head. So, sound has been my soul, and my replacement for those things that others seem to possess so easily.

You may recognise my name.

My name, or more specifically my surname, is also a dual thing with one side missing. One side – the American side, I guess – is the missing, the despised. The obverse is me, Lorin Suliyanto, American by birth and youth, but adopted by Great Britain in early adulthood, as one of its own, a celebrated member of its artistic community. And I should say *Professor* Lorin Suliyanto, as that *is* my title. I am…

No, let me start this again, with due artifice. I subliminally understood it was a sorry idea to start this in the evening: a boondoggle endeavour if ever there was one, without proper prep.

The Sadness is coming – I can feel its breath – and I should retire before it catches me and ruins tomorrow's work. Let's try again in the morning.

CHAPTER ONE

BEGININNGS

Hello. Welcome to Beckington. Do please come in. It's so very nice to meet you. Yes, leave your shoes in the vestibule. There. I don't get too many visitors. The occasional journalist of course, when I have a premiere coming up. Those interviews are always either staggeringly mundane or alarmingly cerebral. But we can discuss all that hoo-ha later. For now, would you care for a cup of tea? Or something stronger? It is nearly 11am after all, and technically legal! Through here is the bar, and it's a *wet* bar, too. Unusual, these days, I've found. Help yourself. Glasses are just there, in the cupboard by the piano.

Oh, that old upright? I don't play that, no. It used to belong to John Lennon in actual fact. I picked it up at an auction in Kensington. Can't recall when. In America they call them *vertical* pianos! Imagine that! What a digital-age tag for an old upright! The lavatory is down the hall – last but one door on the left. I keep my awards in there so that guests like yourself, and you *are* a guest, can pick one up and mime an acceptance speech in the mirror, post evacuation. Do pardon my dry humour – I'm always like this in the mornings. Indeed, very much a morning person. Definitely not a *Morgenmuffel*! Oh, I *am* silly. Let me show you to your room. I'll take these smaller bags.

My name is Professor Lorin Suliyanto, and I am a composer, and more precisely a proud British composer. I am that rarest of intellectual beasts: the modestly (some would say inexplicably or undeservedly) popular classical composer. I press the British angle for a number of reasons – they have adopted me, an American by birth, they have given me a very comfortable life, but most importantly, here in Britain my name is my own. Obviously, the Internet vultures make the connections, but a wise musical mentor once told me, "by all means let a bad review spoil your breakfast, but *never* let it spoil your lunch". He was quite right, naturally. Ignore the chatter of the dismayed multitudes. In many ways, oddly, Britain is more welcoming of those with unusual names. And names mean something. My forename, Lorin, is of English origin – another auspicious Anglo-tie – and means Laurel. With its intimations of victory – the wreath – it has served me well I feel, in reinventing myself on a new continent. My mother had some vague English blood, it is true, but saw herself as an American of Scandinavian descent, and my father was a first-generation Philippine immigrant. How my mother – ever the dreamer – loved unusual names. Look at mine, Lorin, and my brother's, Byron... The mild innocent poetry of these names.

Growing up in Story, Wyoming, in the foothills of the Big Horn Mountains, I saw my forename as an indicator of my mother's formality, her *artistic* formality. Because not very many people realise that my mother was the well-known, and broadly respected, visual artist Selina Colas. Seen as something of an old-fashioned goofball or disconcerting eccentric in Story, she will feature later in *our* story, as she debunked to these present shores with me, and continued her career without a hiccup, before coming out as a somewhat flamboyant lesbian in her later years. Yet most people still do not know of our familial relationship. She, amazingly, managed to escape the connection.

Another aspect of my assumed Englishness was that, unlike my mother, I took to the language with zeal – and I am doing rather well, don't you think? Would you, dear guest, have figured that I was not originally from here? Dash it all, yes, that *figured* gave me away. You will notice the occasional Americanism creeping in here and there. I now see that I used the word *goofball* earlier... Yes, and *boondoggle* – very well noticed! Try to think of it as a charming quirk, like those insincere words that give away novice screenwriters, yet make it into the final cut.

My brother Byron of course... No. Not now. We must continue. We *must* get to the story I want to tell you first. That's why you're here, in the end.

My father I hardly knew. He made a handful of threadbare appearances throughout my childhood (and he makes an appearance here too, later on), but it is enough to say that I was born – during a storm – in a Domestic Abuse Refuge in New York, under the shadow of the Brooklyn Bridge. It was on England's Avenue, and I smile to this day at that fortuitous and presaging fact.

My earliest memories are there – the restaurants on either side of us, Da Roberto's and The Lords' Rendezvous (Italian and Chinese respectively), the smells, the lonely kindergarten my brother and I attended on dusty old Barrow Hill back in the balmy early 80s. There I go again – kindergarten rather than nursery. We were there, in a little flat (apartment/unit) until I was five, when my mother had made enough money from her tortuous and scintillating artwork that we could disappear to Story, Wyoming permanently.

So, until his appearance later, I'll give my father two sentences. Here they are. 1. Rodrigo Suliyanto opened a café in 1971 that later grew into five, and then twelve, and provided enough money for his two sons, at least until his ex-wife became more successful, and took over the finances. 2. He should never have had children, and many Americans wish he never had.

My mother Selina, six years gone now, used to tell me, "Lorin, sometimes the most beautiful and bright creatures are born during a storm. It's so the bad creatures are distracted and don't notice them. Never dwell in your distress. It's all just cover for your wonder". As I said before, quite the dreamer. I'll come back to her at points during this narrative, just as she comes to me at unbidden moments, my quaint fragile painter momma. But as she said herself: "I am not fragile like a flower, I am fragile like a bomb".

Ah, you've joined me, how nice. I see you've availed yourself of the bar. What is that? A Negroni, I see. With Campari and vodka? How delightfully decadent. I don't drink myself anymore, but don't let that stop you. I always used to say to guests, "If you don't have a drink in your hand in this house, then it's your own goddamn fault". I trust you had a good rest? Excellent. And that your bedroom will be sufficient for the stay? All good then. Do find a comfy seat – I recommend that one – just gently swipe the cats to the floor – hey, *hey*, no spitting at our guest! How odd – they're normally so friendly and peaceful. I guess they're not used to newcomers. I do apologise. Right. Take a seat and we can tidy up any loose ends and move on to the main event. Would lunch at 2 be agreeable? Fine, fine. I'll get Hollis onto it right away.

– Hollis?

You wait here while I go and see where she is. It is so nice to have a guest here again you know. It really is. I mean that most sincerely. Now. Help yourself to another drink. Why not, the day is yet young. Put your feet up, and I'll be straight back.

I suppose, before we proceed with the story of what happened last summer, I ought to say a final few words on what England means to me. Call it gratitude, if you will, call it arse-licking if you must, but here goes.

My title – Professor – would have been unthinkable in my birth country, simply because of... well, you guess why. A quick Google search of my surname followed by a U and an S explains everything. In Britain, being an Honorary Professor of the Royal College of Music guaranteed me almost half-a-million pounds per year for one lecture every three months. But more than this, much more than this, Britain has given me the best kind of celebrity to have – a calm recognition for doing something forgivingly obscure to a very high degree – Fame not of the face or personality, but Fame of the talent. And I feel I *can* say talent now – for too long I was shy of it. But I have the awards, the operas performed in major houses around Europe (though of course not The Met, or anywhere in the US), the film scores, the TV dramas, the adverts... But my proudest achievements remain my 7 commissions for the BBC Proms at the Royal Albert Hall, and in particular the oratorio I produced for Queen Camilla's Coronation. *Produced* is the correct word – I didn't *write* the thing, it seemed to roll off the many assembly lines of a vast musical factory. Utilising three extra brass ensembles on top of the already bloated orchestra (contrabassoons, Wagner tubas and full organ for starters) and two massed choirs, it was Mahlerian in vision, and spent seven ravishing months at the pinnacle of the Classical Charts until sadly dislodged by Symphony No. 2 *'The Blistering'*, by one of Ringo Starr's grand-daughters. I wasn't sore at all – to be dethroned by a Beatles descendent was yet another example of my innate Englishness, I felt.

But further, and forgive me if I've said this before, England was my haven. And I never felt any need (or want) to leave her for any substantial time, and I never did. Until last summer that is, as you shall see.

And that crisp morning in late May last year, when I left the house and approached the taxi idling at the gate, what do you think I heard? Yes, an unaccompanied saxophone drifting down the drive. For a man who sees signs and connections so readily, why did I not turn around then? Because subconsciously, I think I knew there were unsatisfied demons that had to be fed, now my twilight years were beckoning, if I was to have any peace, anyplace.

– Hollis? Say, Hollis, where on earth have you got to?

The only thing – and I mean the *only* thing – that I have ever resented – to any extent – about Britain, is the fact that I have not yet (so far as I know) been considered for the position of Keeper of the Queen's Music, or the Musician Laureate if you will. And my agent would have heard if there had been a whiff of rumour or any tabloidal murmurings taking place in the shadowy corners of concert halls – he's the best in the biz, and you'll get to meet him soon. And it wasn't truly resentment anyway. That's too harsh a word, and I am a humble soul at heart. And there's always *some* imperfection, some minor defect in even the most perfect design. One can never have everything. And I suppose, being Queen Camilla's favourite living composer, I *am* the keeper of her music, if the unofficial one.

– Hollis? Where the devil are you? Hollis?

REPUTATION

It was May 27th last year when I found myself saying goodbye to Hollis, my elderly Swedish housekeeper, and her cadaverous Glaswegian husband, Dunn. I didn't know him well, but Hollis had been in my employ for 15 years, and she had proven herself valuably discrete in that time, and also a kind and solemn presence. So far as I knew, she had never heard a note of my music, and that's how I liked it. If I had ever had the good fortune to have a family of my own, I believe I would have roundly discouraged my offspring and wife from familiarity with my work. But...

It was the wrong way round – I was saying goodbye to them, but they were inside my house, and I was out, on the wide gravel path leading down to the steel gates that had been erected in 1866. I was due to be away for five months and, while still keeping her on salary, had given them the bonus of having the run of the place with me gone.

And what a place – I had bought it after my mother's death, mostly, I must admit, with the proceeds of a posthumous sale of one of her most celebrated works – *Touching The Chimp* – a sale which became an auction when buyers proved alarmingly volatile in the face of

Selina Colas's late genius. Set on the outskirts of Oxford, Beckington had seven bedrooms, a barn conversion that became my composing and oft-times recording studio, a wine cellar that resembled a cave and boasted a small swimming pool at one end... Hollis, who had been with me almost ten years by then, was so taken with the place that she and Dunn (they were childless; he ran a tree-cutting business) relocated from London, where I'd had a town house in Blackheath. I wagered there were more trees for Dunn's men to trim up the M40.

It was a phone call that January that had started these events into motion. My agent, Malcolm Landrith, called with news of a big new commission by a private individual, with the potential for future endorsement and sponsorship down the line – straight up, it was a 7-figure sum for a 25-minute orchestral piece. It seemed a breeze, a no-brainer. But there was a catch, and then an even bigger one. The private individual wished to remain anonymous. This was not in itself necessarily unusual, or even worrying. Malcolm had had his lawyers and accountants check out the offer, and apparently it was legitimate: the money was there. But then came the bigger catch.

The private individual was insisting that the piece be composed in the US. A luxury apartment in a colossal glass block (owned by the individual's company) overlooking New York Harbor was to be mine for however long the composition would take. I would have a generous weekly stipend, a grand piano (of course), cleaners and caterers, and anything else I may, whimsically, decide to specify. A classical composer with a *rider*? What a desirably preposterous proposition! Malcolm sensed me flinch, and my subsequent hesitation. Soothingly, he said, "Lorin, look, I know how you've always maintained you'd never return Stateside after the, well, er, the, *what happened*, but there need be no publicity about you personally being there... You say yourself that it's Fame of the Talent you have. Let it *be* that".

Reluctantly, and I add *very*, I was sold.

So that May morning I lumbered to the taxi and began my journey to JFK International. I remembered little of New York, save for our hideaway on England's Avenue, and toddling up Barrow Hill on mineral gasoline mornings, and noodles from the Lords' Rendezvous. Everything else was... mere impression, smudges of memory. My apprehension began to ease when, a half-hour before we were due to touch down, the pilot announced an unseasonal storm ahead, and to expect turbulence. Yes, my apprehension eased, because my mother's words came back to me: "...sometimes the most beautiful and bright creatures are born during a storm. It's so the bad creatures are distracted and don't notice them... It's all just cover for your wonder", and perhaps this trip wasn't going to be a tortuous rebirth after all, but rather a pleasant and productive sabbatical in pleasant and stimulating surroundings.

Malcolm Landrith was true to his promise and was there to meet me at the gate. He had even, presumably in a flash of comedic inspiration, had a sign made, complete with a thin wooden pole to hold it triumphantly aloft, as if for a homecoming of sorts. ENGLISH MUSICIAN was stencilled across it in chunky black letters. Malcolm knew the score, and he knew I would baulk and bolt back across the dismal Atlantic pond at the slightest hint of my true identity becoming known. But before I reached that meeting, and indeed the second I disembarked from the plane, it was the smell of the place that brought those distant babyhood impressions hurtling back.

When you're there even an hour you cease to notice it, but the smell of New York is *something*. Even in the airport it was there, like the throb of life, or death if you were inclined to look at things top-down, rather than bottom-up. I think everyone on earth (or at least those who live with independent minds) has this switch that happens – for me it was around age 38, in 2009 or 2010 – a switch when death becomes tangible, and intrudes permanently on the balmy days before. The smell of New York is perhaps too ineffable for syntax, but I'll give it a go. Attempting to describe the indescribable – that old fool's game. Okay.

The smell of New York is – in no particular order – garbage on a polite breeze, sizzling street meat, horse shit, laundry and BBQs from hidden backyards, damp concrete, piss (whether human, animal or other), vent fumes from the sides of buildings (lending them a living, breathless quality unlike sedate, healthy British ones), car exhaust, fish markets, marijuana, pizza, success, manhole steam, subway restaurants and Nuts 4 Nuts carts, dead dreams, forgotten sex, and insecure pride. None of these are truly pleasant, but in New York, and all together, they're irresistible. We're a long way from Wisconsin, Toto. We're not in Story any more.

JFK itself was a major disappointment. Foreign visitors to NYC – we've only been here fifteen minutes and already those Yankee acronyms are taking over – often arrive fully expecting the celluloid experience.

It's all they know. We've seen the movies. But JFK was as generic as any other major airport, and minus the charm some of them possess. I was immediately struck by the nonchalance, even insolence, of the staff, who acted as if they'd rather be anywhere but where they were. Then the luggage trolleys: designed to frustrate. Then the huge Old Glorys, tethered by twisted steel ropes to the slanting roof, motionless above variegated crowds. My mood, which had lightened, if you recall, during that brief storm before landing, began to sour again. But at least it wasn't technically *late*. It felt late to me, of course, due to my unfamiliar accomplice, jet lag, but it wasn't.

I knew that I'd be deftly directed into some bare room and detained for a while – as I saw it, The Suliyanto Clause would feature in any transatlantic travel for me. And so it proved, but then came the arduous run-in with the sniffer dog. I had half expected this hurdle as well – due to the pesky kittens I'd had to 'hot desk' my work station with for the last month, everything I now wore must have smelled in need of much closer inspection by a dog trained in olfactory cunning. The golden beast circumnavigated my suitcase, then jumped up and put its paws resolutely on my chest. I am not a tall man – five eight as we say back home, 68 inches here – and it was an intimidating specimen, although apparently friendly enough. Despite my subdued and feeble protestations – I had resolved to be as courteous as possible at all times during my Stateside job – about kittens and misunderstandings and not being in possession of drugs or other anti-American contraband – how ridiculous I must have sounded! – I was escorted to another bare room and instructed to disrobe.
  – Completely?
  – Let's see how we go, shall we?
  – Ok sir. And is it necessary the other gentleman be here also?
  – Yes. Start now, if you will.
  – Here?
  – Unless you want to do it out there in Starbucks. Your choice, pal.
  This was delivered without a trace of a smile, and a flat dead gaze. I un-shouldered my jacket...

In a private email – naturally such views would not be dared espoused aloud – a fellow composer once wrote to me that

> ...humour will be bred out of Americans by sheer diversity. Anything witty is bound to offend someone. I reckon they'll reach the point where nobody will dare say anything at all...

And I was reminded of this at JFK, because it did seem to be a place of utter humourlessness. Incidentally, and I must mention this because it provided mirth while also being aesthetically pleasing, the same friend (a Norwegian, if that is of note) had achieved international acclaim due to doing no actual work: he had simply given permission for his Concerto for Orchestra – composed 17 years previously (!) – to be used in a Hollywood horror franchise that had become wildly, indeed hysterically, popular. And thus his haunting Concerto for Orchestra ("barely a student piece, to be honest", he wrote to me: "I'd forgotten about it. And now it's all anyone talks about... Ah, the mystery of the dots...") had become that summer's *de rigueur* soundtrack.

On his way from one promotional event to another, he told me he passed through a smallish American town that, beside its WELCOME TO... sign, had another which read: We Like Who We Are. "You know, Lorin," he wrote, "I quickly realised that people who like who they are will very quickly stop liking who you are."

In the end I was allowed to keep my underpants and socks on, and didn't have to do anything invasive, or more invasive than standing nearly naked in a foreign land with two inscrutable strangers. The dog seemed much more interested in the pile of my clothes than in my body, so no drugs were suspected of being concealed therein. As I dressed, the interrogator (the other man had not uttered a word) gave the sheets of paper in his hand a last, almost regretful glance-over and said

– I guess we know why my colleagues over there had a talk with you. Are you...?

– No, no relation.

With a tiny nod, he signed the last page and motioned for me to leave. Inwardly cursing the kittens, I made my way onto the main concourse and waved to Malcolm Landrith.

As we left the airport I gathered my nerves and whispered inwardly *I am not fragile like a flower, I am fragile like a bomb... I am not fragile like a flower, I am fragile like a bomb...* Then the yellow Ford Freestar swallowed us up and headed toward the harbour.

To Be Continued...